THE
STORY
TELLER

doubleday

New York   London   Toronto   Sydney   Auckland

THE STORY TELLER

a novel

Arthur Reid

PUBLISHED BY DOUBLEDAY
a division of Random House, Inc.

DOUBLEDAY and the portrayal of an anchor with a dolphin are
registered trademarks of Random House, Inc.

Library of Congress Cataloging-in-Publication Data
Reid, Arthur.
   The storyteller : a novel / Arthur Reid.– 1st ed.
     p. cm.
   1. Authorship–Fiction. 2. Authors and publishers–Fiction.
3. Publishers and publishing–Fiction. 4. Truthfulness and falsehood–
Fiction. 5. New York (N.Y.)–Fiction. I. Title: Story teller. II. Title.

PS3618.E53S76 2003
813'.6–dc21

2003051947

ISBN 0-385-50621-X

PRINTED IN THE UNITED STATES OF AMERICA

September 2003

First Edition

1   3   5   7   9   10   8   6   4   2

This is for the members of the Labor Day Club

Victoria and Si

and Alexandra and Dennis

"It is the friends that you can call up at

4 A.M. that matter."

—MARLENE DIETRICH

And, of course, for Jessica and Dave

Acknowledgments

Writing a book can be a little like running a marathon underwater if it weren't for the help and encouragement of others:

Steve Rubin, who opened the door and kept the faith.

Jason Kaufman, an editor of insight and skill who was always there to make sure we got both the small and the big things right.

Owen Laster, whose hand was always steady and, most important, for the many years of friendship.

Jonathan Pecarsky—whatever the question, he always found the answer.

THE GIFT

But what is it to be a writer? Writing is a
sweet wonderful reward, but its price? During
the night the answer was transparently clear
to me: it is the reward for service to the
devil.

—Franz Kafka, letter to Max Brod,
July 5, 1922

One

My name is Steven King and I'm a writer. As you can see from the spelling of my first name, I'm not the guy from Maine, though this story starts there. Professionally, I use the name Steven Konigsberg. That's what my great-grandfather Shmuel Konigsberg was called when he landed in America in 1898. He became Sanford King in 1908 when he opened a dry goods store in Binghamton, New York, with a friend from Cracow, Poland, Chaim Hirsch. Hirsch in turn became Charles Stagg, and their store was called King and Stagg, of course.

About four years ago I was at a very low point in my life. I had just turned thirty-two, and aside from a couple of stories published in small literary magazines, I had yet to see my work in print. In fact, the first two novels I wrote attracted enough rejection letters to make a fair-sized book themselves. Strangely enough, I had a literary agent, Stuart Amster, a hotshot who represented a number of famous and very well paid novelists. Why did he stick with me, a writer who had brought in nada over almost ten years of writing? you may ask. Family pressure—Stuart's my cousin.

I was a disciplined and serious writer, putting in four to five hours a day working on my new novel. The lack of literary success was offset by a wondrous development: I met Tina Blake, tall and lithe, with dirty-blond hair and a profile that was meltingly pretty. She was twenty-seven and taught elementary school, and I fell in love immediately with her soft but strong fem-

ininity, mixed with all-too-uncommon strength of character. I had never experienced the feeling I had for her: it was all-enveloping, scary yet affirm-
ing. I was swept away and it felt wonderful.

Even so, I knew I had to leave the poisoned atmosphere of Key West.
The suffocating combination of oddballs and would-be writers, each with
an angry story to tell, became too much for me. Is this the way I'm going
to wind up? I had repeatedly asked myself in a small, frightened voice.
Thank God, Tina was willing to go with me to a small town on the Maine
coast, Boothbay Harbor, where I had spent summers as a boy. She understood why I had to leave, and she began looking for a teaching job there.
Tina is an optimist. "Everything will work out," she would say with a smile,
about big or small events, from the flurry of rejection slips I continued to
receive to moving northward into the unknown.

I had spent five perfect summers in Boothbay as a kid at camp. I knew I
could live there cheaply, and I hoped I would find the quiet of the place, a
summer resort that hibernates for a good eight months a year, more con-
ducive to finishing my book.

I landed a bartending job at the Rusty Scupper within two days of arriving in town. The Scupper is housed in an old fish processing building on
the west side of the harbor. The bar was made up of two dories set on a
platform, planked over, and shellacked to the gleaming patina of an ice-
skating rink. The place serves your standard surf and turf cuisine, but the
food is simply prepared and really quite delicious. My customers, aside
from in- and out-of-season tourists, were a solid group of lobstermen, local
business owners, and older folks who came out less for a drink than for
some conversation. Unlike Key West, the freak quotient at the Scupper was
pretty close to zero. My customers drank mostly beer and whiskey, some
white wine, and the occasional martini (with a decent splash of vermouth).
I had brought along my copy of *Mr. Boston's Bar Guide*, but I had little reason to use it. I could go for weeks without making a cosmopolitan or a
mojito.

I quickly became close to one of my regulars, who was older than my father. His name was Ben Chambers, and this story is as much his as it is
mine.

We discovered right away that we had something important in common:
we were both writers. To my great good fortune I also found in him a know-

ing and generous critic. He was willing—even eager—to read my latest pages, and his instinct about what was good and what was not was always on target, even if I wasn't happy about what he had to say. He would show up at the Scupper between eight and nine each night and most of the time would close the bar with me. He was a talker, but a real good one. He appeared to be in his early eighties and apparently had done a little bit of everything. Since serving in the navy during World War II, he had worked as a story editor at MGM, a tutor to a set of sisters whose parents owned the biggest rice farm in California, a photographer who specialized in shots of cats and dogs, a crop duster in Canada, a florist, a carpenter, a furniture maker, a logger in the Pacific Northwest, an ambulance driver in San Francisco, and a stockbroker in Miami. I'm probably leaving out a few occupations, but this is enough to give you an idea of the kind of life Ben had lived. And he had been a writer. By his calculation he had written twenty novels, not counting a bunch of plays, screenplays, and short stories. He had even written a few children's stories. None of them had been published. And though I handed Ben sections of my new novel to read as I wrote them, he never let me look at any of his stuff.

"That's all behind me, Stevie boy. Way behind. But take my word for it, they were all pretty damn good. Well written, if I do say so myself, and also commercial as hell."

Of course, I didn't take Ben's word for it. Though I thought he was one of the most interesting and honorable men I had ever met, I figured that his description of his writing career was fiction.

"I'd love to read one of them someday."

"Maybe you will."

"What I find so damn strange is that you never sought to have any of your work published. I'm desperate to get my stuff into print."

"I've told you all this before. I used to love to write—to create my own private world and fill it with people who interested me. It was heaven. But I only wrote for myself. An artist should only write for himself. Once I put down the stories I had to write, I never looked back. I loved the process of writing. Period. That's all behind me now."

"You never made any money from it?"

"Who needs fame and riches? It just clogs up your life; it's like putting molasses in a gas tank. All it gets you are greedy agents, rapacious publishers, dumb producers, and crazy fans. And then you have to deal with the IRS. The joy comes from writing, not publishing. It's the only thing I disagree with Samuel Johnson on."

"How so?"

"Dr. Johnson said that no one but a blockhead ever wrote, except for money."

Ben and I did most of our serious talking out on his lobster boat. Once or twice a week, whatever the weather, I helped him haul in his traps. I could listen to Ben all day. He had lived in Boothbay Harbor for ten years, and he set his traps as a sideline, not a full-time job. Actually, the majority of the lobsters Ben hauled in, he gave away. Most of the professional lobstermen didn't like the part-timers, but that didn't hold true for Ben, who was loved universally, it seemed. The year before, a young lobsterman named Dave Howell had fallen overboard while hauling his traps, alone in his boat. They didn't find his body for almost a week. Ben quickly organized a bake sale, a concert, and a raffle to benefit Dave's wife and little daughter. That's Ben.

We were out past Fisherman's Island, and Ben had just finished pulling his last trap. He moved around the boat like a man twenty years younger. He was half a head shorter than me, and the little bit of gray hair left on his head circled the crown like moss. He had a short stubbly beard, and his arms were ropy with long muscles. What you remembered most after meeting him for the first time were his eyes, a bright blue of the hue you see once in a while on small wildflowers that grow in the spring.

"Let's take *Boswell* over to Christmas Cove and have a hamburger and a beer. How does that sound?" he said.

"Just perfect."

"Want to take the wheel?"

"Sure."

As he lighted his pipe, I slid behind the steering wheel and pointed the bow toward Ocean Point.

"I read the pages you gave me last night," he said as he pulled slowly on his pipe. "You write like a dream, but I have the same problem as I had with the last pages you gave me."

"Which is?"

"Your hero. Teddy. The reader has to like him more."

"Teddy's me, Ben."

"That doesn't change what I said. If a reader doesn't like the central character of a book, you got problems."

"What else?"

"I saw that Beth was leaving him in the last section."

"So?"

"Your reader wants to be surprised. You can't tip your hand that way. Get me?"

I might have had doubts about Ben's own writing, but his critical faculty was always on target.

Two

Exactly one week later my agent and cousin, Stuart, zoomed in to say hello. Though he knew as much about boating as I did about igloo construction, he had bought a fifty-foot powerboat and was cruising up the coast. Luckily, he had hired a captain to pilot the thing. Dutifully, I went to the marina to admire his new purchase, christened with a sense of humor I didn't know Stuart possessed, *The Floating Commission.* Before I even stepped on board, he told me it had cost him $849,000. He then proceeded to give me a tour, which centered on his high-resolution TV hooked up to a satellite dish. The TV was secreted in a sea chest at the foot of the bed in the main cabin and rose with a whirring of gears, like the periscope on a submarine. Stuart was accompanied by his girlfriend of the moment, Ricki, a woman I guessed to be in her late thirties. Ricki appeared to have had enough plastic surgery to qualify for the witness protection program. Fortunately, she didn't talk much.

I took the night off and per Stuart's instruction booked a table at the most expensive restaurant in town, the Point Inn. Tina was supposed to visit me that weekend from Key West, but her mother was in the hospital, so I had to face Stuart alone.

"I just wrapped up a four-book deal for Tim Fisk at Random House. Guess what I got?"

"I have no idea, Stuart."

"Come on. Just guess. It was hard/soft. U.S. and Canada. No foreign."

"A million."

"Jesus, Steve, get with the real world. Tim's last two books came on the *Times* list at number seven. Guess again."

"I still have no idea."

"How does two point six million sound?"

"Wow. Over two and a half million bucks for four books."

"No, shmuck. That's two point six per book. It's a ten-and-a-half-million-dollar deal."

"Jesus."

Stuart smiled generously, giving me another wide-screen view of his new implants (total cost $17,750) as he stroked Ricki's shoulder. Though we're first cousins, Stuart and I have little in common. I'm six feet tall and still thin enough to wear belts I bought when I was an undergraduate. My hair is a very dark brown, which looks almost black in any room that doesn't have fluorescent lighting. It's straight and pelt thick, just like my dad's. My prospects for the future look solid, since Dad, at seventy-one, still has all his hair with just a scattering of gray at the temples. Tina thinks my eyes are my best feature. She says they're the color of a pool that has a good filtration system. I take that as a compliment. Stuart is short with a neck worthy of an NFL lineman. His eyes are small and cat-fur gray. He lost his hair in his twenties but now has a Maginot Line of plugs bristling an inch above his eyebrows. Though he's only six years older than me, he looks double that. But he was a success, and I was tending bar at the Rusty Scupper.

It was when we were sipping our espressos that Stuart got to the question I'd been dreading.

"So, cousin Steve, how you coming with your new book?"

"Pretty good."

"What the fuck does that mean?"

"It's going along well," I said hesitantly.

"When will you finish it?"

"Soon."

"I'm not your probation officer, for Christ's sake. Level with me. I promised your mother that I'd sell this one. And believe me, I'm going to pull every lever and press every fucking button in the business to get you into print. Tell me you at least have a good story going in this one. I need more than an Iowa Writers' Workshop character study. I need plot. A strong plot.

The publishing business has changed. The lit stuff is tougher today to sell than rap music at a Klan rally. Do you hear me, cuz?"

"I hear you, Stuart."

"Great. Now, how about an after-dinner drink? A little Sambuca for you, Ricki, my dear?" Stuart asked as he gently rubbed her inner thigh with the back of his hand, smiling so extravagantly that the overhead spots pinwheeled light off his gleaming new implants.

Three

The bar was quiet, thank God. The regulars were strung out like ducks in a shooting gallery, drinking their beers and whiskeys and minding their own business. Lucky for me. Tonight I knew I'd be unable to play my standard role of buddy/therapist/confidant. Maybe they all sensed I couldn't handle the usual heart-to-heart that took in everything from child support payments to the merits of one SUV over another. Maybe I looked as non compos mentis as I felt. Stuart had kept me up late last night—plying me with more Poire Williams and additional tales of his success as an agent. I paid for it with a massive hangover that had taken me all morning to scuttle. I couldn't even grind out half a page of my novel, and the more I looked at the empty screen, the more depressed I became. I was racking up some clean glasses when I heard someone speak my name. It was Stuart.

"Hey, cuz, I'm here to say good-bye. We're taking off for Camden tomorrow morning, about seven. You don't need to come down and wave us off."

We both laughed.

He told me some more about his itinerary, a ditto of what he'd told me last night, then grabbed Ricki's hand. "Remember my promise—you get me the manuscript, I'll get you a publisher. Deal?"

We laughed again, though mine sounded more like someone being strangled.

Ben arrived at the bar around nine. Most of the steadies had departed, leaving the place almost entirely to Ben and myself. The night before, I had told him I was having dinner with my cousin the hotshot agent, so he must have known what he was in for. I gave him every painful detail.

He nodded and made murmuring sounds of sympathy. "Maybe Stuart has something," he began slowly after I finally wound down. "You're aiming for posterity. You want perfect sentences. Elegant sentences. Forget it. Bring your writing down to earth. Give your readers stories—that's what they want. Something that grabs hold of them. And give them characters they care about, characters they can actually root for. That's what it's all about. Haven't I told you essentially the same thing?"

"Yes." I hung my head, feeling like a child.

"Come on, Stevie, cheer up. You have talent. Loosen up and give it a chance."

"I'm going to try, Ben. I really am."

We both fell silent. Ben stirred his drink and took a swallow.

"I'm going to make it an early evening and push on home," he said after a while. "I don't feel so hot. I think I'm getting a cold. See you tomorrow." He slid off the barstool and headed for the door, but he didn't have far to go. His old saltbox was only a few hundred feet away.

I wasn't able to close the bar until one, so I killed the time thinking about the chapter I'd gotten stuck on that day, and how to lift it out of its rut. Chapter by chapter I'll pull the book together, I vowed to myself. For the moment I felt hopeful, jotting down ideas I could use on the backs of napkins.

When I got home, I checked my e-mail. Tina's mother was home and feeling a lot better. In a week Tina would fly up, and we could start looking for a larger house for the two of us.

I thought my place had charm, but it still was not much more than a shack. When Tina visited, we had to concentrate on not bumping into each other.

The next one came from my mother, and I knew it would be about the great Stuart, my agent.

> *Your Aunt Florence says Stuart is excited about the book. He told her you'd be finishing it soon. Daddy and I can't wait to read it. We're so proud of you. XOXO, Mom.*

The last e-mail was from Quentin Bass, my old prof and mentor from the Iowa Writers' Workshop. Did my troubles as a writer start with him? Quentin was feeling blue. His latest girlfriend—a student, what else?—had just moved out, and his new novel had been rejected by his publisher. Seems that since his last novel four years ago, his editor had left to go work at an Internet start-up and the publishing company had been sold to a Dutch media conglomerate whose main interest was in children's books. Quentin's agent was not sanguine about selling the book. Quentin's e-mail contained lots of typos, a sign that my old professor was drinking again.

I pulled myself up from my computer, feeling lower than ever. I fed my Lab, Chester, a bone I had bought at the supermarket that afternoon. I barely managed to get my clothes off before collapsing into bed for a long night of dreams that thankfully didn't feature my cousin Stuart.

Four

When Tina arrived for a long weekend, my mood reversed itself. It had been almost two months since we had seen each other.

As I waited for her at the Jet Port in Portland, I clutched a small bunch of wildflowers that I had cut in Ben's backyard that morning, held together with a twist from a box of Baggies. I knew Tina would get a kick out of my handcrafted bouquet. Then there she was, smiling and waving like a kid coming home from camp. Her skin was smooth as a silk tie. As the other passengers slipped past us, we stood there locked together, our hands roaming over each other's body—and not very discreetly.

On the way to Boothbay Harbor, Tina filled me in on some things that somehow hadn't nudged their way into our almost daily phone calls, long as they were. (Thank God for seven cents a minute!) The Bath school system had offered her a job that was a bit more challenging and better paid than Boothbay, but half an hour farther away. She was wrestling with which one to accept. She brought me up-to-date on the bar where I used to work (recently sold and rechristened Margarita Village) and on a few of my friends from the group of literary malcontents I had hung out with. The youngest of the group, Curtis Bedloe, a.k.a. Curt Bedlam, who could quote almost all of T. S. Eliot, had written a screenplay that one of the stars of *ER* had optioned. Now he was $25,000 richer and the toast of the group. Another, Geoff Beerman, had just had a poem published in the *New Yorker* but had fallen off a wharf and was now in traction.

On the way home we stopped at the Sea Basket, a small seafood diner just outside of Wiscasset. We had other things on our mind, but this would be Tina's first lobster roll in three months. When our order finally arrived, we gobbled it down, then jumped in the car and sped on to Boothbay Harbor.

The next morning we met Ben for coffee before setting out with him to look for a house to rent. Ben had lined up Millie Merton, Boothbay's best real estate agent, a short, intensely energetic woman in her late sixties who spoke in the staccato bursts of a flight controller. As we all piled into Millie's immense SUV, it was obvious that a big part of her agenda that day was Ben. She sat him up front next to her, and every remark she made was addressed primarily to him. Millie, we learned quickly, was a widow, and it was obvious that Ben had been in her crosshairs for quite some time. Occasionally, Ben would turn back to us with a simple smile and shrug, conveying both his affection for and his exasperation with Millie.

Like any smart real estate person, Millie showed us the best house last. First we looked at a quartet of sad, dark houses, all larger than mine, but aside from being in our price range, there was nothing good about them. Then Millie took us to Southport Island, connected by a swing bridge to Boothbay. She pulled into the driveway of a white Cape with green shutters that sat on a small cove and had a flagstone deck in back canopied by a latticed grape arbor. Upstairs there were two sunny bedrooms and another on the first floor that could serve as a study for the two of us. The kitchen had a butcher-block island, and all the appliances seemed to be new. This was the house. We knew it without saying a word to each other. The monthly rent, however, was a good eight hundred beyond what we could afford. I started to tell Millie that we loved it but couldn't swing the rent, when Ben draped an arm around my neck and walked me outside.

"This is the place for you and Tina."

"I know it, but it's beyond our budget."

"I sensed that, but I have an idea."

"I write and tend bar, Ben. I'm not cut out for robbing banks."

"This is both legal and very dull, but it pays enough for you to manage this place. Also, it won't take too much time each week. You'll still have plenty of time for your writing."

Ben went on to tell me that he needed help putting together a mailing list for a newsletter he was thinking of starting. Then he'd need someone to help him write it. The hourly pay was much more than I was making at the Rusty Scupper. I didn't know what to say, so I just hugged him. Did Ben really need my help? Probably not. Did he have to pay me so generously? Certainly not. But that was Ben.

That night we went to Ben's house for dinner. He quickly enlisted us as kitchen help. Tina chopped the cabbage, carrots, and green peppers for Ben's incredible coleslaw, and I was assigned to the mandoline to slice potatoes for *pommes frites*. The main course of this quintessential Maine dinner rested not so quietly on a table by the stove, where the pot was beginning to steam: three one-and-a-half-pound lobsters Ben had pulled from his traps an hour before. He had two bottles of Sancerre in a big ice bucket on the counter, and before too long we'd finished the first one.

"Have you ever noticed that cold white wine tastes even better when you pour it from a bottle that's been in an ice bucket?" asked Ben as he held the contents of his glass up to the light. "The sound of the ice when you take the bottle out makes all the difference. And don't forget the curtain of ice perspiration on the bucket. Just looking at it can almost quench my thirst."

This led to a toast to ice buckets, to friendship, then finally, a toast to Ben from me and Tina.

"How come you didn't invite Millie tonight?" Tina asked Ben, winking at me.

"Millie's a good woman, Tina. She's already buried two husbands, and from what I hear they both had smiles on their faces as they rested in their coffins. Benjamin Mortimer Chambers appreciates the Millie Mertons of this world, but he knows that's best appreciated from a distance."

After another toast, this time to Millie Merton, Ben put the lobsters into the pot.

When they were ready, we cracked the shells in the sink to let the water run out and sat down to consume them. This spurred Ben to give Tina a short course on lobstering: where to set the traps, how often to check them, what bait to use, and what was the minimum size lobster you could keep. Then he shifted to the osprey nest we'd see from the terrace of our house when we moved in.

"Ben, is there anything you don't know?" asked Tina, leaning across the table to kiss him on the cheek.

"Well, finding someone as lovely as you, that's eluded me so far."

"Did you ever fall for anyone? I mean really fall."

"Once. In California, many years ago. You remind me of her."

Then Ben opened a small bottle of golden Château d'Yquem, which he poured into chilled tumblers.

"Steve has told me that you're also a writer."

"Past tense, Tina. I used to write. That was a long time ago. Now I'm just a reader. And one of the writers I enjoy reading is Stevie here. Someday you're going to be real proud of him."

At that moment I couldn't have been happier if I'd had a number one *New York Times* bestseller; this was as good as it got.

Five

My weekend with Tina slipped away with the speed of a seal slipping into the water. Tomorrow morning she'd be flying back to Key West for what I hoped was the last time. Now that we had a terrific house to rent, and Tina could pick and choose her next teaching job, the time was fast approaching for us to move in together. Even my dog, Chester, liked the idea. Whenever Tina was around, he quickly stopped following me and hung around her like a long-lost kennel buddy.

On this last night together I decided we should try a restaurant in Damariscotta, where Tina could have one more lobster. She was a lobster junkie, ready to have it every day for lunch or dinner, or both. I like lobster well enough, but a little goes a long way with me; I find it too rich, and too much work to eat. Wrapping pasta around a fork is enough food exercise from my perspective.

Before heading out we sat in my tiny living room and toasted our future with a tasty Pinot Grigio I had found at a local store. Would I miss my cozy little shack? I wondered. I couldn't wait to move in with Tina.

Chester was lying on the floor, biting the leg of my desk, his hind legs splayed out behind him, like a swimmer getting ready to do the breast-stroke. "He's going to gnaw this house down to a nub unless you get him something else to chew on," said Tina.

"He'll have a bigger house to work on soon. This place stops serving at nine, so we better get cracking."

As soon as I started to back out of the driveway, we heard an awful grinding sound from the rear of the car: I knew it was the transmission. For weeks I had been nursing the car along, drowning it in sealer and fluid, but my triage method had finally failed. I could now see where the money I had been saving for a new sound system was destined to go.

We went back inside, and I called Ben.

"My old clunker has decided it needs a little R&R in Minichiello's garage. I have to take Tina to the airport tomorrow morning. Could I borrow your car to take her there?"

"Sure thing," was his response.

The next morning, before I could walk over to Ben's house, he was at the front door waiting to drive us to the airport and wearing a chauffeur's cap he must have borrowed from Boothbay Harbor Limo, which consists of three beat-up station wagons. He was all smiles and radiated energy.

As we inched our way across the bridge leading into Wiscasset, then north through Bath and Brunswick to Portland, we didn't talk much. Tina and I held hands. I was already missing her. As we approached the airport, Ben broke the silence. "I've been thinking, Stevie, about the new pages you gave me from your novel. I'm beginning to like the main character. I don't know exactly why, but he seems much more sympathetic."

"You know why, don't you? I'm changing him in the ways you suggested," I said, smiling broadly.

"Whatever you're doing, it's working."

"I agree," said Tina, thumbs up.

As we entered the road to the airport, Ben glanced back at me. "I've also been thinking about your title. *The Pulse of Time* is a little stiff. I think if you changed it to *Time's Pulse*, it might flow better."

It was almost a throwaway line, but he was dead right. At one stroke my novel took on a new weight.

"Time's Pulse," I repeated. "I like it. No, I love it. It makes all the differ-ence."

At the airport Tina and I jumped out of the car. As soon as we'd untan-gled ourselves from each other and whispered, "I love you," I returned to Ben, my chauffeur, my critic, my friend.

"Here's my Portland agenda," he said. "First, a whirl around the museum to look at the Whistlers, then to the Old Port for lunch and browsing the shops. Sound good so far?"

"Couldn't be better."

When it came time for lunch, we headed to a small former warehouse with a severe brick exterior and wonderful food. After we ordered, I said to Ben I hoped I'd have as much energy as he did now when I reached his age.

"I'll bet on it. Actually, it's funny business being in the seven-and-seven part of life."

"The what?"

Ben laughed. "That means I wake up at least seven times a night to take a leak and take seven pills in the morning. But who's complaining?"

When we got our drinks, I raised my Heineken to Ben. "To no com-plaints!"

"About anything?"

"Right." I was still feeling exuberant about Ben's reaction to my new pages and the gift of the new title, but I didn't want to turn the lunch into a seminar. I looked around the restaurant and then back to Ben. "You grew up in New England, didn't you?"

"Yes, indeed, but not around here. I grew up in Massachusetts, Haver-hill. It's a working-class town near Boston. My father and mother had a gro-cery. The four of us lived above it."

"Four?"

"I had a brother, Tom, two years younger. He was a great guy."

"But you managed to tear yourself away?"

"Well, yes, like Marco Polo, I was anxious to get going. But I went back to visit often. I loved them, you see—a sentiment not necessarily standard issue."

"And your brother. Where did he wind up?"

Ben didn't say a word for what seemed like an eternity.

"Tom died in a car accident when he was just thirty-four."

"Oh, I'm so sorry," I blurted out.

"You didn't know about it, Stevie, no need to apologize. I don't mind talking about him. In fact, I almost like it. It sort of brings him back. I like to think of us as kids, racing our bikes, playing ball, climbing trees, pulling pranks on our neighbors and friends. I had a lot of friends, but Tom was always my best pal."

"It must have been tough."

"It was awful, but . . . it's a long time ago now. My parents, bless their hearts, finally managed to accept it. So have I."

We headed home and were planning to meet several hours later at the bar. The place was packed for the finals of the Cuckholds Light Dart Tournament. A month after I started working at the place, I'd started it, with six teams of four people to a team. Ben was appointed by unanimous vote the league commissioner and chief referee. That night the top two teams, the Empty Pot and the Sea Urchins, were competing for a gold-plated trophy and a free dinner. Wearing their satin team bomber jackets, the teams were primed for the final competition. The Empty Pots were made up of four young lobstermen, while the Sea Urchins fielded a team that consisted of a dental assistant, two firemen, and a CPA.

Ben had called about an hour before I left home to say his cold was still bothering him. He didn't sound himself, so I told him I'd drop by after I closed the bar. The competition that night was spirited, and the winner wasn't decided until a little after eleven, with the Sea Urchins winning by fourteen points. I was able to close the place a little before one, then headed out for Ben's.

"You don't look so good, Ben."

He was lying on the couch, propped up by a couple of pillows, a green blanket pulled up to his neck, though the room was as warm as a greenhouse.

"A writer can do better than that, Stevie boy. How do I really look?"

"Well . . . you look like shit."

"For a guy my age, looking like shit isn't really that bad," Ben answered, then coughed, a deep, rumbling sound, like a heavy sack tumbling down a flight of stairs.

"You should see a doctor."

"It's just the flu. Vitamin C, echinacea, ginger ale—that's the recipe for me. I'll be back to form by tomorrow. In fact, how about going out with me to check some pots?"

"Sure."

"Stevie, do me a favor and get your ass off my trunk. You'll cave it in. Sit over there in the wing chair. The one by the fireplace."

"Hey, is this one of the famous manuscript trunks?"

"It is."

I went into the kitchen to get a glass of water, and when I returned to the living room, Ben was asleep. I straightened his blanket and turned off the lights except for one in the kitchen. My hand was on the front door when I stopped to look back. Aside from the sound of Ben snoring, the house was quiet. To this day I don't know why I did it, but I went over to the trunk and opened it. Sure enough, it was filled to the top with manuscripts. I took one out and held it up to the dim light: the title page read *Juno's Dance*. Ben had told me more than once that one day he would let me read his stuff. Why not now? I'd return the next day and put it back when he wasn't looking. It was just innocent curiosity that drove me—wasn't it?

I didn't start reading the book until almost two. The date on the title page was November 1964. The title didn't refer to ballet or any kind of formal dancing, but to a man named Tony Juno, who came from a family of high steelworkers. In his late twenties Tony had a particular way of walking on the steel beams that were suspended tens of stories above the ground— that was Juno's Dance. I knew nothing about high steelworkers, but before I was ten pages into the novel, I was hooked. I cared about the characters who, to a man, were sympathetic and involving. I wanted them to succeed. The narrative, also a wonder, took me from crisis to crisis with the pace of a bobsled hurling down an icy chute. Every twist and turn was a surprise. When I finished, I just sat in the chair, the book's almost four hundred pages resting comfortably on my lap like a large cat. Ben hadn't been kidding. He was a masterful storyteller. The writing was simple in the best sense: clear, direct, and unfussy. I knew I had to tell him that I had read the book. I also knew that I had to persuade him to publish it. It was wrong to let a book of this power sit in a trunk. I didn't know how I was going to do it, but I had to make him understand that others had to share his gift.

Six

I had finished *Juno's Dance* a little after eight that morning. I was drained, but so excited that I wanted to go right over to Ben's house and talk to him about it. Today would be round one. I didn't fool myself that it would be easy to persuade him to let it be published. Ben knew what he wanted and didn't want, and he didn't flip-flop. The only thing I had going for me was that I was the only person in years, maybe decades—or ever—to have read a word of his. And I loved what I read. Wouldn't that give him a buzz? Weaken his resolve? Just a bit?

I glanced down at the novel resting on my lap. What about the other manuscripts? Were they as good as this one? I had a hunch the answer was yes.

I phoned Ben to tell him I was coming over, but I got his machine: "This is Ben. I can't return your call unless you leave your name. That's the way it works. Hope to talk to you soon. And remember what La Rochefoucauld said: 'Old men love to give good advice to console themselves for not being able to set bad examples.'" The message was a good sign. Ben must be up and about and feeling better.

To kill time while I waited for him to come home, I ran some errands that I'd put off for as long as I could: the Laundromat, dry cleaning, the supermarket. About a half hour later I stopped at Ben's. When I rang the bell, there was no answer. The front door was locked, so I went around to the back and tried the kitchen door. "Ben, are you home?" I called as I stepped in. In the deep silence of the house I began to feel uneasy.

I headed to the living room, and there I saw him, asleep on the sofa, just as I had left him. "Hey, Mr. Chambers, didn't you hear me? It's late. It's time to get up."

I reached over to shake him, and as soon as I did, I knew something was awfully wrong: I could feel a chill through his shirt. His face was cold. In shock I checked his pulse, though I knew there was no point. Ben must have died in his sleep. I felt faint, as if I had taken a hard body blow, and collapsed into a chair next to the sofa. Tears filled my eyes. I leaned over and took his hand in mine. How was I going to get along without him? No critiques of my writing. No company at the bar. No warm, generous friendship. "How could you do this to me?" I said out loud, my voice trembling.

I had to do something. Call an ambulance? No, there was no need for that. The police? I leaned over Ben and gave him a kiss on his forehead, then pulled the blanket over him.

I started to make the call, then stopped. The manuscripts in the trunks: what would happen to them? The police, God knows, might seal up the place for weeks until Ben's estate was settled. Would they take an inventory? Probably not, in a case like this, and even if they did, would they know what the bundles of pages were? Someone might toss the trunks out. I couldn't let that happen. Though I had read only one manuscript, I sensed they were all good and, at the least, important to the memory of Ben. By God, I was going to see that they were published.

I brought my car around to the back of the house and, armful by armful, removed the manuscripts from the two trunks and put them in my car, throwing the empty trunks in after them. After depositing the load at my place, I went back to Ben's and called the cops.

Seven

The next day I got together with a few of Ben's close friends at the Rusty Scupper, and we planned his memorial service for the following week. Ben had been very clear in what he wanted. What took time were the two or three, and in one case four, drinks we each had. During the day I talked for over an hour with Tina, who tried valiantly to minister to my spiritual flu.

That night I dreamed that Ben and I were flying a kite off the pedestrian bridge that crossed the lower part of the harbor. A wind suddenly kicked up and whipped around us, flattening our shirts to our bodies. It became so loud that I couldn't make out what Ben was shouting at me. He was screaming, and all I could hear was the wail of the wind. Just like that, it stopped, and when I looked around, Ben was gone. Then I heard his voice: it was faint, coming from a distance. Finally, I looked up and saw him, holding on to the kite and waving at me. He was smiling. I tried with all my strength to pull him down, but he kept drifting farther and farther up into the sky. Then he was gone.

The following morning I packed my suitcase and, together with Chester, got into my car, back from the garage with a rebuilt transmission. I'd placed one of Ben's manuscripts on top of a pair of jeans and some shirts. This one was titled *The Judgment*. I stopped at the Scupper and dropped off a note that said I had to go away for a few days. Didn't say where, didn't say why. Where do you go when you feel like a lost kid? To your folks, of course.

It was late afternoon when I got to my parents' place in Elmira. They weren't there, but my trusty house key still worked. I put Chester out in the backyard and went up to my old room, which looked exactly the same. My mother had painted it since my college days, though she kept the same color. The top of my bureau was covered with trophies won in high school and camp (mostly for swimming, a few for badminton), and my tape collection (all of Dylan, most of the Dead) still lined the top shelves of the bookcase. The place even smelled the same, a combination of curtains and bedspread laundered into submission and a floor that had absorbed more wax than a tango salon. Proust had his madeleine, I had my old room.

I plopped down on my bed and started to read *The Judgment*. Once again, I was immediately hooked, this time on the story of two brothers, Tim and Evan Boland, heirs to a huge international construction business, and the woman who came between them. I was a hundred pages into the manuscript when the door flew open and Fanny and Phil King, a.k.a. my folks, charged in. They were still wearing their golfing outfits, and before I could raise myself up, I was engulfed by a series of kisses, hugs, hair tousles, and shoulder pats.

"Seven cents a minute for long distance these days, Stevie. How come no call?"

"Relax, Phil, the important thing is that he's here," said my mother. "There's nothing wrong, is there?"

"No, Mom. Everything is fine."

"Let's get to the important issue. What would you like for dinner tonight? You have a choice of brisket, southern fried chicken, or pasta with peppers."

"Why don't *I* ever get a choice, Fanny?"

"Because you're sweet, but your son is adorable."

My dad and I laughed. We had heard that remark many times. Where else could a thirty-two-year-old unsuccessful writer go where he'd be smothered with kisses and called adorable?

.   .   .

That night I had two portions of the brisket, two of the mashed potatoes, and one of the broccoli au gratin, which I washed down with three glasses of a Finger Lake merlot my father had been given by an old customer.

"There's something wrong with the broccoli?" my mother asked.

"No, Mom, it's great. I've eaten enough for three condemned men. Give me a break."

"That's not very funny, Stevie."

"I think it's funny, Fan," said my father, leaning over to give me a pat on the back.

"Well, I don't."

That ended that discussion. My brother, Larry, and I had always thought of our parents as judges, with my mother sitting on the high court. My father, who was an excellent pool player (we'd had a table in the basement since I was a little kid), invited me to a game of straight pool. I begged off, since the combination of the drive and the mega-meal made everything but sleep a remote possibility. Chester was waiting for me in my room, grinding away at a huge bone my mother had given him. I picked up Ben's manuscript, but at that point nothing could have held my attention. I turned off the light and went blissfully to sleep accompanied by the sounds of Chester patiently tunneling into the wonderful world of marrow.

The next morning at breakfast the interrogation began, alternating between my mother and father across the breakfast table.

"So how's everything going with you and Tina? And when are you going to get serious with her?"

"When are you going to finish the book?"

"You know, Stevie, you can live a lot cheaper here and still be able to write. I'll fix up the guest room into a study for you."

"Working even part-time at one of our stores would be easier and pay more than being a bartender. Give it a thought."

"What do you eat there in Maine? You look skinny."

"Your car looks like something the Okies used to get to California. Why don't you take your mother's car back with you? I'm getting her a new one in a few weeks."

"You know there's nothing wrong with accepting a little cash from people who love you. What's wrong with living better? There are a lot of people in India who wish they had parents like us."

Since I'd been in high school, Fanny and Phil had been frustrated that I didn't match their "give" with enough "take." I was determined to make it without their help, so I turned down the car and the money, for at least the second time.

My dad wanted me to play golf with him. Though I liked the game and hadn't played in over a year, I begged off to work on my book. He didn't argue with me and left after I promised to play pool with him that evening. After I took Chester for a walk, I holed up in my room and continued reading Ben's manuscript. The book got better the more I read. The characters grew before my eyes, and the plot became more and more intricate without ever seeming to be manipulated. The ending was a surprise, and then there was a coda that topped it. It was late afternoon when I finally finished. Carefully, I put the manuscript back in my bag and went for a long walk. I couldn't get the book out of my mind. It was amazing how Ben could control his material without the reader (me) ever feeling that what happened was anything but inevitable. I couldn't wait to get back to Boothbay Harbor to start reading the rest of Ben's work.

Before dinner my dad and I went down to the basement for our pool match. My dad was good, always better than me, but I could still give him a game. He took the first one easily, but then my stroke came back, and we played close enough for me to nearly win one game. We took a break for beer, and it was then, after he cleared his throat twice, that I realized he was about to give me "the speech." This had been carefully worked out with my mother, who had without a doubt critiqued and honed the message. Though most of the words were also probably hers, I'm sure she felt he was the proper messenger.

He sat down on an old armchair that had once been in the living room, took a swallow of beer, and began.

"Steve, I'm about to go over some familiar territory, but please hear me out. You know that your mom and I love you a lot. Of course, that goes for Larry, too, but our love for you is different. I guess that's because you're our youngest. Aside from the time you dropped my watch in the lake, or that time when you backed my car into that landfill near the club, you've never given us a minute of aggravation. Now, we don't pretend to understand the arts. We're both from families where the only 'Art' we knew was your mother's uncle on her father's side, Art Shamstock. He died before you were born. The only writer we've ever known is you. We think what you're doing is terrific. And from the little bit that we've read of your work, we know that you have talent. Real talent." He paused for another swallow of beer. "We don't have to tell you, but you're in a very difficult profession. We know you'll make it, though it won't be easy. So here's our idea. You keep writing. That's a must. But instead of bartending, you move back here and join Larry in running the business. We'll work it so you'll have plenty of time to write. I'm sure Tina would love living here. She seemed to like the place the last time she came here with you. I've worked this out with Larry—he's all for it. If things work out, and I'm sure they will, you and Larry will someday be equal partners. We have six stores now, and they're all doing well. With you and Larry working together we'll soon have ten, maybe even a dozen. Now, you're probably thinking, how can I continue to write while working in the stores? That's a valid question. I did a little research into this. Did you know that the poet Wallace Stevens worked all his life for an insurance company in Hartford? And the writer Louis Auchincloss—I don't know if that's how he pronounces it—has written a ton of books while still working as a lawyer. And I'm sure there are lots of others. What do you think?"

I rested my cue on the table and went over and gave my dad a hug. Then I told him I'd think about it, knowing even before I spoke the words that I would never take him up on his offer. One way or the other, I had to make it on my own.

Eight

Ben's memorial service was held three days later. Neither the police nor anyone else who knew Ben could locate any relatives. A few of us got together and planned the service. Though we didn't know Ben's religion, if he even had one, we decided to hold the service at St. Andrew's, mainly because it had a great view of the harbor. The place was full. It wouldn't have surprised me if half the crowd owed Ben money. He was the easiest touch in town; if you were short, you went to Ben.

There were four of us who spoke. Leon Fisk had been a lobsterman for over forty years and had sold Ben his boat; Grace Neumann, who worked in the post office, was Ben's regular bridge partner; Arnie Mosely played golf with Ben and owned the liquor store in town; then there was me. The eulogies were warm and simple. What you got from all of them was that we had lost a guy who was special, a man who really would be missed.

Ben wanted to be cremated and have his ashes scattered at sea. He had told us this a number of times, so that's what we did. Ten of us got into Leon Fisk's boat, the *Nellie G,* and headed out to Damariscove Island, a string of other lobster boats behind us. Once we got to the lee side of the island, Leon Fisk cut the engine.

"Ben," said Leon as he held the small urn containing Ben's ashes, "you loved the sea, and I believe the sea loved you. You treated it, and all other things, with respect. I hope you know how much we cared for you, old buddy, and how damn much we're going to miss you." When Leon tipped the urn, a misty fog of ash caught on the breeze and carpeted the swells that softly rocked the boat.

On the way back in there wasn't much talk. We passed around a flask of Scotch until it was empty and looked back at the boat's wake as the island got smaller and smaller.

Later that afternoon I tried to write. I knew I wouldn't get a decent sentence done, but I didn't know what else to do. The four big stacks of Ben's manuscripts that I had taken from his place sat in my bedroom closet. I wanted to start reading them, but the time wasn't right. Why had I taken them out of his place, anyway? I thought I knew then, but now I wasn't sure. What I needed was more time to think. I was scheduled to work that night, but the thought of going into the Scupper and not seeing Ben was hard to handle. Though I had known him for less than two years, he had become an important part of my life. I had never had a close friendship with someone that much older. Suddenly, I felt a whole lot younger, and very lost. When I spoke to Tina the day Ben died, she said something that kept reverberating in my head.

"Steve, Ben was not a father to you, but he was more than a friend. He was what you'd like to be, and what someday maybe you will be. People like Ben step into our lives once, if we're lucky."

Then I heard the doorbell ring. Had it been ringing for a while? I had been somewhere else, far away.

In the doorway stood a tall man in a gray suit holding a battered briefcase. He was in his sixties, maybe older, with short gray hair cut military fashion.

"Steven King?"

"Yes."

"I'm Hamilton Cray, a lawyer, from Wiscasset. I was Ben Chambers's attorney. May I come in?"

Hamilton Cray sat down on my new wicker rocker, the one decent piece of furniture in the place. He sat in it stiffly, his feet fixed solidly to the floor. I don't think the chair would have rocked if we had been hit with a quake that was 7.8 on the Richter scale.

"Do you have any idea why I'm here?" he finally asked me.

"No, Mr. Gray."

"It's Cray."

"Sorry."

"It's about Ben's will."

I immediately pictured Ben's boat. He knew how much I liked it. God bless him, I thought: he left me *Boswell*.

"About four months ago he came into my office and asked me to change his will."

I nodded, still visualizing the boat, Ben and me in the wheelhouse. I'll take good care of it, Ben. Don't worry, I'll treat it just the way you did.

"He didn't have a large estate: the house, which had no mortgage; an IRA worth a little over . . ."

Cray droned on while I saw myself steering *Boswell* out past Fisherman's Island, heading to Monhegan for the day.

"Did you hear what I said, Mr. King?"

"What?"

"I said he left everything to you."

"Everything?"

"That's right. Estimating the sale price of his house and its furnishings, the boat, and his IRA, I'd say that the estate's value will be in the neighborhood of three hundred thousand dollars."

"That's incredible."

"He cared for you a lot, Mr. King. I guess he looked on you as the son he never had. He also named you his literary executor. Do you know the work he's referring to?"

"He told me that years ago he wrote a bit. Poetry, I think. I imagine I'll turn some stuff up when I make an inventory of his things."

Why was I lying to Cray? Ben left me everything; the novels were now mine.

"You'll get a copy of the will after probate, but I wanted to read this section to you." Cray dug around in his briefcase. It was big enough to hold a couple of phone books from major cities. " 'In respect to my literary output over the years, I direct my heir, Mr. Steven King, to handle it in the manner that I've indicated to him in numerous conversations. This work has a special importance to me, and I value it as the most important thing I am entrusting to him. I have full confidence that he will treat this work in a manner I would approve of.' "

"That's it?"

"What do you mean?"

"That's all he says about the . . . poetry?"

"Just what I read to you, Mr. King. The rest of the will is pretty straight-forward."

After Cray left, I went and took a beer out of the fridge. I never drink in the afternoon, but today was different. Very different. I looked at the pile of manuscripts in the closet. "An artist should only write for himself." That's what he would always say. "The joy comes from writing, not publishing." He used to say that, too. You don't want me to try and publish this stuff: is that what you're trying to say to me, Ben?

I went over to the stack and took one off the top: *Thunder in the Valley*, about a pair of ranch hands in California during the Depression. It was the same length as *Juno's Dance*. I called the Rusty Scupper and told them I wasn't feeling well and wouldn't be working that night. Then I sat down and began to read.

Nine

By the weekend I had read four more of Ben's novels. I'm not an expert on what the publishing business calls commercial fiction, but I knew these were winners. They were the kind of books that immediately jump onto the best-seller list. They depend for their success mostly on plot. Ben's books were much more than that. My own tastes ran toward serious literary work. The kind of writing that concerns itself with character, moral questions, the paths that lives unexpectedly take. The thing about Ben's writing was that he drew on both impulses to take the reader into worlds I had never dreamed of, with people I cared for instantly. I don't know how he pulled it off.

He was also a great researcher. One book, *The Wind Demon*, taught you enough about piloting a supertanker to make you feel you could almost do it. Another, *Beyond the Night Sky*, was about exploring for sapphires in Indonesia. I learned not just about the geology and mining of precious stones but about how the international trade in gems worked. I guess the best way you could sum up Ben's work was that with each book you took a journey that you didn't want to end. I kept wishing that he had let me read his work before he died. I would have given anything to discuss the books with him. How did the process work for him? Where did his ideas come from? Though the settings and characters were completely different from book to book, they shared a common thread: they dealt with people who were totally believable. People you wanted to know. People you cared for.

I decided I had to stop working at the Rusty Scupper. The owners were understanding and didn't even ask me to stay on until they found someone else. This left me more time to decide what to do with Ben's work and to start a systematic inventory of his house to see if he had left more precise instructions on what to do with the manuscripts.

It was strange being in Ben's house without him. He had an orderly mind, and everything was where you'd expect to find it.

I looked first in his desk. Ben wasn't a neat freak, but all the clerical aspects of his life (bills, statements, documents) were well organized. It almost felt as if Ben knew he'd be leaving and made an effort to tie up all the loose ends in his life. I found no diary or journal, nothing to amplify the few sentences in the will dealing with his writing. The rest of the house didn't reveal anything, either.

Tina came up from Key West a few days later. The money I was to receive from Ben's estate would be enough to buy a nice house. I told Tina I wasn't sure I wanted to stay in Boothbay Harbor, so it didn't make sense to buy a place now.

The following night we went to the Rusty Scupper for dinner. Claire and Jake, the owners, sent over a bottle of champagne on the house. The restaurant was quiet, and Tina looked beautiful in the soft light from the candles on the table. Her short haircut perfectly framed the oval of her face, and her dove-gray eyes caught the flicker of the candles and seemed to sparkle at me. I knew I was very lucky to have her. I wanted more than anything to make her happy. As we raised our glasses to the owners, I kept my eyes on Tina. We had skirted around the idea of marriage, but as I watched her now, I knew I wanted to marry her and spend the rest of my life with her. I could think of nothing else.

Looking back now, I realize that I was making a decision on what to do with Ben's books without even acknowledging it to myself, or to Tina. I didn't tell her about the manuscripts—not a word. Normally, there isn't anything I would keep from her. Here was the woman I loved, and I wasn't sharing something this important with her. The day before Tina arrived, I had taken all of Ben's work and hidden it in the basement.

After three days in Maine, Tina had to fly back to Key West, where she was still teaching. After driving her to the airport in Portland, I drove directly to Boothbay Harbor. I opened the back door so Chester could have a run in the yard, where he loved to chase birds, though he never caught them. Then I sat down at my computer and stared at the screen for a few moments before I started to write.

I knew that these words would change my life. How much, and how far they would take me, I had no idea.

I blinked at the utter strangeness of what I had written. With a flick of my fingers I had made a Faustian bargain almost without thinking about it, crossing a moral line I had never expected to confront. My chest tightened and I felt light-headed as I stared at the screen. I had started down a road with no signs, no directions, and no map, heading toward a great unknown. I had never been so unnerved in my life.

JUNO'S DANCE

A NOVEL BY STEVEN KONIGSBERG

Ten

I started turning off the phone, stopped checking my e-mails, and began re-typing Ben's manuscript. I would get to my computer at six in the morning and, with only a few short breaks, stop at eight that night. At first I started to make some stylistic changes, but then I realized that if I kept that up, it would take me much longer to finish. And Ben's prose was so tight and per-fectly pitched that there wasn't anything I could do to improve it, really. I made a few changes, updating references, but there weren't many. I existed on spaghetti and English muffins, Chester on his usual menu of Alpo and Kibbles. I think he enjoyed the process because he likes to have me around. He curled up under my desk and, aside from an occasional romp in the backyard, dozed on and off the entire time I was at work.

A week later I was finished. I took a day off before proofing the manu-script and piloted Ben's boat up to Damariscotta, where I ordered a burger and two beers at a café on the river. I drank only one of the beers. The other just sat across from me, cold and untouched. It was for Ben: it helped me think of all the good times we'd had together.

I reread the book slowly. I had read it once, then again as I retyped it; it was still terrific the third time. Before I took it to the post office, I called Stu-art. His secretary put me on hold, and I held the phone like a statue for a good twenty minutes. Halfway through, his secretary broke in to confide that Stuart was talking with "a very important author." Of course—Stuart's only kind of author. As I waited, I thumbed through the *Boothbay Register*, calculating that reaching Stuart was like trying to get through to a credit card company; it was better to hold on than to hang up and start again.

"Steve!" said Stuart at last, shouting into the phone. "What a deal I just made for one of my new clients. Listen to this: a three-book deal for a half million a book, with a bonus of fifty grand for every week he's on the *Times* bestseller list, with no cap and an additional bonus of two hundred and fifty thousand for number one." He giggled as he mentally added up his com-mission, then remembered he was on the phone with me. "Hey, my favorite cousin, what's up with you?"

"I've got news. I finished my book. I'm sending it to you today."

"Oh, that's great," he said unconvincingly. "I thought you told me you had a long way to go."

"You must have misheard me. I was actually at the clubhouse turn when we had dinner that night. Listen, Stuart, I'm really excited about this book. It's a real departure for me. More plot, more character, and a lot of action. And I mean action with a capital *A*."

"Is this really and truly my cousin talking? I swear it doesn't sound like him. I was expecting another . . . well, literary novel from you."

"Well, get ready for a change. Big-time. You're really going to like this one," I said, laughing with pleasure. "That's a promise."

"I'm liking it already. Ship it down."

"Now, I've just got to ask you one favor. I know you've got a couple of readers around your place, but I want you to read this first. Here's the deal. Just read the first ten pages, and if you're not hooked, well, then you can pass it on. Just promise me that."

"You've got me intrigued, Stevie, you really have. You know what I'm doing right now? I'm looking at my calendar for tomorrow and I'm cross-ing out a benefit I was going to. Tomorrow night I'll order in Chinese and curl up with the new Steven Konigsberg novel. I don't know why, but I sud-denly have a very good feeling about this."

While I waited the better part of a week for Stuart's call—reminding myself again and again that Stuart was a snail-paced reader and I would just have to give him time to inch his way through the novel—I began an inventory of exactly what I had inherited from Ben.

I pulled one of the trunks from its hiding place in the basement and lifted its lid, feeling as if I were releasing a genie into the atmosphere. Then I dragged out the other trunk, placed it next to the first one, and opened it. There was a magical aura to the process that plunged me into a vision of myself as a storybook king, reveling in my secret cache of gold and gems.

I stared at the dusty, yellowing onionskin manuscripts that I had crammed back into the trunks, and gingerly lifted one out. Then I couldn't stop. They had a smell that reminded me of clothes I had worn as a kid. I piled them on the floor according to category: nineteen novels, not counting *Juno's Dance*, which I had ripped into shreds and consigned to the town dump after I retyped it; what looked like detailed outlines of six more novels (had Ben been planning to return to writing someday despite his insistence that he was through with it?); enough short stories for at least two collections; six screenplays; and—this really surprised me—three children's stories.

As I was leafing through one of the screenplays—was there no end to Ben's talent?—Stuart finally called. He was beside himself, on the edge of hysteria. As soon as he shouted out my name, my heart began to pound.

"I have an announcement to make: we have a genius in the family," he shrieked. "*Juno's Dance* is fabulous, the best book I've read in years. I am stunned. I am in awe. You are the real deal, Mr. Konigsberg. Who knew you had a book like this up your sleeve?"

When he paused, I knew I was supposed to say something. I choked out a platitude, but he stormed on, ignoring me.

"Stevie, we're going to make a great team. I'm going to auction this baby. I'm putting together the list right now. I'll probably send it to ten publishers. A dozen years ago I would have gone to seventeen or eighteen houses, but the consolidations have killed them off. Only the top, really top people in each house will get it. We're copying it, and I'll make the calls and get the book out to everyone by early this afternoon."

Before I could say anything, Stuart raced on. "What I think is that you'd better start figuring out how to spend the money you're going to make. No more living on a bartender's salary. You're going to be a very rich man. Take my word for it."

Eleven

As I waited for the next call from Stuart, I kept reading Ben's novels, one every day and a half; and unless I had totally lost my critical faculty, I thought that each and every one was terrific. Two of them had the same hero, Chase Newland, a former ATF agent who runs a small airfield in the Upper Peninsula in Michigan and gets involved in helping people who literally fly into his life. This was a character I could perhaps continue with. Ben's ability, of course, lifted the books out of the genre category. The language, the complexity of the characters, the richness of the setting, all appealed greatly to me. I had an idea for the plot of another Chase Newland book and even wrote down notes for it.

A couple of nights later I had a terrible nightmare, in which I found myself suddenly standing in the middle of my bedroom, with a carpet of thick smoke swirling around my feet. The door leading to the living room was on fire. I went toward the door instead of trying to get out through the window, drawn to the burning door as though it were a huge magnet. Ben's manuscripts were in there! I had to get them, so I kicked in the door. The room was ablaze; the roar of the fire was almost deafening. Through the flames I saw the manuscripts, suspended from the ceiling by a wire; each one was consumed by fire, crackling like logs in a fireplace. When I reached for them, I was assaulted by the rancid smell of hair burning on my arms.

As I grabbed one after the other, the pages exploded into red-hot confetti, all the books reduced to fiery dust.

When I woke up, Chester was at the foot of the bed howling. My pajamas were wringing wet, plastered to my body. I got up to calm Chester, whose barking had awakened me. Good dog, I said to him over and over. Good dog. There wasn't a prayer I would get back to sleep, so I got up, dressed, and took Chester for a walk. Though the sun wouldn't come up for another hour, the harbor was active with lobster boats loading traps and bait. By the time we got back to the house, I knew what I had to do.

I gathered all of Ben's manuscripts and carefully packed them in boxes I had picked up at the supermarket. I drove them to Portland and had Xeroxes made of all of them at a copy shop, which cost me almost eight hundred dollars. On the way back to Boothbay Harbor, I stopped at Big Al's Storage Locker. It was a typical setup where you could rent a small room and have your own key to get in anytime you felt like it. I deposited all the copies into this space: sixty-five dollars for the first month and a hundred-dollar security deposit. Then I drove into town and went to Bay State Bank, where I rented the five largest safe-deposit boxes they had. The assistant manager gave me a funny look; I knew he was dying to ask me what was in the boxes I lugged down to the vault. I still had eight manuscripts I couldn't fit in, so I drove over to the Key Bank in Wiscasset and rented two safe-deposit boxes there.

Later that afternoon when I took Ben's boat out again, there was a slight breeze from the southwest, and the sea was almost flat. I headed for the Townsend Gut and into Gooseneck Passage, then pointed the bow toward the Cuckhold Light. I was now in the Sheepscot River. I set the throttle to six knots and slowly made my way up the river. I couldn't shake myself free of the nightmare I'd had last night. It was clear that I was frightened of losing the manuscripts and with them my brand-new persona, still in the making. It shamed me that the first thing I did after the dream was to physically secure the manuscripts in flameproof vaults, as if this were the only important thing about them. What about the author? The real author–Ben. But after all, didn't the work belong to me? I could do anything I wanted with it: Ben had legally left everything to me. Then why didn't I simply tell Stuart that this was a collaborative effort, a novel by Steven Konigsberg and Ben Chambers? That wasn't exactly true, but it was damn sight better than claiming that the work was solely mine. I still had time to stop this whole thing: a phone call to Stuart would set things right.

The sun was low on the horizon when I got back to my place. One of Ben's novels sat on my desk, the only one I hadn't placed in a safe-deposit box. My plan was to just have one in the house at any given time. I picked up the phone to call Stuart and only tapped out 1-212 before I put down the receiver. I couldn't do it. I needed to be acknowledged as a writer, maybe even to become well known. I had begun to believe this was the only way I could do it. What I was doing was wrong–no argument there. But nothing was going to stop me now. I picked up the manuscript and began to read.

The call from Stuart came the next day. I had been out buying some groceries and saw that there were five messages on my answering machine. They were all from Stuart.

"Stevie, where the fuck are you? We've got to talk. This is very important. Amazingly important. Call me back ASAP."

The other four messages were all left within a period of forty minutes. I felt my heart pounding as I called Stuart back. There was no being put on hold this time. This time I got straight through to him.

"You sitting down?" he asked. Loudly.

I sat down. The receiver felt slick in my hand. I was sweating already.

"Are you there?"

"Yes," I answered in a small voice.

"This is fucking unbelievable. I set the auction date for next Monday. So what happens? This morning I got five preemptive bids. Each one a monster."

"Does preemptive bid mean what I think it does?"

"Stevie, these publishers are crazed to buy *Juno's Dance*. Crazed. I've been jogging between these panting motherfuckers all morning. I finally got the offer I want you to accept."

"What's that?"

"It's for two books. The bid is from Chancery Press. The man who made the offer is Dexter Parch. He's the publisher there, a truly great guy, a real dynamo. I've never heard him so excited. Want to know what he offered?"

"I guess so."

"Guess so? You're the coolest son of a bitch I've ever met. Well, here it is. They're offering a total of three point two for *Juno* and your next novel. They're not even asking for a fucking outline."

"Three point two?" I asked.

"That's million, shmuck. Three million two hundred thousand. My cousin Stevie is rich. And I haven't done badly, either. Who the fuck would have thought it? I love you, Stevie Konigsberg! Got to run now. There are some details I have to button down with Dexter Parch—small stuff. By the way, this offer is for U.S. and Canada only. We still have foreign and film rights to go. I wouldn't be surprised if we go over five or six mil on this before we're through. Now, go out and celebrate. I don't know what the fuck you can buy in that burg, but head out and buy something. A boat—whatever."

Twelve

Tina was the first person I called.

"I have some amazing news, sweetheart. Really incredible."

"What did you say? I can't hear you." She was on her cell phone, which was the only way I could reach her between class breaks. Her phone hissed with static like an angry cat. "I've got to get this thing recharged. Start again, honey."

I raised my voice from a shout to a yell. "I sold my novel. I just got off the phone with Stuart."

"Oh, my God!" she squealed. "That's fabulous! I knew you could do it, I always did. I'm so happy for you, darling. I want to hear all about it." Over the castanets of more static, I heard the pure excitement in her voice. I felt a sudden rush of love for her. I wanted her here with me, right now. I was still so stunned by Stuart's call that anything seemed possible. If I proposed to her now, she could come up over the weekend, and we could be married by a justice of the peace.

"I've got to go, darling, but I'm dying to know how you finished the book so fast. I thought you were just barely halfway through the last time I saw you."

"You're right," I said, scrambling, "but what would you say if I told you I wrote another book? After all, here I was with lots of time. I was stuck on the one I was writing, the one you saw. I had some problems I couldn't work out. So I began a new one, and just sailed along, almost like automatic writing. Everything about it felt right. I didn't tell you because I was afraid it wouldn't work out. I sent it to Stuart because I wanted a reaction. I didn't think he'd go for it so quickly, let alone sell it!"

"This is wonderful, Steve!"

"I love you, Tina."

"Me, too, but I'm losing you. I can barely hear you. Call me tonight."

I had just lied to the woman I wanted to marry. Where was all of this going to take me? Suddenly, I felt a pain, sharp as a knife, cut across my temples, an instant migraine.

A few hours later I was lying on my bed, my head throbbing, still playing back my conversation with Tina, when the phone rang. It was my parents, whose direct pipeline in the form of Stuart's mother, my Aunt Florence, had brought them as up-to-date on the sale as I was. Even so, they asked me to go through each detail and development, step by step. This was a brand-new experience for them, like climbing Annapurna. They kept laughing, and interrupting each other, and comparing it to winning the lottery. "How're you going to spend the money, Stevie?" my dad asked. "Buy a yacht like Stuart?"

After finally signing off with my folks I decided to call my old teacher and buddy at the Iowa Writers' Workshop, Quentin Bass. As I dialed, I was still wondering what and how much to say, but I got a lucky break. Quentin was not in. I left a short message about a book sale, without giving any details.

I needed some fresh air. Perhaps that would help my headache. I looked down and saw Chester, dozing on the floor next to the bed, so I snapped on his leash, and we headed out of the house. Chester would be the first beneficiary of the book sale. I would buy him a new collar and leash, the best Boothbay Harbor had to offer.

"Chester, my good buddy, we're both about to head into a new world," I said to him as we stepped out of the house. "Just keep your paws crossed that this whole thing pans out the way I know Ben meant it to."

He barked wildly, as if in affirmation.

Thirteen

Three days later I drove to the Portland Jet Port to fly down to New York, first-class, compliments of my new publisher, a first (first-class, that is) for me. Before heading out I took Chester to a kennel in East Boothbay where he had stayed once before when I went to Key West to see Tina. He gave me a lackadaisical lick good-bye, then quickly turned away and started to bark at the other boarders.

I had to buy a new suit for my trip. Armani, what else? I put it on my one and only credit card. I was close to being maxed out, but Stuart told me not to worry. My huge advance was divided into three equal installments: on my signing of the contract, hardcover publication, and paperback publication, which would be a year after the hardcover. Stuart explained to me that publishers liked to hang on to their cash as long as possible, so the contract probably wouldn't be executed for a couple of months. Standard practice, he said. Chancery had wanted to make the payment in quarters, but Stuart told me as proudly as if he had negotiated the Dayton Peace Accords that he wouldn't budge. To bridge the gap until I received the first part of my advance, he sent me a check for $10,000 by FedEx. It was equivalent to what I used to earn every five months at the bar!

At La Guardia Stuart hugged me as if we had been separated for twenty years, then led me outside where a limo, buffed to a mirror finish, purred quietly at the curb. As soon as we got in, Stuart reached over and pressed the switch to raise the glass partition that shut us off from the driver.

"Got to be careful who hears what you say in this town. I've had things wind up in the columns that I thought only the person having a drink with me was hearing. How're you feeling?"

"Good."

"Only good? Jesus, lighten up. You're rich and you'll soon be something else."

"What?"

"A famous author, that's what."

I played with the thought for a moment but found it so weird and improbable that I just sat there looking out the window, almost catatonic. Things were moving too quickly.

"You with me?"

I nodded and smiled, or tried to smile.

"Let me bring you up-to-date on the film sale. We've got at least four studios chomping at the bit to buy the book. I have CAA on the coast handling the sale. We've turned down two preemptive offers already because I feel there's more money out there. The auction will be the middle of next week. I think it'll be the sale of the year. Now, do you have any interest in writing the script? If you do, we can make it part of the deal."

I suddenly felt like I was struggling to keep my head above water in heavy surf.

This is what Ben would have wanted me to do, wasn't it? I was so desperate to come into my own as a writer that I could almost hear him say, "It's okay, Stevie. What does it matter whose name goes on the book? This is just going to help you get going with your own work." Stuart wouldn't have cared if I told him my collaborator was Ben, Pamela Anderson, or a space alien. Why didn't I do it? Once I said Ben was the coauthor, my big lie would become instantly manageable. I would still receive the money and the acclaim—all I had to do was tell Stuart. But I couldn't do it.

"Stevie, I need an answer. You want to do the script?"

"No, Stuart. I want to stick to writing novels."

What I should have said is that I wanted to stick to retyping novels.

"We can also push to get you an executive producer credit."

"Not interested. I just want to write."

"I was hoping you'd say that. But I had to touch base with you. Now, let me tell you about tonight. I'll pick you up at the Sherry at seven-thirty. That's where they booked you. A suite with a view of the park. Standard treatment for a soon-to-be-best-selling novelist. Then we'll go to Dexter Parch's loft, where there'll be ten for dinner. Parch and his wife, Vivian, and Axel Guderian, the German who heads up the group that owns Chancery Press. There'll be a few others from the house, marketing and publicity people probably, but Parch and Guderian are the key players."

"Do I have to do anything?"

"Cousin, just think of yourself as Elvis. They love you already. All you have to do is show up."

The hotel suite was bigger than Ben's house in Boothbay. The view across Central Park, with the Hudson River shining in the afternoon sun in the background, was incredible. I must have stayed at the window for a half hour, gazing out like someone who had just left Ellis Island. Immigrants now arrived at JFK, but you get the idea. I had been to New York maybe a half dozen times before, staying either with college friends or at the Y. I had little preparation for this. I walked around the rooms taking it all in: large-screen TV, tape player, DVD, fax, telephone with two extensions. The bathroom had a straw basket containing soaps, shampoos, even a sewing kit. I stripped and took a long, hot shower. Then I put on a terry-cloth robe, the fabric thick as a rug. Suddenly, I realized I was hungry. Room service! I ordered up a shrimp cocktail, a BLT, and two beers, one, of course, for Ben. Before I knew it the food arrived. I started to open my wallet to tip the waiter when I realized that my publisher was footing the bill, so I took a pen and added a thirty percent tip. The waiter seemed very pleased. After he left, I pulled a chair up to the window and started to eat. I could have looked out on the park forever.

After a trip later to the hotel gym, I went back to my suite and took a long, dreamless nap. That evening, as I dressed for the dinner party, I thought about the scene from *American Gigolo* where Richard Gere lays out a dozen shirts and ties and mixes and matches them to get just the right combination. I didn't have that problem because I had one shirt, one tie, and one suit. But after dressing I thought that the guy I saw in the mirror looked pretty good. Did he look like a soon-to-be-best-selling novelist? Maybe, maybe not. What he didn't look like was a bartender.

Fourteen

When the elevator doors opened on the loft belonging to Dexter Parch, the first thing I saw was a cluster of eager, beaming faces crowding toward me. Standing in the middle was a large, well-fed man with a shaven head, dressed in a dark pin-striped suit.

I cocked my hand at the group, as if I were a king greeting my subjects, and anxiously barked out a loud hello. Before I had to figure out what to do next, the well-fed man strode toward me.

"Steven, I'm Dexter Parch," he said, reaching out his hand to me. "Congratulations and welcome to the Chancery family. We are thrilled to be publishing your book, and we know, with total confidence, that it's going to be a huge hit. You are about to become a star, Mr. Konigsberg. A major star."

He turned away from me for a moment and spoke to a waiter.

"André, give our author a glass of champagne. Now," he continued, placing his arm around my shoulder, "I want you to meet the chairman of Mannheim International, the firm that owns Chancery. Steven, say hello to Axel Guderian."

A thin man with a bony face and steel-rimmed glasses stepped forward.

"All my colleagues in Düsseldorf are very pleased that you will be published by Chancery. We now hope that our German publishing company, Mannheim Verlag, will be publishing your book as well. Put in a good word with your agent, please," he said with a thin smile directed to Stuart. "This is my wife, Elsa." A stylish woman in burgundy leather and a heavily made-up face stepped forward to shake my hand with a grip a stevedore would be proud of.

I was into my tenth greeting and thank-you when I heard Stuart whisper into my ear, "Your turn to speak."

I felt as if I were four years old and had lost my mother's hand in a large department store, but suddenly I knew what I had to do. I launched immediately into the opening of the toast I had written out and memorized word for word. I threw in a lot of inflated language, sincere but exaggerated, to make my points. I was "profoundly grateful" . . . "your belief in me is a compliment beyond my wildest imagining" . . . "this is a moment of triumph for me and, hopefully, for you, too," and so on. Of course, I did not forget to thank Stuart, who acknowledged it with a modest bow. After making music of this kind for a while I finally got to the part of the toast I cared about most.

"A friend of mine who died recently, Ben Chambers, a really great man, once said to me that the most important thing about a book is the book itself. I owe a lot of this to him. Once a book is written, it belongs to everybody. I hope very much that *Juno's Dance* will reach into the hearts of all those readers out there we don't know now, but who will be touched by it." I grinned and made a world-encompassing sweep of my arms. "Thank you, Ben, and a big thanks to all of you." My nervousness had evaporated.

I smiled at the group and gestured toward Dexter Parch, who began a round of applause. Applause for me? I had never heard such a sound before, and my face reddened with pleasure. As I let the feeling seep into me, I was surrounded by members of the Chancery staff. "There's a ton of media that wants to interview you," said one woman, obviously a publicist, "but we're holding out till publication. Even with a book as superb as *Juno*, timing is everything."

"Is it true," another woman asked, "that your real name is Steven King?" I gave a quick nod. "That would be a fabulous tidbit to hand out to the columns."

As soon as I answered one question, another one popped up in its place. I basked in the attention and could have stood there luxuriating in it forever. But then I heard someone knock against a glass with a piece of silverware. It was Dexter Parch.

"Ladies and gentlemen and honored guest, it's time for dinner. The dining room is this way." He pointed to a pair of large etched-glass doors at the end of the hall. "Follow me," he said, and that's exactly what we did, a flock of obedient and happy ducks.

Stuart gave me a lift to the Sherry, but I was too exhausted to talk. When we arrived at the entrance, he gave me another big hug. "It's written in the stars, baby. Sleep well."

As I pressed the elevator button, I realized "sleeping well" was not the ticket, at least not for now. I badly needed to clear my head. I headed out the hotel and turned north on Fifth. There were only a few people on the street.

Now that I was alone, the thoughts I had pushed away during the party reasserted themselves. I was thoroughly disgusted with myself. There was no other word for it. How could I have masqueraded as a writer I was not? Even to call myself a writer, any kind of writer, was a lie. I was an imposter, pure and simple. I no longer made an effort to write on my own. The party that night, and the complex publishing machinery I saw getting ready to go into gear with the appearance of *Juno's Dance*, drove all this home to me in a way I could never have observed while living in the hinterlands of Maine. I was in big trouble, first of all with myself, but most of all with Ben. Not to mention Tina, who should have been the first one to hear the truth.

Ben. I could see him clearly and I appealed to him. I didn't know what else to do. How do I get out of this fix, Ben? No answer. But then Ben's voice bubbled up into my consciousness: "The right path is always in front of you." "What does that mean?" I shouted out, scaring a couple walking ahead of me.

I was now in front of the Metropolitan Museum of Art, so I walked up the steps and plunked myself down. The step was strangely soft and inviting, and I spotted only one person entering a building on the other side of the avenue. In the quiet I put my mind into neutral and let it drift, until I realized I had made a decision on what to do about my dilemma.

I didn't have the guts to confess. I thought of Tina, my parents, Stuart, Chancery, and I just couldn't do it. But I could do something else, which was, yes, a compromise: I would publish just this one book of Ben's, *Juno's Dance*, under my name. Screw the two-book contract. As for money, I'd only keep as much as I needed to finish my own book. The rest I would use to create a foundation in Ben's name to help young writers—and lobster-men! I'd call it the Benjamin Chambers Outreach Foundation. This was the answer. Finally, feeling better, I stood up and walked back to the hotel, ready to sleep.

Part

Four Years Later

A NEW LIFE

What does Sinclair know about anything? He's
just a writer.

—Louis B. Mayer commenting on Upton Sinclair's
candidacy for governor of California in 1934

Fifteen

THE CHARLIE ROSE SHOW   Transcript #3156

                                        Taping 10:36:23 EST

CHARLIE ROSE: TONIGHT MY GUEST IS AN AUTHOR WHOSE NAME HAS BECOME
    FAMILIAR TO MOST OF YOU. STEVEN KONIGSBERG, WELCOME TO THE PRO-
    GRAM.

STEVEN KONIGSBERG: THANK YOU, CHARLIE. GOOD TO BE HERE AGAIN.

CHARLIE ROSE: YOU FIRST JOINED ME A LITTLE MORE THAN TWO AND A HALF
    YEARS AGO. YOU HAD JUST PUBLISHED *JUNO'S DANCE*, A NOVEL ABOUT A FAM-
    ILY OF HIGH STEELWORKERS. IN THREE WEEKS IT HIT NUMBER ONE ON THE
    NEW YORK TIMES BESTSELLER LIST, WHERE IT STAYED FOR ALMOST A YEAR. IT
    WAS MADE INTO A MOVIE, WHICH WAS NUMBER ONE AT THE BOX OFFICE
    FOR FIVE WEEKS, A COUP IN THAT CHANCY BUSINESS. THE PAPERBACK ALSO
    BECAME NUMBER ONE. HOW DO YOU EXPLAIN THIS?

STEVEN KONIGSBERG: I CAN'T.

CHARLIE ROSE: I'LL TRY TO DO IT FOR YOU. I IMMEDIATELY FELL IN LOVE WITH
    THE BOOK, BUT, I'LL SAY RIGHT OFF, YOU DON'T SEEM CUT FROM THE SAME
    CLOTH AS YOUR CHARACTERS.

STEVEN KONIGSBERG: YOU CAN SURE SAY THAT AGAIN! *(LAUGHTER)*

CHARLIE ROSE: HOW DID YOU GET TO THE SUBJECT OF HIGH STEEL DAREDEVILS?

STEVEN KONIGSBERG: I'M A PRODIGIOUS READER OF EVERYTHING. FROM COMIC

BOOKS TO PHILOSOPHY TO PERSONAL STORIES OF PEOPLE WITH UNIQUE AND COMPELLING LIVES. IF MY CURIOSITY IS PIQUED, I RESEARCH THEM INTENSIVELY, AND PRETTY SOON I KNOW IF I HAVE THE GOODS TO MAKE A BOOK. WHAT I TRY TO DO IS TRANSPORT THE READER INTO A WORLD WHERE HE OR SHE HAS NEVER BEEN BEFORE.

CHARLIE ROSE: DO MANY PEOPLE KID YOU ON THE FACT THAT YOUR NAME IS ACTUALLY STEVEN KING? AND ISN'T KONIGSBERG WOODY ALLEN'S ORIGINAL NAME, TOO?

STEVEN KONIGSBERG: I MET WOODY ALLEN FOR THE FIRST TIME RECENTLY AT A KNICKS GAME, AND WE BOTH HAD A GOOD LAUGH AT OUR RESPECTIVE HANDLING OF THE KONIGSBERG NAME. MY GRANDFATHER SHMUEL KONIGSBERG CAME TO THIS COUNTRY, LIKE SO MANY OTHER IMMIGRANTS, TO FIND A BETTER LIFE. HE ALWAYS SAID, "IF YOU'RE GOING TO PURSUE THE AMERICAN DREAM, YOU SHOULD DO IT WITH AN AMERICAN NAME." SO LIKE MANY OTHER AMERICANS, I GUESS I HAVE A SPLIT PERSONALITY AS FAR AS MY NAME GOES. BUT I ENJOY BOTH THE KING AND KONIGSBERG PARTS. IN FACT, MY DRIVER'S LICENSE AND ALL MY PERSONAL I.D.'S ARE IN THE NAME OF STEVEN KING.

CHARLIE ROSE: FASCINATING. IS THERE A WRITER WHO HAS ESPECIALLY INFLUENCED YOU?

STEVEN KONIGSBERG: THERE ARE MANY, BUT THE MOST IMPORTANT IS PROBABLY CHARLES DICKENS. DICKENS WAS A GENIUS WITH WISDOM ENOUGH FOR EVERY WRITER, OR READER, WHO CHOOSES TO ENTER THE WORLDS HE CREATES.

CHARLIE ROSE: YOU HAVE CERTAINLY ENTERED THAT WORLD. *TIME* MAGAZINE OFFICIALLY DUBBED YOU "THE STORYTELLER" IN A COVER STORY. THE YEAR AFTER *JUNO* YOU PUBLISHED *THE WIND DEMON*, ABOUT THE OVERSEXED CAPTAIN OF A SUPERTANKER. LAST YEAR YOU PUBLISHED *BEYOND THE NIGHT SKY*, ABOUT SAPPHIRES IN SOUTH AFRICA. BOTH WENT IMMEDIATELY TO NUMBER ONE AND STAYED THERE FOR OVER THIRTY MONTHS. AND NOW YOU HAVE ANOTHER BOOK COMING. DO YOU EVER TAKE A VACATION?

STEVEN KONIGSBERG: RARELY!

When the taping ended, I hightailed it down to Seventh Avenue and caught the first taxi uptown. Tucked into my briefcase was a transcript of a show I had done the week before. As soon as I got to my office, I would file it in my archives, where I keep copies of all my videos, transcripts, and print coverage, now so voluminous that it took up two entire file cabinets. I organized the material so that I could use it as a quick reference to what I wanted to say—and what I didn't. I had never yet gotten stuck in a corner, listening to words come out of my mouth that might reveal my secret in some way. I came close during an interview last year in Detroit, and the memory of it still made me queasy. The talk show host asked if *Juno's Dance* was the first novel I had written, and instead of saying yes, I started back to my own first novel. My unpublished novel! He started to look at me in a funny way, which caused me to stop in midsentence, as if I had been hit in the gut. After a pause long enough to recite one of Hamlet's soliloquies, I got back on message.

I was back at the San Remo in no time. It gave me pleasure every time I walked into the elegant lobby, which soothed me when I was anxious and reinforced my mood when I was flying high.

As I put my key in the lock to my apartment, I heard noises from inside. It was my assistant, Fred Jaggers, always on time, who showed up for work at nine. His job was to do everything I didn't want to do: answer the phone, make reservations, handle fan mail (several hundred letters a week), and take care of all my other correspondence.

"Morning, Fred. Any messages?"

Fred handed me a clutch of Post-its and I flipped quickly through them. The callers were all familiar or expected, except for one—Wayne Woodley. He had telephoned yesterday, the day before, and the day before that. He was always cryptic with Fred.

"What did this Woodley say?" I asked.

"Same as before—that he was in New York and really wanted to see you. Had to see you, was what he actually said."

"I'll take care of it myself," I said nonchalantly, folding the message in two and jamming it into my pocket. There was something about this guy that felt odd, but I didn't want Fred to sense my uneasiness. "I'll check my e-mail, then we can go over the other stuff."

I didn't have much for Fred. A couple of invitations for readings—predictably as exciting as a two-day-old bagel—had to be turned down. Chancery had forwarded to me, with no comment, my German publisher's jacket proposal for their edition of *Beyond the Night Sky*, a dark abstract that resembled a large handful of mud thrown against a wall. Who knows what works in Germany? I initialed the jacket proof and gave it to Fred.

"Call Dexter Parch and find out where he wants me to meet him for lunch. And call Louis and make an appointment for me midweek." Louis, my tailor, was making a couple of suits for me out of some fabulous worsted plaid I had bought in London the month before. "Tina will be home from Spence around two. It's one of her early days. Tell her I think we can leave for Roxbury around five or five-thirty. I'll check in with you later this afternoon. And Fred, remind me tomorrow to go to Tiffany's. Next week's our third anniversary, and I want to buy Tina something nice."

As soon as Fred reached Parch, I headed to my office, which was located in a small apartment in a brownstone half a dozen blocks away. This was where I worked on my own books—and copied Ben's. I kept whichever manuscript of Ben's I was working on locked in a small and highly sophisticated safe in a locked closet. The front door was outfitted with two locks, one a dead bolt, and a burglar alarm. I had not installed a phone, though I always had my cell phone with me if I needed to make a call. What I liked about the place was that no one could reach me and that my work, and Ben's, were safe from prying eyes.

The only person who had been to my office was Tina, and that was because she'd asked to see it. "What a snug spot, sweetheart," she said, looking around, then giving me a big kiss. Altogether she was in the room little more than five minutes. I could count on her not to come knocking on my door. She was excited by my success, but what mattered to her most were the fourth graders she taught at the Spence School.

As I walked to my office, I found myself once again pondering the last couple of years. The apartment in the San Remo, our weekend place in Litchfield County, the condo I bought my parents on Marco Island, the mortgage I paid off on my mother-in-law's house in Key West, my eight-figure account at Goldman Sachs, everything I had I owed to Ben. For the most part, I let this overwhelming fact wash over me. After all, hadn't I made all this happen? If the manuscripts had remained piled in Ben's trunks, would my silent partner and I have ever joined the pentagon of superwriters: Grisham, Clancy, Steel, King, and Crichton?

By the time I reached my office, I had shaken off thoughts of Ben and was ready for work. It turned out to be a terrific morning. Before leaving to meet Parch I had written a page of my own book, a good page. If I could keep this up, I wouldn't have to go back to retyping Ben's book for another few months. What I really wanted to do next was to use a book of mine—a genuine Steven Konigsberg—as the new addition to my (and Ben's) oeuvre.

Dexter Parch was already seated at his usual banquette in the Four Seasons Grill when I arrived. His first flute of champagne was almost full, so I knew I wasn't late. After I sat down, the maître d' hurried over to shake my hand. Several publishers at other tables nodded to us as I settled in.

We gossiped about the continuing fortunes of *Beyond the Night Sky*, all good, and about a feature piece that *Time* was planning that would tie in with the publication of the next book. They were already lining up people to interview for the piece and had tentatively entitled it "Steven Konigsberg Takes Another Giant Step." Since Chancery always put my manuscripts on the fast track, it was not too soon for them to start the publicity machine working. When I handed in a manuscript to Dexter, everyone at Chancery focused on my book. Every division of the company, from design to copy-editing, from advertising to sales, put what they were doing on the back burner and began to prepare for the publication of the next Konigsberg novel. If Chancery were a Roman galley, you could hear the drumbeat getting louder.

Dexter Parch didn't like to waste time on things like lunch. I roamed around the menu until I spotted the crab cakes; they were my favorite, hands down. Parch ordered a well-done hamburger and a baked potato, the same meal he ordered every day without variation. After coffees we wrapped things up. This was just a touching-base meeting, stroking of the star author. Chancery needed my books the way a diabetic needed insulin; they had good years and poor ones, but every year that they published a Konigsberg novel was a very good one.

When we left the restaurant, Parch climbed into his town car and I turned toward Park Avenue, thinking I would walk north for ten or twelve blocks before hopping a cab. As I turned, a short, thick-chested man I had never seen before came over and planted himself in front of me.

"I'm Wayne Woodley," he said. He wore a topcoat that was too small for him and a drab olive fedora pushed down on his head. "We should have a cup of coffee," he said with an unconvincing smile.

"Sorry, I'm too busy," I said, and quickly turned away.

"You know," said Woodley, "I just read your book *Juno's Dance*. It was real good. As good as when Ben Chambers dictated it to me twenty-four years ago."

Sixteen

Woodley followed me inside a small bar on Fifty-third just off Lexington, where I found a table in the corner. The bartender was setting up clean glasses while having a heated discussion with his only customer on the merits of breast implants. Wayne Woodley wanted a beer, and I ordered a Dewar's. Double. All I'd had to drink at lunch was grapefruit juice, but I knew I needed a real drink now.

Woodley clicked his glass against mine.

"To a mutually beneficial relationship," he said.

I let the remark pass. Woodley looked to be in his late forties, though he still wore his reddish hair in a military-style crew cut. He was built like a packing crate, and though the years had added a generous padding of flesh, I could see that there was still a core of strength inside the shiny, off-the-rack coat he wore.

"You know, Steve, I'm a great fan of yours. You don't mind me calling you Steve, do you?"

I nodded and took another swallow of my Scotch.

"I've read all of your books, Steve, and I want to tell you that I loved each and every one of them."

"I have a doctor's appointment to go to, Mr. Woodley, and would appreciate—"

"You can call me Wayne."

"Fine. You see, Wayne, I'm a little pressed for time."

"Of course. Now, where was I? Oh, yes, your books. I really want to talk to you about one book. I was just out of the service," Woodley continued, signaling the bartender for another beer, "when I met Ben. What a great guy. Hard to believe that this was almost twenty-five years ago. I had just arrived in San Francisco and was flat broke. A guy I met told me he knew someone who needed a manuscript typed–that someone turned out to be Ben. He had a little apartment on Russian Hill with a terrace that had a great view. On nice days that's where I worked. You see, I had been a typist in the army. I also learned shorthand. Gregg. Wonder if anyone uses Gregg these days? Well, Ben had broken three fingers and his right wrist after being thrown from a horse in Golden Gate Park. He always wrote the first draft by hand. I also took some shorthand when he revised parts of the novel. God, I thought *Juno's Dance* was the best book I had ever read. What characters. And the dialogue. Absolutely terrific. Now, I admit it was a long time ago, and I'm sure you've added stuff that wasn't in the version I typed up, but it seemed awfully like the *Juno's Dance* I worked on. So I just have one question for you, Steve." Woodley took a long swallow from his glass and then carefully placed it in the center of the coaster. "Why isn't Ben's name on the book?"

He stared at me with the sly, confident look of a cat about to play with a mouse.

"I'm not following you," I said after finishing my drink. I felt emboldened by the Scotch and had to restrain myself from ordering another.

"Cut the shit, Steve. You follow me better than a bird dog. What the fuck are you doing here? Ben Chambers wrote that book and I can prove it."

"How can you do that?"

"I have a copy of the original manuscript. It's old and yellow, with Ben's handwriting on almost every page. I don't know why I kept that onionskin mother, but I think it will prove to be worthwhile."

"Do you know that Ben left his entire estate to me, including *Juno's Dance?*"

"Of course I do, Steve. I even have a Xerox of Ben's will, courtesy of the Boothbay Harbor probate court. Cost me thirty-five dollars."

"I don't think anyone will believe you, Wayne," I said.

"Take a look at this," Woodley answered as he slid a piece of notepaper toward me.

There were four telephone numbers neatly written on the paper.

"What's this?"

"Just a few numbers I've collected. The first one is Liz Smith's. The one after that is Don Hewitt's. He's the producer of *60 Minutes*. You probably know him. The next one down is—"

"What do you want?"

"Bingo. I knew you'd get there eventually. After I read *Juno's Dance*, I got me a subscription to *Variety* and *Publishers Weekly*, to keep up with your success, you know, see what it amounted to in dollar terms. You've made a shit-load of money off that book, Stevie boy."

"This is getting tiresome. How much?"

"I'm getting real tired of living in Louisiana. New Iberia is nice, but it's awfully small. I'd like to get a job up here, let's say a job with you. I could be your assistant."

"No way. I might be willing to pay you, Woodley, even though the book is mine and I doubt that anyone would believe your story. I'll pay you enough to move from where you're living, but forget about coming here. That's a nonstarter."

"I want twenty thousand a month. Also, I want medical coverage and an IRA. I think it'll turn out to be a lot cheaper for you financially and emotionally than having all your fans find out that Ben Chambers wrote the book."

I dropped two twenty-dollar bills on the table and stood up.

"I'll need a couple of days to think this over."

"Why don't we say one day? Tomorrow."

I started to walk away from the table.

"And I'll call you, my friend. You remember that I have your number, too, don't you?" Woodley called out, laughing, as I pushed the door open and stepped out onto the street. He was the embodiment of my worst nightmare—and now he was here, almost literally on my doorstep.

Seventeen

Tina stared out the window of the limo as we crossed the park, heading to the YMHA, where I was going to give a reading from my new book—or rather Ben's—which I still called a work in progress since I hadn't finished retyping it yet. I had discovered that my readers loved hearing a piece of a book before it was "finished." It whetted their appetites for more and made them feel in the know.

Reading at the YMHA always gave me a thrill. It was such a classy, intellectual, creative place: one evening, the Emerson Quartet playing Beethoven; then Susan Sontag discussing feminism in Indonesia with Gloria Steinem; the next evening (drumroll here)—me! I knew Tina loved it, too, but you wouldn't guess it from the way she was behaving. I could see the powerful grip of resentment scrunching her shoulders.

"Come on, Tina, lighten up."

No answer.

"I know what's bothering you. It's so silly."

Tina whirled around and faced me.

"Silly, you say." Her voice was as tight as a tuning fork. "This says everything about the way we're living now. We're right across the park. You can almost see the YMHA from our terrace. All we had to do was hop in a cab. Instead, you have to go and hire a limo. It's so . . . showy."

"It wasn't me, it was Chancery. They insisted. But so what?" When she got this way, it really annoyed me. "You know the saying, 'If you've got it, flaunt it.'"

"I know that's supposed to be funny, but it isn't, because I'm beginning to think you really mean it."

"Tina, how about calling a truce?" This was becoming a ridiculous conversation. Unfortunately, it was a lot like others we had been having lately.

"Okay." She sighed.

"I love you so much, you know," I said, pulling her toward me. I did, I truly did; the only trouble was that in this last year the love had been submerged in a thicket of grumblings from Tina about all aspects of our new life. Everything I bought, Tina turned her back on. I had just spent thirty-five grand on a photograph by Vanessa Beecroft that Tina called pop porn. The tennis court I was building at our country place was something I did to keep up with our neighbors, she declared, since I played like Dom De Luise and had no intention of improving. There were times I would think that Tina had been happier with Steve the bartender living in the rented shack in Boothbay Harbor.

I looked away from Tina and out the window just as we pulled up in front of the YMHA. The driver opened the door and I slid out and held out my hand to my wife.

"The next time we come here, we'll take a horse and carriage. But the carriage will be small and the horse lame," I said, laughing. Tina joined in, and on a brief gust of good humor we sailed inside.

The auditorium was packed. As I headed through the door to the right that led to the greenroom, I spotted Dexter Parch with the Chancery publicist.

"Meet you backstage after the reading. I booked a table for all of us at Cipriani for afterwards," he called out.

I would have about ten minutes to greet the organizers of the reading and collect my thoughts. I planned to read from the opening chapters of the new book, *Raptor's Flight*, and I knew it would not disappoint my fans here, or when it was published.

I couldn't get Wayne Woodley out of my mind. What should I do? I asked myself again, though I knew the answer. I would pay him. What else could I do? It would be $240,000 a year, a lot of money, but not if it meant getting him out of my life. And I certainly could afford it. I would put him on the payroll as a researcher, with one proviso: he absolutely could not live in New York.

The applause lasted for well over a minute when I walked onto the stage.

"Good evening, ladies and gentlemen. First, I'd like to thank Matt Trainor and Punch Hutton for organizing tonight's event and, most of all, for inviting me back to read in this marvelous auditorium. It's humbling to think of the great writers who have read from this stage over the years. I'm going to read to you the first two chapters of my new novel, *Raptor's Flight.* Let me tell you a little about the book before I begin. *Raptor's Flight* is a book about the world of—"

I stopped abruptly. There in the audience, sitting dead center in the third row, sharing my moment of triumph, was Wayne Woodley. He was grinning as if he had just won the lottery, and in a way I guess he had. For a moment I didn't think I could go on, but the prospect of what that would mean was even scarier than Woodley. Finally, I faked a deep bronchial cough, took a long drink of water from the carafe on the lectern, made a lame joke about the start of the New York flu season, and started in again, looking everywhere in the hall except at Woodley. It felt like the longest reading of my writing life.

Eighteen

In the four months since I had struck my deal with Woodley, I had heard not a word from him. The checks went out to him monthly, and that was that. With each one he endorsed, his face became fuzzier and less scary. He was officially a full-time "researcher" for my company, Boothbay Literary Ventures, Inc. I included him in my medical plan, but on the IRA, I wouldn't yield an inch.

It was Monday and I was on my way back to New York from our place in Connecticut, where Tina and I were happiest and where I only worked on my own writing. I had a date that afternoon to talk with Dexter Parch about *Time's Pulse*, the first piece of my own writing I had ever shown him. *Raptor's Flight* had been published three weeks earlier, and already it was leaping up the bestseller list, like a countdown for a rocket—three, two, and, this coming Sunday, number one. It was an optimum time to test Parch's feeling for me as a writer of a different kind of book than what he was accustomed to.

Whenever I thought of Woodley's sudden appearance, I was amazed at my naiveté. It hadn't occurred to me that the publication of Ben's books might catch the attention of someone from the past who would know that the material I was publishing under my own name was in fact not mine. Since Ben had been so secretive with me, I never imagined that anyone else had read his books. Of course, who would have thought of Ben with a broken hand in need of a typist? Woodley infuriated and angered me, but I knew I had no choice except to pay him what he asked for, and pray that it was enough to keep him quiet. Once I told myself again that there were no other Woodleys waiting to pounce on me, the headache retreated like a stray cloud on a sunny day.

I still thought constantly—and fearfully—about what it would be like if the truth came out. The glamorous, successful life I had built up for myself would disintegrate instantly. There was really no defense for what I was doing, and I couldn't expect much sympathy or even understanding. Once I had typed my name as the author of *Juno's Dance*, my authorship assumed legitimacy. It wasn't something I wanted to waive away, though I knew I was getting in deeper with the publication of each book. The ache in my gut told me what my lie had been doing to me. If I confessed, I would still be a rich man, thanks to the books already published. The manuscripts that had been in the trunks were legally mine, but in the end where would it leave me? What would everyone think of me? Tina? My parents? Stuart? The people at Chancery? My fans? Most frightening of all, the media? The *New York Post*, most bloodthirsty of all, would run a story like this for weeks. Why kid myself—I would be a total disgrace. My promise to myself (and Ben) that I would publish only one of his novels had lasted until *Juno* hit number one on the *Times* list. Then without another thought I was busily retyping the next novel. It was like having sex for the first time: even if it wasn't as good as you thought it would be, you had to do it again. At least I could pat myself on the back about following through on my promise to set up a foundation in Ben's name. The Chambers Outreach Foundation now had a bank balance in the Wiscasset Savings and Loan of over $3 million. But was that enough? Hell, no.

I took several deep breaths, forcing my mind back to Parch and his reaction to *Time's Pulse*. I could hear him in my mind: "Steve, this is a departure, but it's a marvelous surprise. The characters are rich and the story . . . I didn't know you had it in you. We'll put it on the list immediately." This was the response I desperately yearned for. I broke away from my fantasy and focused on the road again; I was getting near the end of the Saw Mill River Parkway and would soon be in Manhattan. I didn't have long to wait to see if my dream would become reality.

. . .

An awkward silence fell between Parch and myself almost as soon as I sat down at his table at the Four Seasons.

"Steven, you look good," Parch said as he buttered a roll.

I was too anxious to play conversational tennis with Parch, so I jumped right in.

"Well, what do you think? Did you like it?"

"Yes, I did. Quite a bit," Parch began slowly, carefully picking up his roll as if it were a Fabergé egg. He took a bite and chewed stolidly before he spoke again. "But I think it's something your fans, your millions of fans, will find confusing. Too confusing, I'm afraid." He paused again. "I have an idea, though, and I think it's a good one. Why don't we publish it under a pseudonym?"

At first I was crushed, but as Parch continued, I gradually came around to the idea. The only important thing was that the book be published. Did it really matter if my name was on the book? Once I'd agreed, Dexter quickly moved ahead.

"No one can know this book is by the world-famous Steven Konigsberg," said Parch, eyeing me sternly.

"Of course."

"I will be your editor. I'll personally handle all aspects of the publication. We'll set up a new personal corporation as the copyright owner. What name should we use for the author?"

It came to me in an instant.

"How about Chambers Benjamin?"

"Unusual, but like all your ideas, perfect."

"When will you publish it?"

"Soon. Later this afternoon make a date with my secretary for us to meet next week," he said. "Now, let's put Chambers Benjamin back in the closet so I can show you the full-page ads for Steven Konigsberg's *Raptor's Flight* that we'll be running next week in the *New York Times*, the *Wall Street Journal*, and *USA Today*."

Nineteen

The publication party for Quentin Bass's new novel, *Let the Rook Fly Away*, was held at the restaurant of the moment, Boeuf avec Boeuf, which was located in a large former meatpacking plant south of Canal Street. The waiters, all wearing aprons with large faux bloodstains made of crimson silk that were randomly sewn on, weaved through the crowd with trays holding flutes of good champagne. The champagne was Cristal because I was paying for it. Quentin didn't know that, nor did he know that I had also twisted a number of arms to get his book published. First I had hectored Stuart to take Quentin on as a client.

"Jesus, Stevie, no one is publishing this lit shit anymore. Your friend Bass has two whole chapters on how the fucking grass sways in Iowa."

"That was a nice royalty check we got from Chancery last month, wasn't it, Stuart?" I said to him not so gently. I was now Stuart's number one client by a greater distance than Secretariat won the Derby. Stuart could bitch and moan, but in the end I knew he would take on Quentin's representation.

It was tougher with Dexter Parch.

"First off, Steve, I don't like the book. Not an iota. I would have put it down after a chapter if you hadn't asked me to read it. Yes, there's some good writing here and there, but there's no story. The book has as much drive as an escargot after it's been crammed back into its shell."

"I've told you before how important Quentin Bass was to my becoming a writer."

"Thank God you didn't model your writing after his."

"It's vital to me that Quentin's book gets published."

"Please, Steve, anything else you want you got it. I really don't want this book on our list."

"For starters, I'll completely subsidize its publication."

"I still don't want to do it."

"That would include my putting up the money for a hefty advertising budget."

"Is there any way I can talk you out of this?" Parch asked.

I looked at him hard and paused for a long beat before I replied. "Not if you want to continue to publish me, Dexter."

Game, set, and match.

I also worked behind the scenes to get Quentin a teaching post at NYU, where I had recently given the school, through the Chambers Outreach Foundation, $200,000 to set up an annual creative writing prize. He was just about to be sacked by Iowa for drinking and having a few too many "conferences" with his female students. But I didn't stop there. I got Quentin an apartment in the Village and put him into a substance abuse program that actually helped curtail his binge drinking.

How did my old teacher and mentor react to all of this? Poorly. He was angry with Stuart for not getting Knopf or Farrar, Straus to do his book. Chancery was fine for commercial writers like me, but not for Quentin's finely sculpted prose. He was pissed at Dexter for not printing more copies. He was mad at me for . . . well, being successful. He believed that if a writer attracted a large audience, he was a priori a sold-out hack. Tina couldn't understand why I persisted in helping him.

"Okay, so once, quite a few years ago, he convinced you that you could become a writer. But what else has he done for you? He's a mean, nasty drunk who—"

"He's cut down on the drinking, Tina. At least give him that."

"Fine. But answer this: has he given you one word of praise about your own books?"

She had me there. Quentin, in fact, had never even mentioned the books. And the thank-yous for what I had done for him were damn few. But I didn't kid myself about why I was helping him: it was my way of paying off the gods for not letting me become Quentin Bass, another minor literary novelist with too few readers and too much booze in his blood. I knew it was Ben who had actually saved me from that fate, but the all-too-real vision of Quentin produced a powerful mixture of guilt and fear that chilled me more than the frigid waters of Boothbay Harbor.

Finally, the time had come for me to introduce Quentin to the couple of hundred people who had turned out. It's not hard to attract a crowd if you offer enough champagne and decent hors d'oeuvres. Chancery had included my name on the invitation, and that probably contributed to filling the place. I told the group about my years as a writing student in Quentin's classes, and how much his own writing had inspired me. I went on about how much I admired his work, particularly his new book. Quentin came on for a fast handshake, no hug; then he was off, reading the first chapter of the novel, then the second. The audience was beginning to stir. I could see that Quentin intended to read the third chapter, maybe even the whole book. Dexter had the presence of mind to hop onto the improvised stage, applauding like a maniac and loudly thanking Quentin. It was a perfect moment to slip out. My driver was double-parked in front and I hopped in. I had asked Tina to come to the party, but she had begged off. Actually, she'd said, "Thank God I have a lesson to plan." Then I asked her if she'd like to meet me at Da Silvano for dinner.

"Why can't we have a nice, quiet dinner at home, Steven? We hardly do that anymore. I'll make a meat loaf, with a hard-boiled egg in the middle, the way your mother makes it. I can't offer you the people who would certainly come to the table asking for your autograph. All I can serve up is the meat loaf and myself."

Tina was in the kitchen when I got to our apartment.

"Perfect timing. The meat loaf is almost ready. You light the candles and open some wine. I finished my lesson for tomorrow, so a little wine is in order."

As I brought her a glass of wine, I pressed myself against her back and softly kissed her neck.

"Not even your meat loaf tastes this good," I said, nuzzling at the point where her neck met her shoulder.

"I dare you to say that after your first bite. And I don't mean me."

During dinner I recounted what had happened at the party. Tina particularly liked the scene of Quentin reading from his novel.

"I always thought that Dexter could think on his feet. Imagine if he hadn't jumped on the stage. Quentin would still be reading. God, what an ego."

After dinner I helped Tina clean up. I had wanted us to hire a full-time housekeeper for a long time. After all, we had a maid's room that was situated at the back of the apartment. We'd never know she was around, but Tina would not hear of it. Having a cleaning woman come in three times a week was more than enough, she told me again and again, until I gave up.

"I just got the DVD of the director's cut of *Juno's Dance*. Let's watch it and then I'll give you one of my patented back rubs. Who knows where that might lead?" I winked at Tina.

"Not tonight, hon. I've had a hard day and I need a solid eight. I was really dragging today."

She gave me a kiss on the cheek and headed off to our bedroom. After watching about ten minutes of the film, I turned it off, and I went to the bar in the pantry and poured a brandy. The first swallow of the smoky liquor relaxed me. Then I sat down in my favorite chair and picked out a book from a pile Dexter and other publishers had sent me. *The Pre-Raphaelites Reconsidered*: a little Rossetti, Millais, and Morris would be a perfect way to wind down the clock. I didn't get through five pages before I put the book down and joined Tina in bed.

Twenty

As I was looking over the *Times* and finishing breakfast, my private line rang. Tina and I had two other phone lines, both in her name, but only a few people had the number for this one: my folks, Stuart, Dexter, Quentin Bass, and a few other close friends. I picked it up on the first ring.

"How's my favorite author?"

Woodley! Obviously, I hadn't wanted him to call and reach Tina by mistake, so this was the number I had given him. The sound of his voice caused me to feel as if a big man were squeezing me from behind.

"Wayne. How are you?" I asked in a voice that didn't sound like my own.

"Whenever I'm in New York I feel great."

"I told you when we made our arrangement that you were not to come here."

"Well, a few things have changed."

"Like what?"

"I've been having a run of bad luck day trading. Fucking techs been kicking my ass pretty good lately."

"What has that got to do with me?"

"I thought you were a smart guy. You're slower on the pickup than Ray Charles at a singles bar. Let me say it so that even you will understand: I need more money, Mr. Konigsberg."

"You're getting two hundred and forty thousand a year, Woodley."

"Chump change. I just read in *Publishers Weekly* that last month you signed a new four-book deal with Chancery. They estimated you got over six mil a book. That doesn't include film rights, foreign sales, you name it. So don't tell me about how much I'm making. You keep that shit up and I'm going to get pissed off."

"Take it easy."

"We need to talk. Tonight. How about seven at the bar at the Four Seasons? I've always wanted to go there."

The Four Seasons! That would not do at all. Then I remembered a small bar, the Final Draught, in the East Village, where I had met my Dutch publisher the week before. There was a very good chance no one there would recognize me. I told Woodley that I was going to be downtown and that I'd meet him there.

"Avenue B? Where the fuck is that?"

"Just give the cabdriver the address. He'll get you there. See you at seven."

I got to the bar fifteen minutes early to find Woodley waiting for me.

"This is certainly not the Four Seasons. More like the One Season. How the hell did you find this place?"

"A foreign publisher brought me here."

"You and I are the only ones here without a bone through our nose. Jesus, what a crowd."

"Keep your voice down, for Christ's sake."

"Why? You think one of these fruits got the balls to come over here and tell me to shut up?"

A waitress, dressed in black with a silver chain that connected her nose to the corner of her mouth, came over to take our order. I ordered a vodka straight up and Woodley a beer with a Scotch on the side.

"Stay inside during a thunderstorm," he said, laughing at the waitress.

"Very funny," she answered without turning around.

"I've got a dinner to go to tonight, so let's cut to the chase. What do you want?"

"What every other red-blooded American wants—a piece of the action."

"What are you talking about?"

"I'm tired of being on a fucking allowance. I want a slice of the prime rib."

"You're talking like a crazy man. But I'll tell you what I'll do. I'll up you a thousand a week."

"You must be kidding," said Woodley, deadpan.

"I certainly am not. Do the math. That's fifty-two thousand more a year—nothing to sneeze at."

"Steven, I guess you didn't get the drift of what I just said. I want a piece of the show, and I want it now."

Anger welled up in my throat; I couldn't swallow. For a moment I couldn't speak.

"What's wrong? Cat got your tongue?"

"Don't try to be cute, Woodley. You can't pull this off."

"Just watch me."

"All right," I said, taking a deep breath. "What do you really want?"

"Well, for now, twenty-five percent of your total take, after taxes. With a weekly draw of twenty thousand."

I was stunned into silence.

"And don't cry poverty," Woodley went blithely on. "I know what you're making. I don't have to be a CPA to guess what your tax return looks like."

As Woodley talked his way through my successes—and income—in the last year, my heart began to beat wildly. What was I going to do with him? What was he going to do to me? A flash of fear, almost like heat lightning, further stoked my anger.

Trying to buy some time, I said, "I need a few days to work this out. It's complicated."

"No, it isn't. It's simple. If you want me to keep my mouth shut, you'll give me what I want. And soon."

"I'll be in touch at the end of the week," I said with as much nonchalance as I could muster.

"Make sure you call me tomorrow, Mr. Konigsberg. I'm really running out of patience. And, by the way, I have the private number of the executive producer at *Dateline*. Also, for local flavor, I know how to reach all the right people at both the tabloids. They'll cream for this. You'll make Woody Allen look like a jaywalking story."

I stood up and headed for the door.

"One more thing. I'm staying at the Plaza. A lovely suite, with a great view of the park. I instructed them to send the bill directly to you. I knew you'd want me to do that."

When I reached the corner to look for a taxi, I stopped suddenly, turned around, and began to walk back to the bar. Who the hell was Wayne Woodley to threaten me this way? Let him unmask me. I could handle it. Eventually, I'd make everyone who counted understand why I became Steven Konigsberg, best-selling author. When I reached the Final Draught—all I had to do was walk down three steps and enter the bar—I stopped. I could see Woodley through the window. He had ordered another round, and he seemed to be both sneering and smiling at the same time. I desperately wanted to walk in and confront him, bash him in the face, if it came to that. But I knew neither Steven Konigsberg nor Steven King could do it. I felt gutless and weak. I walked slowly back to the corner, where I hailed a cab.

Twenty-one

As luck would have it, my folks came to town the very next day. They're
nuts about the theater, so I had arranged for us to go every night. Tina
called in sick two days in a row so she could take them to museums
and show them around town. Since I had a lot to do on my own book to
get it ready for publication, I stayed home during the day to work. As I
was now a famous author, they understood. Additionally, I had also fallen
behind in retyping the next Ben book, which meant I was working from
eight to six. When I got back to the apartment each night, there were no
fewer than three calls from Woodley on the machine. They became more
and more threatening as his alcohol intake increased over the course of the
day.

"Konigsberg, you're beginning to piss me off. This is no way to treat a
valuable collaborator. We need to get our business done. Remember that
French movie about driving the nitroglycerin through the jungle? Well, I'm
getting a lot like that nitro—very unstable. I could go off big-time anytime
now. Get your fucking act together and call me real fast."

The Plaza had also called a few times: Woodley was running up bills like
a sheikh from the Emirates, and they kept checking with me to make sure
it was okay. Only the best champagne and bordeaux for Woodley—enough
to bathe in. And then there were the charges in the shops in the lobby. He
wouldn't need a new outfit for quite a while. There was nothing I could do

but tell them that it was fine: just send the bill to me. I was swinging between fear and a rage that pounded at me like a jackhammer.

The morning after I saw my parents off, I called Woodley.

"About fucking time. I was debating whether to call the *Enquirer* or
Oprah first. Who do you think has the bigger audience?"

"You can knock off that kind of talk, Woodley. I can meet you tonight."

"That's mighty white of you. I was beginning to get a case of cabin fever
here at the Plaza."

"I hope the case of Cristal helped keep that at bay."

"I wasn't fortunate enough to have your kind of education. An unlet-
tered guy like myself needs different ways to pass the time."

"Where and when? And don't say the Four Seasons."

"You make me feel like an ugly gal you like to bang but won't bring to
the party. Anyway, I've been to the Four Seasons already. Liked it a lot.
Tried to charge it to you, but I forgot to get your approval in advance. You
know there's a place here that I've always wanted to go to."

"I can't wait to hear."

"Coney Island."

"Coney Island? It's not summer."

"So fucking what? I'll be there at nine."

"Where? I've never been there, either."

"There's this old roller coaster ride I've seen in the movies. It's called the
Cyclone. I'll meet you there. After we settle our business, you can buy me
a hot dog."

I told Tina that I was going out to see a movie. She was at her desk in the
library working on her lesson for the next day. Without looking up she said
she'd probably be asleep when I got back. I had made a point of seeing
twenty minutes of a French film that afternoon just in case she asked me
what I was going to see. I also read a couple of reviews on the Internet, so
I could discuss it with her the next day if I had to. I leaned over and kissed
her on the back of the neck, inhaling her warm, sweet essence, and headed
out for the garage.

It was a cold, windy night, more like autumn than early spring. I punched in Surf Avenue as the destination on the GPS in my car and got there in under forty minutes. The place was deserted, so I had no problem finding a parking spot across the street from the ride. Woodley wasn't there, but luckily I had brought a copy of the *New York Review of Books* and was able to read it by standing directly under a streetlamp. I was midway through a review of a biography of Hemingway (yes, another one) when I looked up and saw a meter maid writing a ticket for my car. I dashed across the avenue and confronted the young woman.

"Excuse me," I said in a warm tone. "I just stopped here for a minute to pick up a friend. I was waiting for him across the street." She didn't look up and just kept writing. I couldn't keep the testiness out of my voice. "I was talking to you just now."

"The sign behind you says no parking from seven to ten. It's nine-eleven," she said, pulling up the sleeve of her brown uniform and glancing at a cheap plastic watch.

"Can't you give me a break? I was standing across the street, damn it, just waiting for someone."

Finally, she looked up as she handed me the ticket. She had a round young face, shiny as a button.

"If you want to plead not guilty, just read the back of the summons." With that, she walked off.

I crumpled up the ticket and tossed it away, cursing to myself as I walked back across the avenue. The ticket probably cost thirty-five bucks, maybe fifty, and my business manager would eventually pay it, but it still bothered the hell out of me. I knew I was pissed at Woodley, not that poor girl, who was just doing her job. And no sooner had I reached the sidewalk on the other side when a taxi pulled up and Woodley got out.

He was wearing a soft, shiny black leather jacket that wrapped around his packing-crate body as tightly as a cigar band.

"You like?"

"Let's get down to business. I didn't come for a fashion show," I answered.

"I think you'll agree with me when you see the bill that I got a good deal. Feel the leather—it's like a baby's ass."

I began to go down the street that bordered the ride. Woodley, a step behind, started to whistle. Holding hands, a young black couple walked slowly on the other side in the opposite direction. Ahead was the board-walk, the wide wooden walkway deserted except for a few strollers in the distance. Woodley insisted we walk down the stairs to the beach.

"In a couple of months there'll be more people tanning their asses here than vote in my town. Listen. Hear those waves?"

The sand was damp and heavy as cement. I followed him toward the water.

"Let's get this over with. There's no way I'm going to give you a per-centage. I'll jump you to seventy-five hundred a week and a bonus of fifty thousand if the next book performs as well as the one before. That's my best offer."

"You keep this shit up and you're going to have big trouble. You're mak-ing millions. I want a real taste of that, or else."

"Or else what? You blow the whistle, and you'll find the checks stop real fast."

We were near the waterline when Woodley turned and moved to within inches of my face.

"Try to understand this, Mr. Famous Novelist. I never earned more than thirty-seven thou a year until I found you out. But the money you've given me has only made me understand all the years when I had nothing. My face was pressed so hard to the glass looking at the way guys like you lived that I could barely breathe. I'm not interested in being well-off. Fuck that. It's like when you give someone who's dying of thirst a sip of water. That fuck-ing sip just makes them realize that they need a whole lot more. Now it's my time to step up to the plate. Either you really change my life or I'll blow up your neat little world right into the fucking sky."

"Thank you, Mr. Woodley," I said, and then turned my back on him and walked toward the boardwalk.

"What the fuck are you talking about?"

"For helping me to stop living a lie. You go ahead and call whoever you want, I don't care. Ring up the *Enquirer*, the *Star*, and the *Post*. Call Geraldo, Barbara, and Judge Judy. Feel free. Whatever the tabloids write or the TV shows scream about, so be it. Those who really care about me will under-stand. As for the others, as you would say, fuck 'em."

I suddenly felt like running for the sheer hell of it. Now the sand didn't feel heavy. It was like dust under my feet. The wind off the ocean seemed to push me ahead even faster. I could see the light of the streetlamps shining into the darkness under the boardwalk, so I headed for it. I wanted to run forever.

"Where the fuck are you going?" Woodley shouted after me.

"To the light," I yelled, laughing. "To that beautiful light."

"Stop, damn you."

As I neared the gloom under the boardwalk, I slowed down. It was only another forty feet or so, and I could make out small mounds of trash littering the sand, like bodies scattered on a battlefield. When I got under it, the smell of rot and urine was so strong I almost took out my handkerchief. Then suddenly, I was tackled from behind. I hit the ground heavily, spat out some sand, and tried to get up.

"You're not going anywhere, Stevie."

When I managed to turn onto my back Woodley straddled me, his weight pinning me to the ground. Then I looked up and saw that he was holding a gun.

"Unless I hear a new story line from you, I'm going to use this. If serious money isn't going to come my way, you sure as shit aren't going to enjoy yours. No fucking way."

"So now you're going to kill me? Extortion wasn't enough for you?" Strangely, I wasn't afraid—that is, until he pulled the trigger. The shot went into the sand, inches from my head. The sound seemed to bounce around us madly, and though I saw Woodley's lips move, for a few seconds I couldn't make out what he was saying.

"Take my word for it, the next one you won't hear," he said as he pressed the barrel of the gun to my forehead. "Are you having any second thoughts about my proposal?"

"I won't say a word until you move that away." My voice didn't sound as scared as I was.

"I bet you've never seen a gun this close up." Woodley smiled down at me. "I bought this baby from a guy in a bar yesterday. I'm such a hick that the thought of a little protection in the big city seemed very appealing."

I heard the footfall of someone walking above us. I wanted to scream, but I couldn't.

"What the hell is that?" Woodley yelled out, and swatted at something behind him with his gun hand. "Jesus, it's a rat. Oh, no, there's more than one." I could hear the chiseled squeals of the rats as Woodley turned away from me and tried to shoo them away. "Get the hell away, you miserable bastards."

I still don't know how I did it, but as Woodley flailed away, I pushed up with all my strength and shoved him off. He reached for me and we rolled together in the black sand, his hot, fetid breath wet against my neck.

"Hell," he screamed. "The fucker bit me."

He fired wildly, two shots, so close together they sounded like one. I grabbed for the gun. I had to stop him. The next shot could hit me. I tried to pull the gun away, but his grip was tighter than a vise. Woodley fired again.

"I'll kill every miserable one of you," he spat out.

We tumbled like kids on a snowbank, and for a moment I was on top. Woodley pulled the gun away from me and struggled to his feet, pulling me up with him as if I were his partner in a dance marathon. I chopped at his hand, and his arm swung up wildly as the gun went off again. But then Woodley's grip went slack, and he settled against me like a deflated balloon. We fell to the ground. I pushed myself out from under him and lay there, gasping. I don't remember how long it was before I raised myself up and looked down at Wayne Woodley. He looked surprised, as if he had just been told an amazing story. I reached to touch the pulse on the side of his neck, then stopped. In the gloom I could make out a wet ribbon of blood, almost like a clown's makeup, snaking down from his left eye, an eye that was no longer there.

I have no recollection of driving home. What had started out like a nightmare now resembled the plot of one of those novels by the other Stephen King, who understands bad dreams like no other man on the planet.

Twenty-two

As soon as I woke up the next morning, I reached over to Tina's side of the bed, needing to be comforted, though I was still too groggy to realize why. Tina, of course, was already at school.

Then I froze and my eyes opened wide. The memory of last night seared its way into my mind. there was no chance of getting out of the way of it. Woodley was dead, a bullet through his eye. I started to tremble.

I got out of bed, pulled on my bathrobe, and went to the front door to retrieve my copies of the *Times* and the *Wall Street Journal* on the doormat. I searched through the *Times* twice, page by page, first the Metro section, then the rest. There was nothing about a killing under the Coney Island board-walk. But the *Times* was not the right paper for what I was looking for.

I called downstairs to the doorman and asked him to get me copies of the *Post* and the *Daily News*. I managed a calm and friendly hello to Carlos, the elevator man, who brought them to my door. I didn't even wait to sit down before racing through the two tabloids. Nothing. I was puzzled for a mo-ment; then it occurred to me that the encounter had probably taken place too late for the papers to include it.

What to do? The body would be discovered, probably already had been, and immediately reported to the police. The absence of the story from the newspapers was not a free pass to my old life—that was gone forever. A line had been irreversibly crossed.

Maybe I should call my lawyer, explain what had happened, and go with him to the police station. He was well known for his probity, and his presence would vouch for my character and honesty. But that idea was madness, I instantly realized. The police would think I had planned the killing to get Woodley off my back. Any rational person would think that. The sleazy reporters who monitored police doings, waiting for stories with red meat, would be off and running. The whole sordid mess would be spread out for their readers' delectation by evening, the next morning at the latest. What could be tastier than a double scoop of scandal?

I had only one option: cover my tracks. No one had seen the two of us at Coney Island, I was sure of that. I opened the closet and looked at the suit I had worn the night before. It was in remarkably good shape given what it had gone through, but when I turned down the cuffs, sand scattered on the floor like spilled sugar. A trip to the dry cleaner wasn't enough; safer to destroy the suit, though it was a favorite of mine. I scissored the jacket, then the pants, to ribbons; next the shirt. Finally, I grabbed my shoes and socks and threw them on the heap. I got out three black trash bags and divided the clothing among them, then stuffed all three into a large canvas bag. My plan was to distribute them in trash cans around the city. I vacuumed the sand from the floor of the closet and called the garage for my car.

I dropped the first trash bag in Morningside Heights, then stopped at a shadowy side street in the West Twenties. Finally, I proceeded to TriBeCa. As an extra precaution, I made certain there was no one in each vicinity to observe me. Not that anyone would have been suspicious; I was just another crude New Yorker dumping his trash in a public receptacle. Even people in new BMWs did that.

After my last stop I turned onto the West Side Highway and headed north. As I drove, I became more and more elated. No more Woodley. No more payments. No more threats. And no need for guilt on my part. After all, I hadn't killed Woodley. Woodley had killed himself. He fired the gun in the struggle, a struggle that could have led to my own death if he had prevailed.

Before going home I drove over to Café Boulud for a delightful lunch alone. To start things off, I asked the maître d' for a kir royale and toasted the gods for getting Woodley out of my life. I felt so good that I even had a chocolate soufflé for dessert.

Twenty-three

The next day the following story appeared in the *Post*:

> An unidentified man between the ages of 40 and 50 was found yesterday shot to death under the boardwalk at Surf Avenue and West 33rd Street. The victim had been shot once in the head. Detectives at the 60th Precinct said a gun was found by the body of the victim.

I read the piece four times trying to see if there was some subtext that I was missing. Then I checked the *News* and found an almost identical version except for speculation that the murder might have been a robbery gone awry. The *Times* ran something the following day but lumped it together with three murders in the Bronx. I tried to feel sorry for Woodley, but the well was dry. He was a nasty piece of work, crude and brutish, and whatever compassion I had for him had disappeared long before the event under the boardwalk. Was there a family back in Louisiana that loved him? Somehow I doubted it. I knew the best way to put this ugly business behind me was to work, and work hard. So I plunged into retyping the next Ben book and polishing my own novel. The week slipped by happily and productively.

Things with Tina were going better than they had for over a year. At first she had some trouble adjusting to both life in New York City and my new-found fame. She was overjoyed by my success, but some of the trappings and adulation that came with it made her uncomfortable. What she liked best was her teaching and quiet weekends at our place in Litchfield County. Gradually, we both got used to our new world. Our sex life, which had receded a bit, came roaring back. We couldn't keep our hands off each other, like teenagers.

One night we went to the theater. Even the play, a Pulitzer winner that was truly lousy, couldn't dampen our mood, and at dinner I ordered champagne instead of wine. Tina had no school the next day, and she was relaxed. We toasted each other two or three times.

"I've been thinking of something," Tina said after our second glass of champagne. "Or, rather, two things."

"Here's to the first of two things."

We clinked glasses again.

"For starters, what would you think of our living full-time in Connecticut?"

"I love our house, but I like it in town, too."

"You could always come in for a night or two each week. And you'd probably get more work done in the country."

Sure, I thought to myself, retyping manuscripts is always better in the country air.

"I've also done a little checking around with the schools up there. You know, places like Hotchkiss, Kent, the Gunnery. There's a chance I could get a job with one of them."

"What's the second thing?"

"I'll save that for when we get home."

Sometimes when sex is truly amazing, it seems as if you're on a distant planet. Existing in a time frame that moves as slowly as the path of the sun on a hot summer day. Afterward we lay laced together like those vines in the South, not moving, barely breathing.

"That was the second thing," Tina finally said.

"I like the second thing a lot."

"Maybe this was the time. You know what I mean?"

I was still somewhere else, so I just grunted.

"It felt different. Almost as if this was the way it was meant to be."

Then it hit me what Tina was referring to. The baby! Having a child was the only thing missing in our life. We'd been talking about it for a while. Yes, maybe this had been the time. Without undoing the tangle of our limbs, we both fell asleep instantly.

Tina was gone when I got up, not to school, but as a note on her pillow informed me, to a yoga class. As I showered, I realized I hadn't felt this good in a long time. I was finishing up breakfast, looking over the paper, when the phone rang. It was my private line.

"Hello," I said, expecting to hear a familiar voice.

"Could I please speak to Mr. Steven Konigsberg?" asked a man with a strong New York accent. As if I'd sustained a blow to the back of the head, I felt dizzy suddenly, and scared.

"Speaking."

"Mr. Konigsberg, this is Sal Rigano. I'm a detective with the Sixtieth Precinct in Brooklyn. Homicide. I'm near your apartment and I thought maybe I could see you for a few minutes."

"I'm busy right now."

"As I said, it won't take very long. It's concerning someone I believe you know. A Mr. Wayne Woodley. How about I come up in half an hour?"

Twenty-four

I sat immobile by the phone not even blinking. For at least another two very long minutes. I should have known the police would contact me. How could I have thought they wouldn't? Woodley had the Plaza send his damn bills to me. How could I have forgotten that? This detective—what was his name again?—would just ask me some routine questions, nothing that I couldn't answer easily. But hold on. I couldn't see him here. What if Tina came in while he was questioning me? That would be a disaster. I rushed to the phone. Thank God for Caller ID. I punched out the number—by the area code I knew it was a cell phone—and he answered on the second ring. I explained that I had to get something at my office. Would it be all right if we met there? No problem, he said.

Detective Salvatore V. Rigano (that's what it said on the card he handed me) was about my height with long, stylish black hair that shone like tar. His dark brown eyes were hooded by a brow as formidable as a cliff face. He was in his late thirties and wore a well-tailored suit with a blue shirt and a richly patterned tie. He held a large manila envelope which he switched to his other hand when we shook hands. He had the kind of strong grip you knew immediately could become a lot stronger.

"You're right on time. I thought you might have trouble parking."

"Police, Mr. Konigsberg," he said, smiling. "We can park anywhere we want to. One of the few perks we get."

"Well, what can I do for you, Detective?" I said as I sat down on the small couch under the window that looked out on a garden.

"I guess you don't know about what happened to Mr. Woodley."

"Something happened to Wayne?"

"He wasn't related to you, was he?"

"No. He just worked for me."

Rigano looked past me toward the window. He leaned forward and lowered his voice.

"I'm sorry to inform you that Mr. Woodley is dead. His body was found in Coney Island six days ago."

"Jesus," I gasped, as if someone were squeezing me. I thought I hit it just right.

"We believe he was murdered."

"Murdered? How?"

"Shot. It happened under the boardwalk. It looks like a robbery or maybe . . ." Rigano paused and looked down at the gleaming patina of his shoes. "Do you know if Mr. Woodley was a homosexual?"

"I have no idea. I don't think so."

"Do you know if he had a family? We haven't been able to locate any."

"Wayne hadn't been working for me that long. He never mentioned a family."

"What did he do for you?"

"He was a researcher—a very good one."

"Researcher?"

"For my next novel. I'm thinking of setting it in Louisiana. In Cajun country. He knew the area well."

"I wish you were running the police department, Mr. Konigsberg. You're quite generous. Putting up an employee at the Plaza. Not bad."

I gave Rigano a smile and a shrug.

Rigano continued in this manner for another twenty minutes. Most of his questions I couldn't answer, anyway (Did Woodley have a drug problem? Whom had he worked for before? How long had he lived in New Iberia?).

"Well," he said, rising, "I think that's about it. If I have any other questions, though I doubt I will, I'll give you a call. Same when we find the perp."

"Please, keep me informed. What a terrible thing. Poor Wayne."

He stopped at the door. He turned slowly and looked at me with a serious expression. Oh, shit, here it comes.

"Could you do me a big favor, Mr. Konigsberg?" he said as he opened the envelope he was carrying. He handed me a copy of *Juno's Dance*. "You're my favorite writer. I'd love it if you could sign this."

I've never been so happy to autograph a book. The clouds had parted, and now the sky before me was clear. I quickly grabbed two other books off the shelf and signed them, too ("This is for Salvatore Rigano, my favorite fan in law enforcement. All my best, Steven Konigsberg"). When I handed them to Detective Salvatore V. Rigano, he was beaming.

Twenty-five

From the beginning, Quentin Bass and I were more than simply teacher and student. I had had teachers I liked, but none that I could call a friend. He was tall and lanky, about fifteen years older than me, and hailed from outside Detroit, where his father was a worker on the line for GM. For an aspiring writer, aspiring first to put distance between himself and his hometown, the Iowa Writers' Workshop must have seemed like Valhalla. He got his undergraduate degree from the university, then moved neatly into a position as an instructor of creative writing. He climbed the ladder until he reached associate professor, where he stayed until he was asked to leave. I helped to put out the net to catch him before he hit the pavement. If he was thankful, he certainly never mentioned it. But his lack of social graces never bothered me.

Since Quentin's move to New York, we had gotten into the habit of having dinner together once a month. I usually called and set the date, which Quentin would cancel at the last moment. We then started the whole process again, negotiating with each other as if we were planning a summit meeting rather than a dinner. This time, however, Quentin telephoned me. He seemed anxious to see me. We decided to meet in a small French restaurant in SoHo.

Tina, as usual, begged off. She found Quentin pretentious and angry, with the kind of anger she was convinced could boil over like a pot untended on a burner. I couldn't argue with her about that, but it didn't shake my loyalty to Quentin. He was the one who taught me what good writing was all about, as he saw it, and persuaded me that I had the ability to run the course. If it had not been for him, I would have dropped out after a semester and fulfilled my parents' dreams by enrolling in one of the Jewish grad school trinity: business, medicine, or law.

On my way downtown to meet Quentin, I thought about my days in Iowa. Quentin lived in a large, run-down Victorian near the campus. There were always parties on the weekends, with lots of cheap red wine, surprisingly high-quality grass, and women who were mad either for sex or for constant talk of writers and writing. A few, luckily, were mad about both. At that time Quentin was a star. He had just published his third novel, a feat that impressed the shit out of us all. Never mind that his personal life was a mess. His marriage (number two) had ended that semester, and the serious drinking had begun. Drunk one night, he went to punch out a fellow faculty member, and it was only the quick moves of several guys, including me, that enabled us to wrestle him away and prevent a major debacle.

Midway through his second martini, Quentin got to the point of why he wanted to have dinner.

"That book you sent me last week . . . what was its title?"

"*Time's Pulse*," I answered in as neutral a tone as possible. I had sent Quentin an advanced reading galley. Of course, I didn't tell him it was my book.

"I loved it," he said, draining his drink and waving his hand for another. "This is real writing. Totally on target."

"You think so?" I was flattered and excited by what he said. It was what I needed to hear.

"Absolutely. The characters are strong, the writing spare yet lyrical, and the premise, how and why we need to create our own sense of time, extremely appealing. This"—he raised his fork in the air as if it were the book—"is what you should be doing."

I was set to tell him that it was mine when something made me stop. He had never said word one about the three earlier Ben manuscripts I had sent him.

"I'd love to give it a quote, but in my current state I guess it wouldn't mean much." He paused to fish an olive from his glass with his finger, then asked, "Who's the author? I never heard of Chambers Benjamin."

I wanted to tell Quentin it was my book, but the secret I shared with

Dexter—our Manhattan Project—was inviolate. Finally, I mumbled something about Chambers Benjamin being someone Dexter Parch had been carefully bringing along after discovering him at a writers' conference.

"That's hard to believe. Parch's taste is so far up his ass it would take a team of Navy SEALs to find it."

"I think that's unfair. Dexter is a good publisher. He has a wide range."

"Yeah, from shit to horseshit," he said, motioning to the waiter for another drink.

"I think you should go easy on the booze."

"I'll do whatever the fuck I want, Steven Konigsberg. Maybe you're afraid of the truth."

"The only thing I'm afraid of is your falling off your chair."

"Very funny, Mr. Bestseller. You want to know what I think about your Konigsberg opuses? I'll tell you: I find them repulsive. They're all about story, plot, and pace, a pace you relentlessly and calculatingly manipulate like a fucking metronome. There's nothing else: no feeling, no voice, no soul. Though the writing is serviceable—you can't write anything that isn't at least decent—the books aren't serious. They're shams, best-selling machines stamped out like lawn mowers. Something made for one reason only: to entertain! How could you have done it?"

"Done what?" I answered in just above a whisper. I was desperate to get Quentin to tone it down. "Written books that entertain and move people? Stories have been what people want, from the beginning of time. And stories are what people need. When they're good, they buy them. I'm thrilled I'm able to do it."

"Bullshit!" said Quentin, now shouting. Half the restaurant turned our way. I thought I heard someone say at a nearby table, "Isn't that Steven Konigsberg?" "Don't get sanctimonious with me, Steven. We're both too old for that."

"Gentlemen, gentlemen," said an older man with a French accent who suddenly appeared at our table. "Could you please lower your voices? You're in a restaurant, not out in the street."

"Why don't you get back in the kitchen, Pierre?" said Quentin, waving the man away like a child being sent to bed. He picked up his martini and drank half of it in a swallow. "I'll tell you what you're after. It's the money, and of course the fame."

"You're being ridiculous," I said, becoming angry myself.

"No hack can call me ridiculous," he said, shooting up from his chair, which he knocked over. "You don't need me. I'm sure your bulging checkbook is enough to keep you company." As he turned toward the front door, he caught the edge of the table, which teetered for just a moment before crashing to the floor. Dishes, glasses, and food cascaded across the floor in a smorgasbord of Quentin's rage.

"Quentin, Quentin," I called out to him, but he was out the door. I threw some money down on the bar, a lot more than what the check would be, then rushed outside, but there was no sign of him. I started to walk uptown. My first thought was petty and self-centered: would this incident be recounted on "Page Six" of the *Post* tomorrow? So what? was my immediate response. Part of Quentin's behavior was motivated by jealousy, I was positive of it. If he wanted to rile me, he had succeeded brilliantly. My belief had always been that after the next Ben book, I would stop this double life and turn to my own work, the real work. But I kept putting that off. I was in the same fix I'd been in when I first put my name to *Juno's Dance*. A fabulous fix, but a fix nonetheless. Like an addict, I was constantly looking for a "magical cure," something fast and easy that would let me keep the high of being a bestseller novelist while casting off the suffocating guilt and fear of being discovered.

I continued walking north. I'd be damned if Quentin would be the person to make a decision for me. He was envious, pure and simple—so why did I feel lousy? When I realized that I was only a block away from my apartment, I still didn't have any answers.

When I got up to the apartment, Tina asked me how dinner had gone. As I struggled to say something that didn't sound as bad as I felt, she just said, "Why you continue to see him is beyond me. Chester needs a walk. That'll be good for both of you."

Chester was not a city dog and was always straining on the leash whenever he got a sniff of a bird or a squirrel. He loved it in Connecticut where he could run in our fields. I reached down and patted him.

"You were there when I started this whole thing, Chester. Why didn't you say anything?"

As we walked around the Sheep Meadow, I proceeded to tell him about the entire miserable dinner and the sad condition of my soul, but mostly about my tortuous relationship with Quentin Bass. For at the base of our friendship, if it could still be called that, was another secret, one only

Quentin and I shared, dating back to the time I was a second-year graduate student in the writers' program at the University of Iowa. Quentin, whose class on short-story writing was my favorite, quickly became both my mentor and drinking buddy. His marriage to Nan, his second wife, was on the ropes, and the two of us started to spend a lot of time at a favorite watering hole for both faculty and students. Toward the end of my second year a story I had written and rewritten in Quentin's class was accepted by *Prairie Schooner,* a pretty good literary magazine of long standing. "The Path Home" was my first publication in a well-known journal.

"This calls for a celebration," said Quentin when I told him the news. "If memory serves me right, you'll be getting a check for a hundred fifty dollars—at least that's what they paid me for a story last year. A real writer should blow it all on a night of fun."

Quentin decided that we had to set our sights higher than the Wet Trilogy, so we drove in his car out of town to the Branding Iron, a steak joint that was pricey enough to have tablecloths. I had by now acquired, through many nights out with Quentin, a taste for gin martinis, extra dry with two olives—not one, not three, but two. At some point after the T-bone steaks and apple cobblers, and a marathon discussion on the genius of Joyce, we made our way to the bar, where we met two off-duty nurses who liked martinis as well as we did.

When the bar closed, Quentin decided he and I and the nurses should continue the festivities at my place, the second floor of an old brick house a block from the football stadium. He tossed me the keys, and I started to drive back to town. It was the end of March, and the night was typical of spring in Iowa, temperature in the low twenties and still a good half foot of snow on the ground.

My memory of the accident is hazy at best. I don't know what caused me to go off the road. All I remember is the car on its side in a cornfield, lying in an ocean of shardlike stubble, the headlights pointing into the blackness as if announcing a movie premiere. I think Quentin got out on his own, and then the two of us extracted one of the nurses from the backseat. Then we realized that we were missing the other nurse. We found her moaning twenty feet away. She had been thrown from the car, and from the position of her leg, I could see that she had a bad break.

"Steve, do what I'm doing," said Quentin, down on his knees, scooping up a handful of snow and rubbing it into his face. I heard the sound of a police siren in the distance. "This will help wake you up a bit." The explosion of the snow crystals against my skin jarred me into a semblance of clarity.

And then the police were there, two cars and three officers. A minute later an ambulance pulled up.

The cops had witnessed this kind of scene many times before. One came over to us while the two others checked the nurses.

"Who was driving?"

Before I could say a word, Quentin stepped in front of me and said, "I was."

After that, everything seemed to be on fast-forward. Quentin was given the Breathalyzer, which he failed impressively. The nurses went into the ambulance, and Quentin was booked for DUI and driving with an expired license. The cops dropped me off at my place, where I slept through a whole day's worth of classes.

It took Quentin two years before he could get his license back, and though his insurance picked up some of the cost of the nurses' suits against him, eventually he had to declare bankruptcy. The only conversation we had about the accident was a week later over Diet Cokes. We were both on the wagon, though I stayed on it longer than Quentin.

"What happened that night is between the two of us," he said. "If they had nailed you as the driver, you would have kissed your degree good-bye. That's why I did it. I already have mine. No one else will know, and I'll find it very boring if you ever bring it up again. You can be assured I won't."

Quentin was good to his word. The years that followed my leaving Iowa City certainly didn't bring the two of us closer. I also began to see all of Quentin's worst qualities come increasingly to the fore, but I knew I could never abandon him. No one understood why I treated him as well as I did, and, sadly, no one ever would.

Twenty-six

I met Douglas Tern in the greenroom of *Regis and Kelly* a few days later. After I had accepted the role of honorary chairman of the Literacy Partners Benefit Dinner scheduled for the following week, I'd let the head of the dinner committee pester me into going on the show to promote the event. Though I was regularly sought out to help and endorse numerous charities, I found the mission of tackling adult literacy to be a special one. I also felt it was the kind of cause that Ben would have thought worthy. I had done the *Regis* show twice before while promoting my book. I was scheduled to be the last guest, so I had a chance to watch the monitor and observe the person preceding me.

Douglas Tern was a well-known private investigator who was publicizing his first book, *A Very Private Eye*. I had read about Tern a number of times in the tabloids. He seemed to be in the middle of almost every other high-profile scandal. He had a large organization that was based in half a dozen cities, and the title of his book seemed to be amazingly accurate. He was willing to talk about his techniques and methods, but not a word about his numerous famous clients. I loved his firm's motto: "We keep our eyes open and our mouths shut." His approach didn't seem to be the recipe for a best-selling book, but I thought Tern was a rare guy in a somewhat sleazy business: he appeared to be honorable. And then something clicked inside my head. Tern was the man I needed. I had to meet him as soon as possible.

A few minutes later he came into the greenroom to retrieve his briefcase. He walked directly over to where I was sitting and said, "I just want you to know, Mr. Konigsberg, that I'm one of your biggest fans. It's a real honor to meet you."

We had lunch later that week at Lupa, an Italian restaurant in the Village that was a favorite of mine. Though mobbed for dinner, the place was quiet for lunch. Like diplomats, we had a ritual exchange as soon as we sat down. I handed Tern all my books, signed, in a large envelope. He handed me his book, with an awkward smile. I could see he felt the exchange was uneven. I opened the book and read, "This is for Steven Konigsberg. A new friend who, hopefully, will become a good one." Though he had known many celebrities in his lengthy career, I could see that sitting down with me for lunch was a special occasion for him. I realized that what Tern was responding to was not really me, Steven Konigsberg the typist: he was basking in the reflected glow and heat of Steven Konigsberg the celebrity. It made him feel special to be with me. I had even noticed the change in my parents. They looked at me differently and were constantly bringing in friends and neighbors to meet me whenever I visited them. If most people want to be a celebrity, even more want to meet one.

We chatted for a few minutes about publishers and publicity tours (Tern was off to the West Coast the following day), then family (he was a devout Catholic with six children).

"When I saw you on the *Regis* show," I said, taking a sip from my glass of wine, "I was impressed by your discretion."

"Thank you. It's the principal tenet of my business."

"The best way for you to know what's on my mind is for me to tell you a story about a man who was very important in my life. His name was Ben Chambers." Tern leaned forward, his eyes locked on mine, a look of rapt concentration and excitement stamped on his face.

Slowly and carefully, I told Tern the story of my relationship with Ben, going into how we met and how close we became. Then I got to how he willed everything to me, leaving out, of course, the manuscripts in the trunk. I recounted the many occupations Ben had had during his life, and every detail about his past that I could remember.

"You see, Doug, I loved the man."

"I can understand why. He sounds like he was an amazing person."

"What I'm getting at is that for all I just told you, I realize there's so much more about Ben Chambers that I don't know."

"I think I know where you're going."

"Good. When you love someone, you can't know enough about them. I want you to find out everything you can about Ben. Do you think you can help me?" I asked as innocently as a kid crossing the street alone for the first time.

"Do you mind if I take a few notes?" Tern removed a thin black leather notepad from his inside pocket. Tucked in the binding was a gold pen.

"Before you write, Doug, there's one caveat: I don't want anyone who was important in Ben's life to be contacted directly. I just want to know something about them: who they are, where they live—that kind of thing. You understand."

"Of course."

No, you don't, but I'm glad you think you do.

"I could see you were a decent guy from the moment I met you. You don't want to upset the lives of these people from your friend's past. It's commendable."

Yes, and I also didn't want them to know that I was checking up on them. If there's another Wayne Woodley out there, I wanted to know about him before he showed up at my door with a big smile and his hand out.

"This is going to be expensive, Steve. There are quite a few years and territory to cover. Compiling this kind of dossier takes a lot of people and a lot of time."

"I figured that would be the case."

"Now, I'll need as much info as you can give me. Social Security number is a must. Military ID would be great, too. And if you could possibly also supply his . . ."

As Doug Tern continued with the laundry list of data he needed to do his job, I felt a wave of satisfaction wash over me. I had always thought of myself as a pretty smart guy, but maybe, just maybe, I was getting a little bit smarter as things went along. It was a comforting thought.

Twenty-seven

I spent six hours in my office working on the outline of my new book and starting to retype Ben's next one. It was a long book, almost six hundred onionskin pages. (All but four of his books were written on onionskin; the paper was almost as fragile as a spiderweb, and each sheet had the smell of a damp basement.) I didn't know when I would publish it, but I had gotten to the point where I hated the retyping process. Working on them well in advance in small bursts seemed an easier way to do it. I didn't even go out to eat. Our housekeeper, Maria, made me a tuna fish sandwich and, like a kid in grade school, I brown-bagged it.

When I got back to the apartment, I went directly to my study, where my assistant was on the phone. He handed me a list of phone messages.

TODAY'S CALLS

1) 10:17 Your mother: Don't forget to call your dad tom'w. It's his birthday.

2) 10:42 Marti Runyan/Chancery: Remember you have a phone interview with Hank Small's Big Show (KQED) on Thurs. They will call here at 3:40 (our time).

3) 11:03 Your mother: Same message as above. (Didn't she call yesterday, too?)

4) 12:11 Stuart: Rec'd check from Paramount. Also, Leigh Fur-

nace (he's set to direct *Beyond the Night Sky*) would like to meet you. Dinner Thurs? Le Bernardin? Would Tina like to come?

    5) 12:18 Javier Miranda-Levi: He's your new Spanish publisher. Staying at the Carlyle. Would love to have a drink, lunch, dinner, etc.

    6) 12:56 Your tailor: The jacket is ready. He's sending it over.

    7) 1:33 Detective Sal Rigano: Needs to talk to you. Call him on his cell. 917-555-0016.

I immediately thought of the old line about an impending execution being a wonderful way to focus the mind: there were another eight or ten calls on the list, but Rigano's name was the only one I saw. I knew I couldn't speak to him from the apartment. The office was the only safe place to make the call.

"Fred, I'm going to take Chester for a walk."

"I just walked him an hour ago."

"Well, I need a walk, and his company will be good. I'll probably get back after you've left. See you tomorrow."

When I got back to my office, I went to the desk and picked up the phone. Then I put it down. There was no problem here. Rigano had just come up with some more info on Woodley. Or maybe he wanted an autographed copy of *Juno's Dance* for his brother-in-law. I closed my eyes for a moment to compose myself, then called the number.

"Rigano here."

"Hi, it's Steven Konigsberg."

My voice sounded a little high to me. I had to lower it.

"Thanks for calling back, Steve."

"What's up?"

That's better. Nice basso tone there.

"A few things have come up—we should meet."

"Sure. What's good for you?"

My basso was now an alto.

"How 'bout lunch tomorrow?"

"I think I can do that. Where'd you like to meet?"

If he said Coney Island, I was going to pass out.

"This might sound a little forward, but I've always wanted to go to the Four Seasons. I've never been there. You think that would be possible?"

"I'm pretty sure I can get a reservation."

There's no chance he'd arrest me at the Four Seasons.

"For the Grill Room?"

"What time?"

I made a reservation for one o'clock and showed up ten minutes early wearing my new jacket, which made me look a lot better than I felt inside. Of course, Detective Rigano was there waiting for me.

"This is great, Steve," he said, giving me his patented bear-trap handshake.

A waiter came to the table with Rigano's Coke and my usual, a mixture of orange juice and cranberry juice. The color, like the sinking sun on a hot August day, usually made me feel good. Now it brought up an image of Dante's *Inferno*.

"Is that Henry Kissinger over there?" he whispered to me.

"Yes. He eats here a lot."

"And isn't that . . ."

Like a tour guide at Colonial Williamsburg, I pointed out the celebs in attendance, a number of whom waved to me when they saw me looking their way. After thanking me twice for the books I had given him, Rigano took out his notebook and brought me up-to-date on what he'd discovered so far.

Woodley, he believed, had definitely been in a fight with another person, presumably a man. That person didn't shoot him. Rigano was sure of that.

"Also, our forensic people found some fibers from someone else's clothing on Woodley's hands."

Thank God I got rid of that suit!

"I've found out quite a bit about Mr. Woodley's past life. I know you said he was a great researcher, but his sheet reads like he was a real slimeball."

I tried to look surprised.

"Married twice. Both marriages ended over physical abuse charges. A kid from each, but it doesn't seem like he was in touch with either of them."

Lucky kids.

"Ten months in L.A. County for assault with intent and two years and change in Danbury for mail fraud. The boy's been around."

Rigano put his pad away when our first course of *terrine de veau* arrived. He had asked me to order for both of us. Sal loved the dish and especially flipped for the little *cornichons* that accompanied it. He took out his pad and carefully wrote down the name of the dish, which I spelled out for him slowly. Our main course, *sole grillée*, he also found wondrous.

"This is nothing like the flounder my wife, Teresa, makes. Damn it, it's good."

By the time we were served our cappuccinos, I was beginning to feel relaxed.

"Do you remember the Son of Sam case?" Rigano asked me as he reached for a petit four.

"Sure. Who doesn't?"

"Do you remember how they nailed him?"

"Didn't a neighbor call the police?"

"No, that wasn't it." He drained his cup and then took another petit four. "They nailed him on a parking ticket."

Oh, shit. Here it comes.

"One of the detectives checked all the cars that were given parking tickets the night of one of the murders. Bingo." I picked up my drink with someone else's hand and took a sip, surprised that I hadn't spilled it all over the table. "On my way over here, you know what I thought I'd be doing now? Reading you your Miranda rights and then, after you settled the bill, taking you downstairs, where I'd cuff you in my car before taking you to be booked." He reached over and put his hand atop mine. "Steve, why didn't you tell me you were there that night?"

I paused long enough to give someone the impression that I might be having a mini-stroke. Sal just stared at me and waited.

"I wish I could answer that."

Now, here's the part that proves that there is a God, or, at least, there is one for Steven Konigsberg. Sal didn't really want me to answer his question. He had already answered it for himself.

"He was shaking you down, right?" I imagine my head trembled slightly in assent. "When I first met you, I spotted you as a good guy. Decent, feet on the ground, regular joe kind of guy. Like me. Even though you're a writing genius, you're still a right guy. You know, Steve, when I started on the force, my first captain said to me, 'Rigano, don't ever forget this: our job is to put the dirtbags of this world away. The good folks, people like us, we have to help.' And that's what I still believe. I've been dealing with the guys like Wayne Woodley since I've been on the force. Mutts like him should be put away for keeps. Whether it's robbery or a shakedown, they just want to hurt decent people. Woodley got what was coming to him. What I'm doing would get me thrown off the force, maybe even indicted, but I don't care. I know in my bones that you're innocent, and I refuse to have a hand in ruining the life of a decent man. I can spot a guy who's guilty from two rooms away, and that's not you. Chances are a jury would find you innocent, but I don't want to take that chance. I really don't care what happened under the boardwalk that night—whether you were even there or not. I know you're a good guy, and good guys have to be protected. No one is going to know that your car was parked on Surf Avenue that night."

At that moment I wanted to hug Sal Rigano, right there in front of Henry Kissinger and every other power broker in the room. I wanted to jump up on the table and shout, "God bless Detective Salvatore V. Rigano. Ladies and gentlemen, save for Ben Chambers, this is the best man I've ever met."

"Thanks, Sal. I don't know what to say. If there is anything I can ever do for you, just name it."

We exchanged another power handshake and looked at each other.

"Your friendship is enough."

"You've certainly got that."

I was about to ask if there maybe wasn't something I could do in a monetary way for the Police Benevolent Association, or maybe even the Rigano family itself, when Sal coughed nervously and said, "There may be one thing."

"Name it," I blurted out.

"You know how much I love your work, Steve. You're really great. But there's another writer I love, too."

Where the hell was this going?

"Who's that?"

"Joseph Wambaugh. I'm knocked out by his police stuff."

"I like him, too," I answered quickly, though I had never read a word of the man's work.

"You see, Steve, I've been working on a book myself. A novel. I think I have a good story to tell, but I don't know if I can pull it off without help. You know where I'm going here?"

"I think I do." I was now trying to control my facial muscles from giving me a smile like an amusement park dummy. "And, yes, I'd love to help you with your writing. It would be a privilege."

Twenty-eight

After we left the Four Seasons, we arranged to meet on Wednesday of the following week. Sal's days off were Tuesday and Wednesday, but on Tuesday he helped out in his father-in-law's butcher shop in Bensonhurst to bring in extra money. I used the week before our first session to read Joseph Wambaugh's work. Sal was right about Wambaugh's police novels. The characters were both gritty and warm, and the world that he created around them was totally convincing. My next task was to read Sal's manuscript, *Grind Squad*. He had dropped off 180 pages the day after our lunch. After reading it I knew that Sal had a long journey ahead of him to become a published writer, let alone the next Joseph Wambaugh. Though his central theme—whether a group of cops in a squad devoted to drug busts in a crime-infested housing project would testify against one of their own in a police brutality case—was a good one, the writing was overblown. Some of the dialogue was sharp and funny, but many scenes went on too long, and I had a hard time differentiating between some of the characters. Still, Sal was doing what most would-be writers never do: he was writing about something he knew and cared about. If Sal's book was a mining claim, it would be one that would require a lot of excavation to expose the vein. But there was no question that the book contained real ore.

Sal, wearing a suit and tie, showed up right on time (no surprise), and after dancing around a bit I came out and told him exactly what I thought about the book.

"Jesus, Steve, that's great."

"What do you mean?"

"Well, you said that there was something there. Coming from you, that means a lot to me. And I love that image about the mine. Well, I'm ready to turn on my miner's light and start digging, if you are."

"I just happen to have my pickax right here, too. So let's get going."

Before I knew it, we had worked for almost three hours. We had gone through forty pages of the manuscript, and Sal probably had fifteen pages of notes that he took on a legal-size pad in a precise, even script. Before he left, I gave him a bunch of books: Fitzgerald's *Tender Is the Night*, Mailer's *The Deer Park*, and a collection of Ray Carver stories.

"I don't expect you to finish all of these by next week, Sal, but try to dip into a couple of them. To write well, you have to understand good writing. These are all very different, but they share a common thread. We'll talk about what that is next week." Sal clutched the books as if I had given him a piece of the true cross.

"This was great. I can't wait for next week."

"Neither can I."

And you know something? I really meant it.

Part

A COMPLICATED LIFE

Writers are always selling somebody out.

—Joan Didion

Twenty-nine

One of my rituals was to inventory my cache of manuscripts, the mother lode only I knew about.

From the beginning of this amazing adventure, I had learned to lie with ease. It was as if I were born to be a con man. Sometimes I wasn't even aware I was lying. Whenever I had the presence of mind to step back from the moment, I had to acknowledge that there was no such thing as one lie. Like dominoes, one falling down and knocking over the next, these lies led to many more. I lied to everyone I was closest to: Tina, my parents, Stuart, Quentin, Parch. I hadn't been on the level with any of them since this journey to fame and riches started. For someone who had once been totally open about everything, the top of my bureau a kind of clearinghouse for my most personal matters—checks, letters, bills, prescriptions—it was a stunning and unsettling reversal.

Though someone else might think it was overkill, I checked on the manuscripts every six months. I had a complete list of the books, numbered according to a simple numerical code based on the name Vanderbilt (since the word is ten letters long and no letter is repeated, it works like this: "V" equals 1, "a" is 2, and so on), as well as by a version of the shorthand Pepys used in writing his diary. This list I kept in the safe in my office with the manuscript that I was currently retyping. Still I had a need to see the manuscripts in the flesh. Like a miser for whom a bankbook wasn't enough, I had to touch my treasures periodically.

I had stored them in a large safe-deposit box in a bank in midtown Manhattan. I felt like one of the old ladies I occasionally saw in these vaulted rooms, the only other souls I ever encountered, who were there to examine their jewels. I supposed that they had their emeralds and diamonds, and I had mine. I'm sure we felt the same when we entered the locked private carrel with the deposit box in hand. Here I would open the large envelopes, each containing a manuscript, to verify my code and the continued presence of the material. I was dead serious about this job, the source of my amazing double life.

In the second box I examined, I came across one of Ben's children's stories, which I pulled out and read right there in the small, windowless room. *The Dam and the Pocket* was predictably charming. It featured a beaver named Brooks, and a wren, Wally. One is a master builder; the other uses whatever he can find for his nest: the eaves of a porch, the top of a door frame, and, in this story, the pocket of a pair of overalls hung on a clothesline. The two animals are great friends, but one cannot understand the other. In the end, of course, they come to appreciate each other very well.

As I held the story in my hands, I wondered: what if I took a break from publishing the novels? A children's book would be a perfect change, and there would be far less chance for a Wayne Woodley to come out of the woods to threaten my very existence. I removed the story from the metal box, took it to my office, and quickly retyped it, which took barely an hour. Brimming with excitement, I carried it home that afternoon. Tina would be the first to hear it.

After dinner, I announced that I had a surprise. Tina sat down on the sofa in the living room with an air of expectation, like a kid at a party. As I read the story, I could see the delight in her face. I knew she loved it.

"I adore it, Steve," she said, reaching over to hug me. "It's so original. I didn't have any idea you were interested in children's stories, or that you'd ever thought of writing one."

"The idea just came to me, maybe because I have a resident expert here."

"Well, maybe . . . but you know that's not it."

"Maybe you're right," I said, grinning.

"I spend most of my time with children, and I couldn't have come up with that story in a hundred years. You can do it because you're a born storyteller. It's that simple. If we lived ten thousand years ago in a cave, you'd be the person who everyone would gather around at night to hear you tell stories. You've written a totally charming book. My fourth graders will love it, but grown-ups will, too. I think I know you better than anyone, but you continually amaze me. Now, give me another kiss."

I kissed Tina softly on the lips and then drew her close. After a moment she pulled away and said, "I hope you know, Steven King, that you make me very, very happy."

"It's a distant second to the way you make me feel."

"You know, darling, this is the first time since Boothbay Harbor you've shown me your work before it was in galleys."

"Well, from now on I will."

"I'd like that. From the time you first showed me something, I loved it. What are you writing now?"

What *was* I working on? I could tell her in great detail of the start I had made on my own new novel, my Chambers Benjamin book. But what book of Ben's was I currently retyping? I had gotten to dislike the retyping process so intensely that I completely disengaged my mind and did the work like a little clerk earning minimum wage.

"I'm sorry, hon, but I was just looking at your eyes. Depending on the light, they seem to go from green to amber. They're beautiful."

"That's sweet, but you were going to tell me what you're working on."

"Right. It's about two brothers who inherit a huge international construction business. Something like the Bechtel Corporation." Very nice touch, I thought. I had just read about Bechtel in *Newsweek*. "I'm thinking of calling it *The Judgment*. How does it sound to you?"

Jesus! That wasn't the book I was retyping. *The Judgment* was one of the first of Ben's books that I read. For some reason it just popped into my mind. The one I was now copying was called *The Dark Rainbow*, and it was about several generations of a family in Sonoma. I'd have to remember to tell Tina sometime soon that I had put the other book aside to write this one.

"I've never understood how you get to know so much about things like wine and construction and all the other subjects you've written about. *Time's Pulse* was mainly autobiographical."

"Ever since I took social studies at Paige Noland Junior High in Elmira, I've loved doing research. I remember the thrill of looking up in the encyclopedia how many bananas were grown in Brazil and the size of the Russian navy. And I still feel the same excitement today researching everything from sapphire mining to how to pour concrete for the foundation of a seventy-story skyscraper."

"Well, I still don't know how you do it. I guess it's just a beautiful mystery. You're a genius, and one day I'll finally get used to the fact. You might have started a little late, but boy oh boy did you make up for it." We eyed each other. Was she going to throw me another question—the kind I couldn't answer? But then she smiled and I relaxed.

"You're really something, darling," she said. "I think I know you better than anyone else in the world, except maybe my mother, and yet you never cease to amaze me. You deserve another kiss."

What she said touched and saddened me, and as I leaned over to kiss her, I thought, here I am astounding the woman I love by passing off someone else's work as my own. But I slept well that night. Very well, because Tina loved the book and, most important, she loved me. The chance of another Wayne Woodley coming out of the past to threaten my world with this children's book seemed as remote as a distant star.

The next morning I took the manuscript of *The Dam and the Pocket* to Dexter Parch. I insisted he read it right there in his office. I left to get an espresso, and when I returned, he was beaming.

"Who would have guessed it?" he said, a shiver of wonder in his voice.

"I didn't see it coming, either, but here it is. I guess I owe it to our place in Litchfield County. It got me into looking at birds. Last year a family of beavers dammed up our stream and flooded one of our fields. At the time it bugged the hell out of me. Right now I want to hug each and every one of those beavers."

Parch immediately called David Hockney and asked him to illustrate it. Hockney responded to the book and started to paint a dozen watercolors.

He turned in his work quickly and the book was rushed into print, with the overnight speed that paperback houses used to publish things like the Pentagon Papers. Even before its official publication date it was at the top of the *New York Times* bestseller list for children's books. And it's still there.

I wondered if Ben would smile down on me if he was looking on.

Thirty

As a famous person (why avoid the term, because that's what I was: I had more Google mentions than the current secretaries of treasury and interior) I was in constant demand to make personal appearances. Most of these requests were from organizations I had no connection with. In the past month alone I had been invited to be a judge at the Miss Junior Teen America pageant in Naples, Florida, a contestant on *Bestseller Jeopardy!* (best-selling authors competing against each other for charity), and a presenter at the PEN dinner to give an award to a writer who had been in lockup for seventeen years in Senegal. I had also been asked to speak at the banquet of the Western Forestry Association in Corvallis, Oregon (the fee was $30,000; the subject was my choice); to appear on a panel at the American Bar Association Convention on "The Novel and Real Characters: The Threat of Libel Today"; to receive the Novelist of the Year Award (a gold-plated cup with a silver library card sticking up from the rim of the cup) from the Four Corners Librarians Association (that's Utah, New Mexico, Arizona, and Colorado); and to cut the ribbon at the opening of the new King and Stagg store (number seven) in Cooperstown, New York.

Of course, due to family considerations, I went to the King and Stagg store opening. I said no to all the others except PEN, to whom I wrote a nice note and sent a check for $2,500.

Here's a sampling of the dinner invitations Tina and I received in the same month: be a guest at a "small" birthday party for Glenn Close (she had a role in the film *Juno's Dance*); sit on the dais for a dinner (definitely not a small one) celebrating Axel Guderian's thirtieth year at Mannheim International, the parent company of Chancery; spend a week at the Palm Beach home of Bitsy Ballot, a textile heiress I'd met twice before, once at a dinner to benefit the Children's Zoo (a favorite of Tina's) and the other at a publication party for her book *Entertaining Très Luxe*, published by Chancery and personally edited by Dexter; and go for a long weekend of skiing at the Aspen home of Brewster Silas, a partner at Goldman Sachs (a round-trip ride in a G3 provided).

Why am I cataloging all this? To show how popular I had become? Of course. To show the exciting and glamorous world I moved in? That, too. But there's something more at work here. All of these invites were not for Steven King, the nice guy who deep down thought of himself as an intellectual grad student and who still maintained subscriptions to eight literary magazines; they were for the other guy, Steven Konigsberg, the fabulously wealthy, best-selling, celebrity author. Like vacationing in rain forests, having a Konigsberg at your dinner table was a way to show you were connected to what was absolutely au courant. And Ben's books had a special cachet: they were commercial, but even respectable critics said they were okay to read. You could have one with you on a plane and not be ashamed of being seen reading it.

Once Tina had asked me, when Steven Konigsberg began to receive applause and riches, why I wanted to live in New York. After all, the real Stephen King still lived in Maine, and Grisham lived in Virginia or somewhere else down South, and Clancy in Maryland or near an artillery range in the general area. So why New York? My only relatives there were Stuart and two cousins, Bernie and Selma Borofsky-King, who lived in Forest Hills, and to whom I wasn't particularly close. My friends from college and graduate school were scattered from coast to coast, with a cadre still living in Iowa City.

Even if I turned down ninety-five percent of the invites, I loved getting them. And by being based in New York, I was rubbing shoulders with more serious writers (and artists, actors, dancers, you name it) than I would if I lived in Maine, Virginia, Maryland, and twenty other states combined. That made me feel more like the serious writer that I desperately wanted to be. Did I feel guilty that Tina would be happier living somewhere else? Of course I did. Was I ready to move? Absolutely not.

Thirty-one

One of the side benefits of being a Chancery author was access to Dexter Parch's opera tickets—or more accurately, Axel Guderian's. The chairman of Mannheim International, A.G., parent company of Chancery, was an opera nut. He had four center orchestra seats to every performance of the Metropolitan Opera, and since he came to New York only once a month, the tickets were usually available. I had started to enjoy opera as a sophomore in college. My roommate, Bert Castleman, came from a musical family (his father was the first violinist with the Cincinnati Symphony). He played operas on his stereo all the time. Within a short time I found myself not only liking the stuff but also, bit by bit, learning something about it. So while our dorm room was surrounded by the booming sounds of the Grateful Dead and Ted Nugent, Bert and I resided in an oasis of Wagner and Verdi, Handel and Mozart.

Parch and I got into the habit of going to the Met. Sometimes his wife and Tina would join us, but this particular evening Parch and I were on our own. Tina's mother was in town, and using money and clout, I was able to get them two tickets to *The Producers*. Gillian, my mother-in-law, was thrilled. Tina had seen it before with me, but was more than happy to see it again. The two opera seats Parch didn't use he kicked back for a tax break to the box office (always keeping the bottom line in mind, even if the resulting tax deduction was small), which resold them and filled them with strangers.

The performance that evening was *Die Meistersinger*, its first production of the season. At the first intermission we went for a glass of champagne. Though operas can last long into the night, they make up for it with generous intermissions.

"Nobody does Wagner like Jimmy Levine," said Parch as we waited for our drinks.

"You're so right. The *Meistersinger* overture lifts my spirits every time. It's a big favorite of mine."

By luck, Parch and I found a corner table, where the general din didn't reach us. We sat down and clicked glasses, falling silent as we savored our drinks. "I have something to thank you for," said Parch after taking a sip from his flute. "You're responsible for a big change in my fortunes."

"I work for you at all times, Dexter. Now, tell me what I've done."

"You helped me get a new contract with Chancery. It's being drawn up. Five years."

"That's terrific. Congratulations."

I raised my glass for a toast, but Parch raised his hand.

"No, no, Steven, you're the one who should be toasted. Here's to what I call the Konigsberg effect. It's the unbelievable success of your books that did it for me. And, best of all, I made a good friend in the bargain. I couldn't ask for more. I cannot think of a time that I have not enjoyed your company."

"That's mutual."

"And there's a lot more I could say, but I'll stop. For now. But there's one thing more I want you to know. The real reason I agreed to sign up Quentin Bass's book was not because of your importance to the firm, but because of our friendship. I knew that it was important to you. And when something is important to a friend, then it's important to me. That is something worth toasting."

"Here, here," we said in unison.

"If we keep up with these toasts," I said, jumping up, "we're going to need more champagne. I'll get the next round."

When I returned with our drinks, we shifted gears and began to talk about the firm, the book business, the competition. I always felt good when I was with Dexter, and though it might be crazy to think so, I believed in my gut that I could tell him anything. What if I told him the books Chancery published by Steven Konigsberg, that got him his new contract and would probably buy him a new weekend house in the Hamptons, were not mine, but were written by somebody named Ben Chambers? I had always been impressed with Parch's self-assurance. He would probably handle my confession with aplomb: he'd keep it to himself, and his advice on how to continue would be on the money. I realized that if I chose someone to tell my secret to, it would be Dexter Parch. Not Tina? The woman I loved and would trust with my life? No. And Stuart? Are you kidding?

The bell sounded, and as we stood up, we spontaneously hugged each other, then headed back inside for the second act.

I felt better than I had in months, and it wasn't just because of the champagne.

Thirty-two

The next morning I got a call from Douglas Tern, the private detective, as I was leaving for my office.

"Steven, I'm holding in my hands a ninety-seven-page report that I think you'll find very interesting."

I know it's a cliché, but I felt my pulse speed up.

"When can I see it? I really appreciate your getting it done so fast, Doug." That was better.

"Since it was for you, I really cracked the whip with my staff. We used all but two of our field offices to do it. Your friend sure lived some life."

"I wish you had known him."

"I'm going to messenger it over to you right now."

"That's great."

"I hope you feel that way when you get the bill."

"I'm sure it'll be worth every penny."

"By the way, I have a favor to ask."

"Ask away."

"Do you think if I include copies of all your books with the report, you could autograph them? They're for my parents."

"No problem. Just show me how you want them personalized and I'll do it straightaway."

"Thanks for your generosity. You're a real gem."

I was thinking "zircon" as I hung up the phone.

An hour later I was in my office with Tern's report. It was contained in a blue leather binder, titled simply "Benjamin Mortimer Chambers, 1912–1999." Taking extensive notes, it took me an hour to go through the first twenty pages. By midafternoon, realizing that I hadn't yet had lunch, I went outside to get some takeout Chinese food. I had no intention of sitting in a restaurant eating roast pork lo mein and reading the dossier. After finally finishing a little before six, I felt I needed a drink. There's a small fridge in the office that I keep filled mostly with Evian and Orangina. But I required more than that. Luckily, I also kept a bottle of Stoly in the freezer. There were a few tall shot glasses in there, too. A white rime instantly circled the glass when I poured the icy vodka in, and the first sip released me from the tension I now realized had embraced me from the moment I opened Tern's report.

When Ben told me about the exotic array of jobs he had held during his long life, I'd always thought he was exaggerating. The report showed that he had actually left out several occupations. In addition to the ones I knew about already, Ben had worked as a court reporter in Orlando and as a radio announcer at a small station in Stanwood, Washington, as well as brief stints as an advertising space salesman for a golf magazine in L.A. and as a manager for a carpet cleaning company in Sacramento. If some children are afflicted with attention deficit disorder, then Ben had the career version of it. According to Tern's research, the longest Ben stayed with a profession was well under five years.

Sure enough, Wayne Woodley's name appeared just at the time he had said he met Ben. At the time, Ben was running a business incorporated under the name Edit Express. Woodley had been paid by the corporation. The business was designed to write speeches, annual reports, and the like. Their letterhead said, "From Writing to Proofreading: We Do It All." Ben had a partner in the venture, Victor Gentry, who was still alive and living in Miami. After the business ended, Gentry worked for seventeen years as a copy editor for Encyclopaedia Britannica. I didn't like the fact that Ben had worked for two years with a copy editor. Could he have read Ben's books? Gentry was definitely someone I had to see.

There were many things in the report that were news to me. Ben, just after the war, had gotten married. Like his work life, this lasted a short time, just over a year. The woman, Claudia Bellows, died a few years after the divorce in a plane crash. They had no children. My attention was also drawn to a man by the name of Lorenzo Buffman, with whom Ben co-owned a house during the time he lived in Los Angeles. Buffman had been a successful sitcom writer in the mid-sixties. Could he have read Ben's novels? Buffman was now living on the other side of the Hudson, and though retired, published a newsletter about TV shows. Here was someone else I had to investigate further.

There was another name that raised a red flag: Flo Wanger. She and Ben had started a furniture company in Palo Alto, C&W Fine Furniture. Ben had been the designer. This relationship was more than just one of Ben's many business partnerships. There was a Xerox of their wedding announcement from the local paper. The wedding, however, never took place. There was also a copy of the lawsuit that Flo Wanger filed against Ben alleging financial misappropriation in the business. The suit was settled out of court, and now Wanger, who was twelve years younger than Ben, ran the business out of Northampton, Massachusetts. The Dun & Bradstreet report on the company, still called C&W Fine Furniture, estimated its revenues at between $25 million and $30 million. It was after Ben split from Flo Wanger that he moved to Boothbay Harbor. It seemed that no one had been closer to Ben than Flo Wanger. I knew that I had to learn more about their relationship.

After a second vodka I put the report into the safe alongside the manuscript I was retyping. I had hoped that Tern would help me put to rest some of my anxieties about dangers I might face from Ben's past. Unfortunately, he was such a good detective that he had instead increased them. There was nothing I could do but get out and investigate. The situation I was in was no one's doing but my own, and my continuing silence had boxed me in.

Thirty-three

A loud grinding noise rang in my ears, deafening me. I didn't know what it meant, but I had to put a stop to it. In the dream I realized where the sound was coming from: one of Ben's trunks; but before I could reach the latch, the lid exploded and a flood of manuscripts cascaded out, engulfing me, as if I were drowning in a whirlwind of swirling paper. They pushed against my body, the pages fluttering like the wings of insects. Thousands of manuscripts were now piled above my head. I gasped for air, but onionskin pages choked me. I tried to scream for help, but all I could get out was a strangled sob. I now knew what the old onionskin smelled like: earth that encased a coffin–the smell of death. The weight of the manuscripts was pressing me farther and farther down. There was darkness all around me: I was completely lost and thoroughly buried.

I groaned and snapped out of the dream.

"Are you okay?" Tina mumbled, then turned away from me and fell back to sleep.

When Chester saw that I was awake, he crept up closer from the foot of the bed. I stroked his ears, and within seconds I was asleep again, the nightmare pushed back into a safe dark corner.

.   .   .

The next morning I didn't have as easy a time of it, because I couldn't shake the dream. I was back where I'd started from last night, exhausted and anxious. So much for my short respite. At least Tina was at work already.

I needed to do something, anything, to break away from where I was, so I got up and rolled out my exercise mat. I would do something good for myself and concentrate on that, but it didn't turn out that way. With each leg thrust I heard the sound of the paper spewing out of the trunk. This was hopeless.

I went to the kitchen and made a cup of coffee and sat down at the table. I moved my spoon back and forth in the inky, fragrant liquid, trying to make my mind a blank by focusing on the steady motion of the spoon. It didn't work. I could not escape from myself, and the closer I looked at who I had become, the less I was able to countenance the image that stared back. What I needed was somebody to talk to. This was pop psychology at its most basic–talk it out and you'll feel better–but how could I test this cliché? From the beginning I had confided in no one, and now it seemed too late.

In the last year or so I had toyed with the idea of seeing a therapist, but how could I find one without tipping my hand? Could I dare talk to one about what was bothering me? The answer was a firm no. Most of all I was terrified of a leak. I could see the gossip column headlines now: "Steven Konigsberg Seeing a Shrink. Is It Research, or Is It a Hidden Secret?"

I looked down at the floor at Chester, who was as close to me as the table allowed. When he saw I was watching him, he began to thump his tail. "Chester," I said to him, "you're the only one I can talk to." I stroked his head and ears, stood up, snapped a leash on him, and headed out to Central Park.

My favorite place was north of Strawberry Fields, in a secluded area with few benches and almost no other people. I could see the circular drive, but only at a distance, and a corner of the lake beyond it. I let Chester have a good run, with me on the other end of the leash (I might be a fraud, but I was still a model, law-abiding citizen). When I finally sat down, Chester stretched out at my feet.

In a low voice I began recounting my dream and what I thought it meant. Chester never took his eyes off me. His end of the dialogue was unconditional love. After a short while I raised my head and saw two young women at the edge of the lake looking at me and giggling. It was clear I was the object of their amusement; I guess it was funny to see a man having a discussion with his dog. They were too far away to recognize me, so I relaxed. After a moment I smiled and, lifting Chester's paw, waved back at them. My dilemma was ridiculous, and I had to acknowledge that fact before I groped my way to a solution.

Thirty-four

I stopped doing book signings after *Juno's Dance*. My first signings stoked my ego: the lines of people clutching books, the eager looks of expectation, the eyes that focused on me as if I had shamanic powers, were all heady reenforcement of my newfound fame. Maybe it was because I had never had any interest in getting someone's autograph, but I started to find the whole scene most unsettling. Though the majority were friendly and literate, there were always a number who were off-the-wall. Most of them were harmless and only slightly unhinged. Others, however, were just a step away from being measured for a suit where the sleeves are tied in the back. The ones who upset me the most were those who had known me, however fleetingly, in the past.

"Make it out to Claude Kayfleck, please."

I had only gotten as far as "All my best—" when the man continued in a much louder voice.

" 'Kayfleck' used to come before 'King' in Miss Pacini's French class at Paige Noland Junior High. Does that ring a bell?"

I looked up to see a beefy, red-faced man in a cheap blue suit. His smile revealed a row of uneven teeth as small as corn kernels.

"Of course. Claude Kayfleck. How you doing, Claude?" I answered with a totally insincere smile.

"You used to call me Kayo back then."

"Kayo—how could I forget? Living here in town now, Kayo?"

I had more of a recollection of the man who gave me a shoeshine in Miami seven years before than I had of Kayo Kayfleck.

"I'm back to being called Claude now, Steven. And, no, I live in Cherry Valley. That's near Cooperstown. Where my kids live with the ex."

Some people in the line were beginning to get restless. I heard someone mutter, "Get that blimp to move along, ferchristsake. I've got to get back to the office."

"Sounds great, Claude. Love to chat with you, but I think this really isn't the time."

"How about some coffee afterwards?"

"That would be tough for me to do," I said as I handed the book back to him. "Maybe some other time."

"You left the 'e' out of 'Claude,' " he said, his voice now approaching a shout.

"Gee, I'm sorry. Here," I said, reaching out, "give it back to me and I'll—"

"Forget it, Mr. Big-Time Novelist. I guess the first thing they teach you when you become famous is to forget your friends." Claude Kayfleck wheeled around and sent a five-foot pyramid of *Juno's Dance* tumbling onto the floor. But he wasn't finished. At the revolving entrance door he stopped and screamed, "Fuck you, Steven. I didn't really like you in junior high, anyway."

There were others: a counselor from summer camp; a rabbi with colossally bad breath who prepared me for my bar mitzvah (his breath was still in the germ warfare category); a teacher from fourth grade who said that she had predicted my talent back then; a much-tattooed biker who used to cut our lawn in Elmira; and, scariest of all, an enormously obese woman in a specially built wheelchair who told me, and the rest of the people waiting on line, that I'd asked her out to the prom but she had rejected me.

Dexter understood my decision to beg off and said that book signings at my level weren't that important, anyway. The publicity and sales department at Chancery didn't see it that way and were always pestering me with events, like book and author luncheons, that had signings attached to them. But I held firm and didn't do another signing until I published *The Dam and the Pocket*.

The prospect of seeing crowds of little kids had changed my mind. Tina and I were so anxious to have a child that we went to see a fertility doctor, though there was no reason: the doctor felt that Tina had a good chance of becoming pregnant fairly soon. We didn't ask how soon is fairly soon: just those words were good enough for us. Tina's equipment, he told us, was as good as a showroom BMW, and my sperm count was as high as a tech stock before the crash. "You don't need me. You're both in perfect shape. As they say at NASA, all systems are ready for liftoff. Just keep working at it, and I assure you it will happen." Though neither of us had ever considered it work, now we went at it like college kids on spring break.

The Dam and the Pocket signings were always scheduled in the afternoon on days when there was a school holiday. This one, a Monday, was held at the Barnes & Noble opposite Lincoln Center. I arrived with two publicists from Chancery a half hour before the announced starting time; there was already a crowd of kids with their parents that wrapped completely around the block. I was ushered into the manager's office, where I had a cappuccino and signed some books for the staff.

The signing started right on time and was scheduled to last an hour and a half. The only thing I feared at these signings was picking up something from the kids who were either blowing their noses or coughing like Violetta in the last act of *Traviata*. The children came in enough sizes and colors to satisfy the art director of a Benneton ad. There were also a fair number of parents and grandparents on line, too. I always kept a running count of the most popular names at each signing, and in this one Vanessa and Nicholas were far in the lead. The children generally didn't want my signature in the book, but rather those of Brooks Beaver and Wally Wren. I was only too happy to oblige. After the first signing I went out and had two rubber stamps made, one with the imprint of a beaver's paw, the other of a wren's foot. I enjoyed stamping my ink pad and pressing the images down hard on the page with a flourish.

Finally, the line had dwindled to the last few. The publicist passed me a slip of paper that said I had signed 424 books. A new high. I was contemplating lunch when I looked up to see an attractive woman with thick, long black hair and a pleasant smile. She placed a book on the table in front of me. "Could you make it out to June Bowers, please?"

I only had a chance to write "Best wishes—" when she leaned in and whispered, "Actually, Mr. Konigsberg, why don't you just sign it 'Ben Chambers'?"

Thirty-five

June Bowers was staying at the Bodenheim, a small, hip hotel in TriBeCa. She wanted me to meet her at the Power Pocket, a gym in the basement there.

"Let's meet at six-thirty. Please be on time, Mr. Konigsberg. I'll explain when I see you."

My stomach was tied in a Gordian knot all day, and I stayed away from both the apartment and my office. I called my assistant, Fred, to tell him I was going to be in the library doing research. Then I wandered around for a few hours trying to convince myself that I would easily work this out; yeah, just the way I worked it out with Wayne Woodley. I sensed that June was a lot smarter than Woodley. Maybe she would be easier to deal with than the unlamented Wayne. To kill some time, I went to see an Iranian film at the Angelika, but I kept seeing June Bowers and not the subtitles, and within ten minutes couldn't follow the plot, which centered on a tiny Kurdish town with poor cell phone reception.

I walked over to the West Village and into a bookstore, where all my books were in stock near the front, fitted neatly between Stephen King and John Grisham, my fellow travelers in bestsellerdom. One of the clerks recognized me, and I wound up signing copies for the staff. Then I bought a copy of Boswell's biography of Johnson for my library in Connecticut and a new book of short stories by Ann Beattie, a favorite of Tina's. As I left the store, the manager asked if I would have my picture taken with the clerks. So I stood there while they commandeered one of the customers to snap the photo. Would anyone, no matter how perceptive, be able to read into my forced smile that I was scared witless about meeting with this woman?

I got to the hotel a half hour early, and I went into the bar, the Gigablyght, at the back of the lobby. The walls of the place were covered in bloodred leather, and it had about as much light as a mine tunnel. It was filled with thin young women in black, half of them with tattoos on their shoulders. The men were also in black, many with shaven heads. I squeezed my way into a corner at the bar and asked for a double vodka on the rocks, my drink of choice when terrified. After I swallowed half of it, I tried to regulate my breathing and think clearly for the first time that day. I was about to order another double when a trusty switch somewhere in my cortex clicked on and told me to forget having another drink and get down to business.

The Power Pocket was obviously a "serious" gym. There were a few treadmills and stationary cycles, but the heart of the place was weights, weights, and more weights. Aside from a few people with normal physiques, probably hotel guests, almost all the others wore huge leather belts that wrapped around their abdomens. They had triceps that flared out from their bodies like flying buttresses, and they walked with a rolling gait, as if they were on the deck of a boat in a mild chop. The clientele was exclusively male, except for June, who was dressed in shorts and a T-shirt. There was a small juice bar in the lounge area. I ordered a Coke and then took a seat and continued to watch June and her friends. After a dozen more lifts she went to the corner of the gym and started doing curls with hand weights. Several repetitions later she stopped and started to stretch out. When she finished, she got up off the mat and headed over toward where I was sitting. I looked at my watch: six-thirty exactly. She stopped first at the juice bar and ordered a towering glass of a concoction the color of pond scum.

June sat down opposite me and didn't say a word until she drained her glass. Though she didn't seem happy drinking the concoction, she walked back to the counter and ordered another.

"What are you drinking?" she asked.

"Just a Coke."

"My sister says that stuff's poison. She likens it to pouring lye on your favorite begonia. According to her, it corrodes your insides and gives you gas."

"What are you drinking?"

"It's called Protein Mint. It doesn't taste so great, but it's real good for you. Let me order you one. Hey, Drake, blend up a Protein Mint for my friend."

"Sure thing," answered the young man behind the counter.

Within moments the noxious-looking drink was in front of me. I took a swallow: it was as thick as rubber cement and tasted like a fish tank that hadn't been cleaned for weeks.

"Like it?" asked June.

I nodded my head, since my tongue was plastered to the roof of my mouth.

"My sister, Vera, swears by it. Says it has all the nutrients you need for the day in just one drink. I wish it tasted better."

"So do I," I stammered.

"I want you to meet my sister, but she's in the hospital. She was in a car accident. She's going to get out pretty soon. You know, my sister's an internationally ranked bodybuilder. I'm just a beginner." My mind was so focused on June that I took a large swig of my Protein Mint. Big mistake. "I can't lift much yet, but I'm getting stronger. Someday we plan to compete together."

June didn't seem to have a very strong personality. All the references to her sister seemed to underline an extremely insecure person. I decided it was time to take the lead.

"How did you know about Ben Chambers?"

"Mr. Chambers—we called him Uncle B—was our tutor for almost two years. Vera and I loved him. He also worked for our daddy in the office he had on the farm. You see, our daddy grows rice. Lots of it. Thirty-four hundred acres. Now, Uncle B wrote the story you published especially for us. We made him read it to us pretty much every day. You want to see it?"

June Bowers reached into her gym bag and pulled out a typescript of *The Dam and the Pocket*, protectively encased in a clear plastic folder. It was on onionskin and was exactly like the copy that now resided in my safe-deposit box. The only difference was a handwritten inscription on the title page in Ben's handwriting that said, "To my favorite girls, June and Vera. All my love, Uncle B."

"My sister and I thought this might be worth serious money to someone. Maybe someone like you."

"What do you want?" I was finally able to get out.

"We—I mean Vera—hasn't decided yet. She wants you to think about it. She told me to tell you that you shouldn't think that just because she's a bodybuilder she isn't smart. She has a B.A. from Pepperdine and an M.A. from U.C. Davis, both in phys ed. I have an M.A., too, but it's in history. So you can see my sister is no musclehead."

"I can see that," I said, though I really didn't.

"That's good. Vera has a dream, and I've dedicated myself to helping her achieve it. She wants to be the best female bodybuilder in the world. Her other dream is for me to join her. I've just started to work out, but I know I can do it. I'm a lot stronger than I look. Vera thinks I can get big in no time. Imagine, the two of us atop the winner's platform at the world championship. Two sisters getting the gold. It's never been done."

"Sounds fantastic," I said with little conviction.

"Now, attaining a dream is never easy," June continued. "For one thing, our folks don't understand it at all. They never could see the beauty of it. Now, I love our mommy and daddy as much as a frog loves flies, but they've been of no help. Though Daddy is sitting on a pile of dough, he hasn't given Vera enough to pursue a gold medal in checkers. He just covers medical and car payments. Luckily, Mommy helps out a bit on the sly. So that brings us to you. I came to town to show you our little book and see if maybe you could help. What do you think?"

"Well, what do you want me to do?"

June Bowers reached again into her gym bag and pulled out an index card.

"Here's the number of our checking account at Wells Fargo Bank in San Francisco. I'd like you to wire twenty-five thousand dollars into it. Make sure you do that tomorrow."

I took the card and put it in my pocket.

"And then?"

"I have to give this more thought. I'm not a professional shakedown artist, I just need help in fulfilling my sister's dream."

"What makes you think you're not shaking me down?"

"I haven't threatened to share our little secret. Our daddy always says, 'When a chicken is laying a lot of eggs, talk softly to it and treat it right.' Just like the chicken, we want you to stay productive."

June looked at her watch.

"Time for me to get going. Sleep is an important part of building yourself up. It was nice meeting you, Mr. Konigsberg."

I sat there staring at my Protein Mint for several minutes. Finally, I made it back to the bar upstairs, where a double Ketel One started to do me some good. June seemed decent, and even somewhat embarrassed by the extortion scheme. Unlike Woodley, she was neither irrational, greedy, nor the least bit violent. She was well mannered, and her gentle, slightly southern accent was appealing. This could have been a lot worse, I told myself. I took another swallow of my vodka and realized that I could no longer detect the taste of the dreadful Protein Mint. Things were definitely looking up.

Thirty-six

"I'm so happy you're speaking to the kids," said Tina as she finished putting on some lipstick and threw a cardigan over her shoulders. "They're very excited."

"Me, too," I said, trying to sound enthusiastic.

My mood for the past few weeks had been pretty glum, mainly because I had Ben's manuscript to retype. I kept putting it off. I had wired the $25,000 that June had asked for, and aside from a postcard saying thanks for the money, I hadn't heard a word from her.

"They almost feel as if they know you. I always talk a lot about you. They can't believe they're going to meet the man who wrote *The Dam and the Pocket*. I'm so proud of you, Steven, darling." She put her arms around my waist and gave me a gentle kiss, as light as a butterfly's touch. We both sighed softly with pleasure, a human version of a cat's purr. She stole a glance at the mirror in our hallway and giggled. "Looks like a bit more lipstick is called for."

"You'd better step on it or you're going to be late."

"I'll make it. And you better be on time, too. Remember, eleven o'clock."

"Yes, Teacher," I said, smiling.

As soon as Tina left, I sank down in the chair next to the desk. My hands were sweaty and I could hear my heart beating. What was wrong with me? It was my turn to tell Tina's fourth graders what I did for a living, with as much wit and charm as I could muster. What could be an easier gig? Fathers and mothers of the girls had been recruited by Tina to say how they spent their time between nine and five. I'd been invited into the mix as an honorary dad. The father who'd preceded me was an airline pilot.

A tough act to follow? Not for me. I had spoken to over three thousand at the Booksellers' Convention in Chicago, to wild applause, to thousands more at a dozen colleges, including two commencements, and at many benefits for worthy causes. I had never been unnerved at any of these events. Why now?

The apartment was stuffy. The school was across the park on the East Side. I had plenty of time, so I'd take the long way round, past the Bethesda Fountain, then uptown to the Met, then past its southern facade, looming high like the hull of a passenger liner, where I'd exit onto Fifth.

I arrived exactly on time. While the Spence School receptionist in the office rang up Tina, I took in the sights of . . . girls, lots of girls: tall and short, from five to eighteen, on their own or with a teacher in tow, coughing and sneezing like patients from *The Magic Mountain*, younger ones all dressed in green plaid uniforms with white cotton blouses. I had been buoyed by my walk through the park and looked at the girls with simple pleasure.

As I followed Tina upstairs to the classroom, she said to me, "You know, they love this book, and they've all read it many times. If you wanted to stand in front of them and do jumping jacks instead of speaking, even that would give them a thrill."

"You're funny, sweetheart," I said, giving her fanny a pinch after looking around like a cat burglar to make sure no one else could see. "I'm determined to give them their money's worth."

Tina had brought in the other section of fourth graders, and the classroom was packed with girls. I waved a hello. "Good morning, Mr. Konigsberg," they said in unison, grinning excitedly.

"How many of you have read *The Dam and the Pocket*?" All hands shot up. "And did you like it?" (I already knew the answer.)

"Yeah," they yelled.

"Since you already know the story," I said, "let's skip ahead to a Q and A. Does anybody know what that is?"

Silence.

"It's an old expression meaning questions and answers. 'Q' stands for questions, 'A' for answers. It's a way to get information."

The girls nodded as seriously as grad students in a seminar.

"So this is how we'll do it. I'll ask the questions, and you give the answers."

The girls stared at me, puzzled, then a skinny girl with red hair giggled. In a moment the whole class joined in.

"I was just kidding," I said, laughing. "You ask the questions, and I'll do my best to answer them. Who wants to be first?"

A pretty, chubby girl stood up. "Is it hard to sit in a chair for a long time just writing?"

Then there was no holding them back. Where did I get my ideas from? Did I get lonely and wish I had a friend with me? Did I write all day and skip lunch? Who did I like more, Brooks Beaver or Wally Wren? Were Brooks and Wally still friends? Where do they live? How did Brooks learn to build a dam?

Then came a question that almost derailed me, from a small girl with blond hair and a dusting of freckles across her nose.

"My name is Samantha, and I have a very important question to ask." She stood up.

"Go right ahead, Samantha."

"Will you write another story about Brooks and Wally?"

I felt like an animal caught in the headlights of a car.

"No, I'm afraid not," I finally said.

This was met with a collective groan, as if I had announced that Christmas was going to be canceled. All at once, like a chorus of petitioners, they called out, "Why?" I almost answered, "Because Ben Chambers had only written one." Suddenly, I was bathed in sweat, my shirt plastered to my back like a freshly applied piece of wallpaper. I tried to speak but couldn't. Kids have very acute antennas that detect when an adult is in distress. I could tell my behavior was making them nervous; I just didn't know how to pull myself out of it. I had reached a new low. Here I was lying to a class of little girls who were taught by my wife! This is where fame and fortune had finally led me. I tried to smile, but my face felt as if it had been injected with Novocain. In a moment I knew that all my defenses would be breached, and I'd just stand before them and cry. Then my savior appeared. Tina had stepped out of the classroom five minutes before; now she returned. I pulled myself together, grinned like I was trying to sell them aluminum siding, and said, "That was just a joke. And it was a very poor one. I don't know when, but someday I'll definitely write another Brooks and Wally story. I guess I'm just waiting until your favorite beaver and wren have little girls old enough to go to school here at Spence."

This answer enabled Tina to call out from the back: "Girls, girls, Mr. Konigsberg has to get back to his desk, and you have to go downstairs for lunch. Thank you, Mr. Konigsberg!"

"Thank you, Mr. Konigsberg," the girls echoed loudly, then started to applaud.

Tina had a huge smile on her face, and I wanted to hug her.

"I'll take the girls to the cafeteria. Back in a moment," she said.

Within minutes I heard Tina coming down the hall. I pulled her into a classroom and kissed her before she could say a word. When we pulled away from each other, she said, "Steven, darling, you were fabulous. The girls adored you. You were so warm and nice to them. Someday you're going to make a great daddy."

"I loved them," I said sincerely. "The best audience I've ever had."

"And I know the girls will be talking about you for a long while. I even thought I'd give them an assignment to write a story themselves. Would you judge them?"

"I think I'll take a pass on that," I said, smiling. "I'll stick to writing and let you be the critic."

"I was only kidding. Now, I hope you won't be angry with me, but you have some other fans here who are also dying to meet you. I've made some enemies by only inviting four of them. And I promise this will be more of a snack than a lunch. You'll be out of here in no time."

Tina led me to an alcove off the teachers' lounge, where a small round table had been spiffed up with a tablecloth. Standing beside it were Tina's colleagues, three women and a man. As soon as we sat down to eat, they started peppering me with questions just as eagerly as the girls upstairs. The questions they asked were old hat to me, but this time I had a sour feeling inside. I had enlarged my world, I realized: for the first time ever I had lied to kids. I didn't betray my emotions—I had gotten very adept at playing Steven Konigsberg the famous author—but I needed to get away as fast as I could. One last question came from a teacher (an English teacher, of course), who first professed to be a fan of my books; then cautiously, ever so cautiously, she asked me if I'd ever considered writing a "literary book." This was not the first time I'd been asked that question, and I handled it with my usual aplomb, but what I mightily wanted to do was reach into my briefcase, where I had the galleys of my Chambers Benjamin book, and hand it to her.

I left the school in a dark mood. I was on deadline to finish retyping the next of Ben's books, but I couldn't face it. Instead, I picked up my car and drove across the George Washington Bridge to the Palisades, where I pulled into a viewing area to take in a long swath of the Hudson. The car was in park, and for no reason I started to gun the engine. The sound from the finely tuned eight-cylinder engine was a powerful roar. The nearest car was more than a hundred feet away, so I kept my foot on the accelerator. Though I wasn't suicidal, the idea that maybe things would be better if I just pushed the gearshift into drive was strangely appealing. I could see the car rocket forward, snap the low wooden barrier like kindling, and then plunge down into the icy Hudson. What a headline that would make. Of course, I wasn't going to do it, but if I didn't have Tina, maybe I would have. My performance in Tina's classroom had been a new low. Was there a way to drag myself out of my rich and comfortable hole? What would happen if I did stomp on the gas pedal? Certainly, some people would be genuinely saddened. But what of my spectacular writing career? Would it end?

Perhaps Stuart and Dexter would get together and hire anonymous writers to keep the Konigsberg canon alive. I might become the male V. C. Andrews. Not even death would stop me from turning them out. What would Ben think of that? But there would be a positive side to my early demise. I would no longer have to retype Ben's manuscripts—free at last.

I turned off the engine. It was a bright day, and the river was slow moving and green as a leaf. I settled down and let the beauty of the scene seep into me, hoping it would soften the edges of what I was feeling. Now more than ever in the past year, I had started to feel like a different kind of fraud. Not a plagiarist, but a con man, the writing version of a three-card monte dealer. The dealer had his patter and I had mine. The admission depressed me. I would have to take a break from publishing Ben's books. A real break. I wasn't sure where it would leave me, but I felt sure it was the only way to become my own man.

I told myself that I would tell Dexter the truth tomorrow. Maybe Stuart, too. But how could I tell them and not Tina? No, I had to start with her. She was the most important part of my life. How would she take it? I had no doubt of her love for me, but my confession would certainly shock her. Wrong word. She'd be hurt. Really hurt. I'd have to find exactly the right moment to reveal my secret. Maybe tomorrow, or sometime during the coming week. Timing was the key. I'd have to pick the perfect moment. Once I cleared the bar with Tina, Dexter and Stuart would be easy. Yes, I would do it. It was just a question of when. I started the motor and then drove back across the bridge suddenly feeling a lot better.

Thirty-seven

Fred brought the large envelope into my study, where I was reading the first three chapters of Quentin Bass's new novel, *The Sunset Demon*. Why would I read anything by him after the scene we had in the restaurant? Two days after his blowup, Quentin called me and apologized—sort of.

"It wasn't Quentin Bass talking last night, Steve. It was my old nemesis, Mr. Tanqueray. He's never been a friend of mine. He's always been a nasty, mean prick, and though he's not sorry, I guess I am."

Of course, a large part of the reason for the rapprochement was that Quentin wanted me to read these pages. They were pure Bass: some fine lyrical writing set in a morass of self-indulgent ranting. The book that Chancery had published, and I had underwritten, was doing poorly. The few reviews it had received were lousy. Quentin, predictably, had justifications for this, none of them having to do with him: the bookstore chains didn't give a rat's ass for literary fiction; Parch and Chancery were too busy planning the publication of my next novel to give any attention to his book; and last, but best of all, the jacket art on his book sucked.

"But you told me that you loved the painting on the jacket when they showed it to you."

"I was just trying to be nice. And they printed the thing way darker than when I first saw it. And what about my name? You need a jeweler's loupe to read it. I do have a following, you know. It might not be the size of your faceless hordes, but it's still there."

I put down Quentin's pages and looked at the manila envelope, which had been sent by certified mail, return receipt requested. The return address indicated that it was from Hamilton Cray, Ben's lawyer. I had made Cray, along with Tina and myself, a trustee of the Chambers Outreach Foundation. Periodically, I received reports from him on the foundation, which was run out of his law office in Wiscasset. Instead of a financial report, the envelope contained a note from Cray, attached to a white letter-size envelope.

Dear Steven:

I trust this finds you and Tina in good health. Things are running smoothly at the foundation. The new accountant I hired to keep the books, a woman named Rachelle Broome, comes in twice a month and is a marked improvement over the fellow from Brunswick. I will be sending you the quarterly financials in a few weeks. At this point our expenses and disbursements appear to be running as we expected. No surprises there. I will recommend, however, when we meet next, that we purchase a new computer with the proper software for our needs. Also, a part-time clerk should be considered. Bernice, who does all the typing and filing, is becoming a bit overwhelmed handling the daily flow of inquiries. Real estate agents keep contacting me to inquire if Ben's house will ever be put up for sale. That's your decision, of course, but I'm sure if you decided to sell, it would move quickly. I went over to Blake's Boatyard last week to check on Boswell, *and I'm happy to report that the boat has never looked better. They just finished rebuilding the engine, and they've painted the trim. The color you picked out, I believe it's called teal, looks terrific. It's a shame that you're not here to make use of it. The new extension to the Boothbay Harbor Library, the Benjamin Chambers Reading Room, is well under way and the contractor expects it to be finished by next fall. The town cannot wait for the dedication by their favorite author.*

Now to the main reason for this letter. I enclose an envelope that was handed to me by Ben two months before his death. He instructed me to deliver it to you on the fifth anniversary of his death, which I'm sure you're aware is next week. I have no idea of the contents, but if there's anything in it you might want to discuss with me after you've reviewed it, I am, of course, always at your disposal.

Affectionately,
Hamilton

P.S. I hear you'll have a new book out this summer. I can't wait to read it.

I put aside Hamilton Cray's note and stared at the envelope. There, in all caps, in Ben's strong, clear handwriting, was the following: THIS IS TO BE READ ONLY BY STEVEN KING. Below that was signed, simply, BEN. I went to the door of my study and locked it. When I went back to my desk and picked up the envelope again, it took me a long time to open it. I inserted a letter opener under the flap and carefully cut along the top. The letter was written on two pages from a yellow, lined legal-size pad. For a moment I felt dizzy, so I stood up and went to the window. The traffic on Central Park West was light, and the few, bruised clouds that hung over the park made rain a real possibility later in the day. After a while I sat back down at my desk. There was something in me that wanted to destroy the letter. Between Wayne Woodley, the Bowers sisters, and the festering guilt that seemed to wash over me on a daily basis, I didn't know if I could handle what Ben had to say. But whom was I kidding? I'd give up a vital organ before I'd destroy the letter. With moist hands I picked it up and began to read.

My Dear Stevie:

Surprise! Just like your old Ben to say hello to you from "out there." I guess things are going pretty well where I am since nobody ever comes back to complain, except in a few bad movies. I wish I could give a report on the cuisine or the famous folk that I've met, but since I'm not there yet, I can't do it. By the way, who do you think out of all the people here I'll try to talk to first? My old favorites Boswell and Dr. Johnson? Nah. Napoleon? Not him, either, though I've read everything about him I could lay my hands on. The first person I'm going to buttonhole is Thomas Jefferson. How was he able to learn and do so much? Maybe I'll find out. He loved wine, and perhaps a glass or two will get him talking.

I'm writing this letter a couple of days after seeing my ticker doctor in Portland. The report isn't great. I need surgery, but there's a good chance that it will result in a Ben Chambers quite unlike the one who's writing this. So though the doctor is all for operating—aren't they always—I'm not. Believe me when I say this, I'm not scared. Hey, I've had a pretty good run, and when the old pump calls it a day, it'll be short and sweet, or so says the good doctor.

Stevie, though we've only known each other a relatively short time, I've felt from the first time I met you that we were destined to be friends. I just wish that our show could have had a longer run. I've asked myself what is it about you that I like so much. In some ways I think you're a lot like me. You have the soul of a writer; you're interested in people, and you care for them, too. I also love the way you enjoy simple things. I remember the first time I took you out in Boswell *and we went to Christmas Cove. I could see that you thought that the burger and beer we had out on the deck of that restaurant were the best in the world. If I had a large family, I would still think of you as family. The fact is I have no living relatives and that is why, as you know now, I decided to make you my sole heir. Some might say that I view you as a son. Well, I guess there's some truth in that. The fact is, however, though the age disparity between us is great, I also think of you as a brother. A brother who is both a writer and a bartender—who could ask for anything more?*

I imagine that you came across my "oeuvre" pretty early on. I hope you liked them, or at least some of them. They mean a lot to me. How you choose to handle this work—keep them in the trunks, bury the trunks, whatever—I leave up to you. Friendship is trust, and I trust you.

I hope that you and Tina are married by now. She's a beaut, so take good care of her. The one thing I really wanted to do was be best man at your wedding. When you truly care about someone, you feel that you haven't told them everything you wanted to. But somehow, Stevie, I believe you and I have touched almost all the bases.

All my love,
Ben

I couldn't tell you how long I sat there at my desk. It took Fred's repeated knocking on the door to rouse me from a place I had never been before. I felt as if Ben had been with me in that room. It wasn't the tears in my eyes that stopped me from opening the door: I just didn't want to break the spell.

Thirty-eight

In the days after receiving Ben's letter, I took a lot of walks with Chester. We walked almost completely around the drive in Central Park and all the way to the East River and back. Once I started to walk to Chinatown, but Chester didn't like the sound of midtown traffic, so we turned back. Whenever I thought no one was looking, I would spill it all out to Chester. His breath might be lousy, but he was a great listener.

" 'Keep them in the trunks, bury the trunks, whatever,' " I repeated several times to Chester. "What does that really mean? It's the 'whatever' that I think is the key word. And then what about, 'Friendship is trust, and I trust you.' Trust me to do what? Do what I'm doing? If you're ever going to speak, Chester, now's the time."

I was not myself as I walked the city with Chester. Tina asked me what was wrong. She accepted my explanation that I was at a critical junction with the new book and therefore deep within myself. She didn't ask which book it was that I was working on. Steven Konigsberg or Chambers Benjamin? Fred handed me call lists and Post-its of things to do, but all I could do was walk Chester. On the fourth day Chester put his paws down and refused to go with me. He had had enough. He didn't want to continue training for the Iron Dog Triathlon.

When I finally looked over my calls and mail, I saw that I had gotten a letter from June Bowers. The letter in the envelope postmarked Jakarta was written on hotel stationery, the old-fashioned kind like tissue paper.

Dear Mr. Konigsberg,

We just got here from San Francisco. Vera got out of the hospital a week ago and she looks great. (Photo enclosed.) Strong as ever. It's her first competition in quite a while, but I have a feeling she's going to do quite well. A bronze medal at the least. I'm working out almost as much as my sister and you won't believe the difference in how I look. Take my word for it, your investment in Vera's career is really going to pay off. We're off next to Osaka. Hope all is going well for you and will try to drop you a line soon.

Yours truly,
June

At the bottom in big loopy letters was a postscript:

Mr. K—My sister says you're all right. That's a good beginning. She also told me you drink Coke. Take my advice and stay the fuck away from it.
Vera

The photo showed Vera, looking more angry than happy. Her massive body was crammed into a skimpy bikini, and the oil coating her body almost made her shine.

On my call list the name that appeared most frequently was Stuart's. After each call Fred had written: "Must talk to you" or "Urgent" or "This is really important."

"Can we have lunch today?" Stuart asked when I called him. "I'll break my lunch date. I really have to see you."

"Why?"

"Jesus, Steven, you know why. We've got important business to discuss. Big money business."

"I don't think I can make it today."

"Why?"

"I don't feel like it."

"That's not a reason."

"For me it is."

This roundelay went on for a few minutes until I finally caved.

"Okay. Where and when?"

"My club at one."

Stuart had recently joined the New York Yacht Club. He now ate all his meals at the place and probably even showered there. His new mode of dress was a blazer (with club crest), white linen trousers, and Top-Siders.

"I'm not going anyplace where I have to wear a tie."

This led to more negotiating until I agreed to meet him at a Greek restaurant on Fifty-fifth Street. I got there twenty minutes late and Stuart was pissed.

"I've been twirling my fucking thumbs for a half hour waiting for you, Steven."

"I've always told you to have something to read when you go out," I said. "I never leave the house without a book or a magazine."

"What gives with you these days? Is it the new book? I hope to hell you're not blocked. Please tell me you're not blocked."

The waiter came over to take our drink order. Stuart ordered a Seabreeze, the preferred drink, he told me, of most of the members of the club. I opted for a Perrier after toying for a moment with the idea of getting a Coke, but the vision of the Bowerses rappelling down from the ceiling and snatching it out of my hand stopped me.

"Well," he asked after the waiter left, "are you blocked or not?"

"Not blocked, and my bowel movements are fine, too."

"Very funny."

In the past couple of years Stuart and I had drifted apart. We never had much in common to begin with, and now our only bond, and certainly it was a significant one, was the monetary aspect of my career. Not only was I his most important client but my incredible success had caused him to lose a number of his other productive clients. They complained, like Quentin Bass, that he was spending too much time on me, which was probably true. The Konigsberg industry was a big one, and Stuart saw himself as the CEO of it. He was always ready to talk to the press about my work, or jet out to L.A. to meet with the studio execs there. He had even engineered an executive producer credit for himself on the last movie and now saw himself as a mover and shaker in the Hollywood community. He was even thinking of buying a place out there. His only problem was where: Malibu or Bel Air? Beverly Hills or Brentwood?

After a few minutes of questions about Tina, who never liked Stuart, and my folks, who loved him as family, he got down to the real business at hand.

"You've got to address these offers on *The Dam and the Pocket*. I've got DreamWorks and Disney drooling for it. Now's the time to do the deal."

"I told you before, I'm not interested in selling the film rights."

"Why, for Christ's sake? It could be the biggest deal we've done yet. The book is a natural. It could become a huge franchise. There could be sequels up the wazoo: *Brooks and Wally Go to Africa*; *Brooks and Wally in Orbit*. That kind of thing."

"Why do I have to keep repeating myself? N-O. No. I do not want to sell."

"Well, what about at least letting me peddle the commercial rights? I've got Mattel and Hasbro waving blank checks at me. And that's just for toys. There's a load of companies who want to do calendars and posters. You can't believe the interest."

"It's still no."

Stuart leaned across the table and placed his hands on my arms.

"Steven, this means a lot of money to you and to me. I could really use it."

"Do you need a loan?" I asked, and immediately regretted saying it.

"No, I don't need a fucking loan. But if you don't let me do my job, maybe I will one day. And, by the way, that hurt. You had no call to say that."

"I'm sorry."

We sat there in silence while the waiter cleared the table.

"Will you at least reconsider it?"

"Sure," I said, lying.

In the past I've always tried to understand where I was heading in life by looking down at myself, like a lab technician watching a mouse run a maze. This decision not to sell the film and commercial rights to the kids' book was part of a larger change that I was going through. No doubt it had something to do with June Bowers, but it was more than that. I had recently told Dexter not to use my photograph on the Steven Konigsberg books anymore, and to keep my author's bio as short as possible. Add that to my earlier decision not to promote the books, and even I could see a pattern emerging. It wasn't just that I was withdrawing from the Steven Konigsberg universe; the real question was, where was I withdrawing to?

Part

4

A LIFE OF UPS AND DOWNS

Talent alone cannot make a writer. There
must be a man behind the book.

—R. W. Emerson

Thirty-nine

It's funny how one little phone call can make such a difference. As I listened to Dexter Parch, I felt a surge of joy, something I hadn't experienced for months. He wasn't talking about the Konigsberg mega-selling oeuvre, but about my own writing. What he said came as a complete surprise, which made it all the sweeter. His spies at the *Times* had informed him that in the next week or so they would be running a rave review of *Time's Pulse—my novel—*in their daily edition, followed two weeks later by an even better one in the Sunday *Book Review*.

"Wow! That's amazing. I can't believe it!"

"Believe it, my dear boy, believe it," said Parch in his paternalistic mode, which he enjoyed using with me occasionally.

"Who's reviewing it?" I asked. But really, who cared, if the reviews were as good as he thought they would be.

"Don't know about the daily, but for Sunday it's Quentin Bass."

"Oh, really," I said, remembering our last meeting at the restaurant. I felt a flicker of apprehension.

"Don't worry about him," said Parch benignly. He had always been good at reading my mind, at least the portion I opened up to him. "He doesn't know the book is yours. Nobody does. And no one ever will. Also, my sales reps are very high on it. It's selling well in the independent stores, and it's starting to move at Barnes & Noble and Borders. I've ordered a second printing and paper for a third. Your book's got buzz, Steven, real buzz. I knew it was good, but who knew it would sell? With literary fiction it's always safe to bet against it."

Buzz. I never thought I would ever hear anything like this about my own writing. Just being published was a summit I had prayed I would climb. Actually having the book find an audience was the stuff of dreams.

"That's fabulous, Dexter," was all I could manage to say.

"It's so odd the way things work out," said Parch. "Because Chambers Benjamin is such a mystery man, the Chancery publicity department has been fielding calls left and right about him. Curiosity has positively gotten the better of everyone. They all want to scoop the others by identifying him, which they never will be able to, since the secret is buried deeply."

I drank in every word like someone who had been crawling across Death Valley in July.

"One more thing: you'll be amused to know that your cousin, the great Stuart Amster, is desperate to represent Chambers Benjamin. I'm sure one of his minions touted him to the book. I can't see *Time's Pulse* sitting on his bedside table. No doubt he'll try to follow up the Maine connection, so don't be surprised if you get a call."

The only person who hadn't liked *Time's Pulse* so far was my father. I sent him the book with a note saying it was by a new young writer I thought would interest him. His response: it was okay, but not nearly as good as my novels. My conversation with Dexter galvanized me into deciding I should work flat out on my own new book so I could submit a good chunk of it to him soon. It looked as if I now had two robust writing careers. Five years ago, when I spent most of my time pouring beer and racking glasses, if a friend had told me I would reach this point, I would have suspected him of using drugs.

After Parch hung up, I tried Tina on her cell phone, but she had turned it off. When Fred Jaggers came in with my mail, I wondered if there would be something from June. The last time I'd heard was a card from Seoul, where Vera had tied for the silver in the KBO (Korean Bodybuilding Open).

This time she'd sent me a note by FedEx. I ripped open the large envelope.

Steve—

Hope things are okay and that your cash situation is solid because we need some more money. Vera wants you to wire $50K into the account as soon as you receive this. She told me to say that she wants it in the account like yesterday! Vera is getting stronger all the time and improving with every competition. The gold is not far off. I thought that the enclosed newspaper clipping might amuse you.

As ever,

J

The piece was from a paper in Perth. The headline read: "Bowers Wins Both the Silver and a Whopping Fine." The article related how Vera, unhappy with the judges' decision not to give her the gold medal, first spat on one judge and then proceeded to kick the other two. She was arrested after a struggle in which one policeman broke a finger, and was subsequently fined 160,000 won. The photo with the story showed Vera being led away in handcuffs. She was the size of an NFL running back. June was walking alongside, a look of concern on her face, wearing gym tights and a pullover. She definitely looked a lot bigger. There was no doubt that June was lifting weights.

Also in the mail were reviews of the latest Konigsberg book from my Japanese publisher, in Japanese; three requests to speak; and a request from a men's magazine wanting to know my favorite movie, color, drink, and vacation spot. I tossed that in the wastebasket. There was also a thick monthly statement from my stockbroker that I put in my desk drawer unopened, where it joined the last four in a similarly pristine condition. The rest of the mail I stacked into a neat pile, then left the apartment for my office. Once there, it gave me real pleasure to see my new book on the screen. It was rolling along and I had confidence in it, even more so today than yesterday. I worked until six before running in the park. It was almost seven when I made it back to the apartment.

Right away I noticed the dinner table set for three. I could smell something delicious cooking in the oven, and I could hear Tina in the shower.

I quietly opened the bathroom door and entered with the stealth of a cat burglar. I knew she hadn't heard me. I grabbed at her through the shower curtain, a recurrent reprise of mine of the scene from *Psycho*, and was rewarded with a little shriek. Within seconds her wet face appeared at the edge of the curtain, and we exchanged a long, damp kiss.

"Who's coming for dinner?" I asked.

"Surprise," said Tina.

When dinner was ready and the guest had still not arrived, she looked at her watch. "He's running late," said Tina. "I think we should start without him."

I helped her carry the dishes to the table, a silver cover over the guest's plate (to keep it warm, she said). Before I could even pour some wine, she reached across the table and with a flourish removed the heavy dome. There on the plate sat a jar of Gerber's baby food.

"Yes," she said with a huge smile. "The guest won't be here tonight. But I can guarantee you a date with the guest in no more than seven months."

Forty

When Chancery published *Juno's Dance*, they convinced me to start a website, *www.stevenkonigsberg.com*, which started to get a lot of hits when *Juno* hit number one on the *Times* list. Just like my book signings, it flushed out a large number of people from my past. For a time my assistant had to hire an assistant to take care of the site. I was even contacted by four people who attended Montessori school with me in Elmira. It didn't take me long to tell Chancery to drop any mention of the website on the jackets of my books and a month later to scrap the site completely.

Though my books no longer had a picture of me, and I now did almost no publicity, the people who had known me before the "Konigsberg Explosion" (*Newsweek*, February 21, 2002) continued to contact me. I had given the dreaded Wayne Woodley my home phone number, but a few others were somehow able to get it as well. Some found out where I lived and staked out the entrance to my apartment house the way Mark Chapman had waited for John Lennon. Most tried to contact me through Chancery, who regularly sent up large batches of mail that Fred opened and usually answered in my name. If the letters had requests for money, or seemed more than the run-of-the-mill fan mail, he passed them on to me. That's how Mona Pinchman's letter landed on my desk.

Mona Pinchman had been my definitive dream girl from sophomore to senior year at Winston Braggler High School. Mona had it all: she was beautiful and smart, both a cheerleader and president of the Shakespeare Club (which I joined and was recording secretary for two years). She had a body that would make any sixteen-year-old boy fantasize—a perfect 10 before the expression found its way into common parlance. Mona was voted both Prom Queen and Miss Congeniality, a first for Braggler High. In a school not known for producing whiz kids, she was the only one who won early acceptance to a top school: Stanford. She never gave me the time of day. Mona always showed me her two-hundred-watt smile, but she beamed at everyone else, too. The one time I worked up the courage to ask her out on a date, she told me she had a history paper to write. Mona forgot we were in the same history class and that the assignment she referred to had been handed in two weeks before. Not being great at dealing with rejection, I never asked her out again.

The letter was written in a large, flowing script on stationery that said "Mona Pinchman Rashid" at the top.

> *Dear Steven:*
>
>   *I'm sure you get a ton of letters from people who knew you "when," but what's wrong with my joining the crowd? First off, congratulations, though your amazing success doesn't really surprise me. I always felt you had something special in you, Steven. I remember vividly your work in the Shakespeare Club. You were the glue that held it together. I can't wait to read your next novel. Hope it will come out real soon. I've read them all (in hardcover!), and keep them in a special section on the bookshelf. Right now, I'm living in Cornwall, CT. I come into the city a lot and I was wondering if perhaps sometime we could have some lunch or a drink. I know your schedule must be incredibly hectic and would completely understand if that's impossible for you to do. But as my grandmother always used to say, "You have to ask to know." My number here is (860) 555-5286. If I'm not in, there's a machine.*
>
>   *Your old friend,*
>   *Mona*
>
>   *P.S. I also write a bit, too. Mainly song lyrics and poetry.*

Of course, I called her. Mona wasn't there, but the machine said, "This is Mona. I'm out right now, but I'm very good at returning messages. Please leave one with the date and time. You're going to hear lots of beeps before you can leave your message. Please be patient. Thanks." I left a short message and, surprise, surprise, Mona called me back a half hour later. We settled on having lunch the next day, not at the Four Seasons, but rather a small Italian place, Trattoria Pozzo, in Chelsea. Why? Though I had no intention of pursuing my unfulfilled wet dreams with Mona, there was no sense in going to a spot where there were scores of people who knew me. I was still floating from the thought of becoming a father, and why have someone thinking Steven Konigsberg was fooling around when, in fact, he wasn't?

Though I showed up on time, Mona was already there waiting. Her hair was now dyed a whitish blond and cut short. She was attractive in a studied, overly tended way, but the Mona Pinchman of Braggler High was no more. It wasn't that she had aged poorly, or that her figure had yielded to the laws of gravity, but rather that Mona appeared to have lived life somewhat beyond the posted speed limits. Her tale of the years since she had been Prom Queen attested to three husbands, two of whom had been rock musicians, and two long relationships with men who wound up in prison. Both were now out, however, and she had a court order that kept one of them at a safe distance. She had gone to Stanford, but for only two semesters. At the start of her sophomore year she joined her first husband on a forty-city, nine-country rock tour. She told me her tale while sipping a glass of Evian (she was now in A.A. and sober for almost two years). She left out nothing, neither the abortions nor her stays in detox. She told me her father, Saul Pinchman of Pinchman and Flax, Elmira's largest jeweler, was still alive.

Her mother would still be alive, too, she told me, if Mona hadn't put her through so much. The death certificate might say heart attack, but it should really state, "Caused by Mona's miserable life."

Thankfully, we moved on to what had happened to some of our fellow students at Braggler. Besides me, the other notable success was Monroe Deacon, who played two seasons for the San Diego Padres and was now selling mutual funds in Albany. The most notorious member of our class was certainly Bobby Farro, who had swindled $14 million out of Elmira's municipal employees and pensioners through a Ponzi scheme. He was now serving time in a federal prison in Pennsylvania. This piece of news elated me, since Bobby Farro had made it a habit of shaking me down for lunch money on a regular basis.

After I paid the check, Mona handed me an envelope.

"I think I told you I wrote song lyrics. There are several in here that I think might be perfect for the movie version of your last book. I know it's an imposition, but could you show them to the producer?"

"Of course, Mona. I'd be happy to do it."

We hugged each other on the sidewalk, then I hailed Mona a cab.

"You know," she said as she was about to get in, "I have the use of a friend's apartment in Kips Bay. It could be fun to meet there sometime."

"I'm sure it would be. But I don't think it's the right thing for both of us. You know what I mean."

"Of course, Steven."

I kissed her on the cheek and then watched the taxi slide into the traffic of Eighth Avenue. Jesus, I thought as I walked uptown, that whole thing felt like a scene from a French movie, though I couldn't think of one that was this depressing. Poor Mona Pinchman. I knew that I wanted to work the lunch into my new Chambers Benjamin book. Finally having the girl you lusted for come on to you; nice circularity there. I stopped in a coffee shop and had a decaf espresso while I wrote some notes on the lunch. Because I can be pretty dense at times, the real significance of what I was trying to understand didn't hit me until I reached the park. Simply put, I was incredibly lucky to have Tina's love. Instead of going to my office, I walked toward Spence. I planned to stop on the way and buy a huge bunch of violets, Tina's favorite flower. I'd wait for her outside the school, and when she walked out, I would hug her as if my life depended on it.

Forty-one

I sent June and Vera Bowers the $50,000 they asked for. But screw them. They couldn't hurt me. The specter of Wayne Woodley was nothing more to me now than a ghost story told by children late at night. All was right with the world: I was going to be a father.

Tina was barely two months into the glorious baby-making game, and to anyone other than me appeared as slim as ever. There was some time before we had to make announcements, and until then we decided to tell no one. Tina's mother could be counted on not to spread the word in Key West, though there were plenty of writers there who liked nothing better than gossiping about other writers. My parents were another thing. I wanted very much to give them the news, but if I did, my mother would not be able to resist talking about it to her sister, my Aunt Florence, who would share it with Stuart, who would broadcast it to *Variety*, "Page Six," *Good Morning America*, and Reuters. Restraint was not one of Stuart's strong points.

It was a deep pleasure to keep a secret like this one (so different from some other secrets I had), and we luxuriated in the privacy and closeness it brought us. Dr. Scherer told us there was a new test that could identify a baby's sex even at this early stage. When we found out that Tina was having a boy, we agreed without discussing it or thumbing through baby name books for inspiration that the baby's name would be Benjamin Chambers King. Of course, we also knew that we would call him Ben. Though the baby's name was a given, there were other things to fantasize about: what color his eyes and hair would be, whether he would look more like Tina or me, how to decorate his room. We went about our lives in normal, everyday ways, but thoughts of the baby bubbled up into my mind all the time, and I knew it was the same for Tina.

One morning, early, the phone rang. It was Dexter Parch. I could hear the lift in his voice when he said hello.

"I was going to hold off and call you at a more civilized hour, but I couldn't wait to give you more good news. A publisher's happiest task, I might say, and rare. Remember I said we had ordered paper for a second printing of *Pulse?*"

"Yes?"

"Yesterday I decided to double the printing to thirty thousand instead of fifteen. Thirty thousand, Steven. Your total in print is fifty-five thousand. That's a number to be reckoned with for a literary novel."

"You're not kidding, are you?" I asked, suddenly feeling dizzy as if I had just sprinted up the stairs.

"My head of sales told me he's convinced *Pulse* will make the list in a matter of weeks. And so am I. As an extra dollop—not the right word, though it'll do for the moment—I just got word that German rights have been sold to Droermer, one of the best. So I would say you had a pretty good day, Steven, and it's still not even nine in the morning."

"Amazing," I said, flushed with delight. I was a successful literary author, no doubt about it. Anonymous, yes, but the real thing. One good thought led to another. I had a powerful urge to shout into Parch's ear, "And guess what, I'm going to be a father," but he hung up before I could break the promise Tina and I had made to not spill the beans.

Later that morning, just before noon, Sal Rigano arrived for another writing tutorial. Sal had sent me his revised pages several days earlier. He had turned out to be a quick study. He had cut out most of the bloat, sharpened his dialogue, and developed two new strong plot elements. It was getting to be pretty good, and I told him so.

"Keep this up, Sal, and I'll show it to my publisher."

"You mean it?"

"I'm dead serious."

"That would be so unbelievable. Wait until I tell Teresa."

"Now, let's get back to work."

We worked side by side at my desk for a couple of hours before we called it a day.

"Not so fast," I said as he stood up to leave. "You don't get out of here without another reading assignment. Here's *Double Indemnity* by James M. Cain and *All the King's Men* by Robert Penn Warren. Pay close attention to how these guys develop the plot. Never mind that you've probably seen the movies based on them. They're good, but we're both in the writing game, and it's the original that we can really learn from."

I started to open the door to let him out, then shut it again. "I've been bursting to tell you something, Sal. Something wonderful that I can't keep secret any longer, though I promised Tina I wouldn't tell anyone. She's pregnant. I'm going to be a father."

Sal hugged me, tightly and warmly.

"You're going to be a great father, Steve."

"How do you know that?" I asked, smiling.

"You're a giver. Men who can give make the best fathers. The takers, and there's a lot of them, should become toll collectors and stay away from having kids."

The next day a package was delivered to the apartment. It was from Sal. In it was a miniature policeman's cap and a tiny badge. There was also a card inside that said, "To my favorite giver. Congratulations. From his friend, Sal."

I hadn't felt this moved since I'd read Ben's letter. With a friend like this, maybe I had a shot at getting out of the mess I'd gotten myself into.

Forty-two

The next few months were as good as any I had ever experienced. Tina's obstetrician, Dr. Paul Scherer, said everything looked fine, and that in five months Benjamin Chambers King would be residing with us. Every time I glanced at myself in a mirror, I was smiling. So was Tina. It was time to tell family and friends. I warned Stuart that if he leaked anything to the columns, I'd never speak to him again. He didn't, but he tried half a dozen times to get me to change my mind.

"Your fans would love to hear the news."

"My fans would also love to get a fifteen percent commission on every book I sell."

"That was uncalled-for, Steve."

"You won't hear it again if you drop your role as publicist and stick to being my agent."

There was only one further request for money ($85,000) from June, from whom I received regular updates of Vera's progression in the world of bodybuilding. Once in a while, Vera would throw in a line or two, like this letter I received from Murmansk.

> *Stevie Boy:*
> *I can see from the photo of you in* People *that you need to build up your pecs and abs. You're as scrawny as a hamster's dick. I'm sure you eat*

*way too much junk food. I've enclosed the diet that I follow. Stick to it and
you'll look better, sleep better, and crap better.*

V

They also included a photo spread on the two of them from a bodybuilding magazine. They definitely looked a lot bigger than they had in
the last photo I had seen. Their arms and legs were massive. Though they
were smiling in all the shots, there was also a hint of something else. They
looked angry. I didn't kid myself that the sisters would stay on the road
forever. But I felt so good that even the thought of dealing with them
didn't scare me.

Sales for my Chambers Benjamin book were building. It was now in a
fourth printing. The reviews for the British edition were good, too. I even
got a terrific (though short) review in the *Times Literary Supplement.* The cap-
stone to all this came while I was having lunch with Dexter Parch in his office. Chancery had just hired a chef, and Dexter wanted to show off for me.
A private dining room had been set up in what had been a small conference
room down the hall from Dexter's office.

"I asked the chef to cook two of your favorites, Steven."

"Let me guess."

"Go ahead. Jesus, I hope I'm right. I've seen you order these dishes more
than any others."

"*Vitello tonnato* and pasta with red clam sauce."

"You make me feel like I'm almost smart," said Dexter, beaming.

After we finished the pasta, Dexter handed me a large envelope.

"I think you'll find the contents interesting." I quickly opened it to find a
printout of the bestseller list from the *New York Times.*

"Why are you showing me this?"

"It's this coming Sunday's list."

"So?"

"Why don't you give it a close look. I think you'll like what you find
there."

Suddenly, I saw *Time's Pulse* at number fifteen. I had written a bestseller.
A literary bestseller. Who would have believed it? And the only people who
knew were Dexter and Tina. Oh, and Sal. I knew I could trust him completely, so I'd told him, too. Sal thought it was my best book. That's all the

audience I needed. I stood up and went around the table and embraced Dexter.

"This means a lot to me. Thank you for all you've done."

"No, thank you for having written a terrific book. Different from your others, but terrific nonetheless. Chancery is proud to have published it."

"And you've been very good at keeping our secret."

"Trust me, Steven, it will always remain a secret. And I think the time is right for me to tell you one," he said, lowering his voice. "The best thing about our publishing relationship is that it's grown into a true friendship. I've published a lot of authors, but I can't recall one who has meant what you do to me."

"I feel the same way," I said, beginning to fear what Dexter was about to tell me. Was he sick? Marriage in trouble? About to start a new sex life?

"Steven, my name wasn't originally Parch." Inwardly, I breathed a sigh of relief. This I could certainly handle. "In fact, my father, who is still alive, thankfully uses the name he came here with after the war." He paused. "My real name is Plotz. Until this moment no one outside of my family knows that."

"Konigsberg, Plotz, what does it matter?"

"Well, to me it matters a lot. Your name was already changed to King when you were born. I went through elementary school, junior high, and high school as Plotz. And my first name wasn't Dexter. I took that from a street in Queens. I was born Hyman Plotz."

I might have done some internal damage holding in a riotous salvo of laughter. Inside, I was pleased enough with my steely control to hug Dexter again.

"Dexter, you're family to me. And it's only with family members that you can be assured a secret will be kept forever."

I realized that this was the perfect moment to tell Dexter *my* secret. I had just told him that he was family to me: that was certainly true. My relationship with Dexter was closer than the one I had with my own brother. I trusted him completely. If I had revealed that the books had all been written by Ben, he would be shocked, but once that passed, he would take the secret with him to his grave. We were alone in the room, so there was no chance of anyone overhearing my confession; what was stopping me? "Ben," I wanted to call out, "give me the strength to tell Dexter." But of course, there was no whispered assurance from above, no subtle sign that would have urged me to proceed, so we spent the rest of the lunch discussing the new tennis court that Dexter was building, and the merits of Har-Tru versus Omnicourt.

The next day I received a call from Bruno Mortice. Bruno had directed the film version of *Juno's Dance*, and its success had placed him solidly in the red-hot center of directors who could green-light a film. After exchanging pleasantries, he got down to the reason for the call.

"You know that book you sent me a couple of months back? It was called *Time's Pulse*."

"Sure. I remember."

Now, I have to admit here that I couldn't resist sending copies of *Time's Pulse* to a number of people. Actually, it was over fifty. Each copy included a note from me that said, "I thought you might find this novel by Chambers Benjamin interesting. I always like to give first novels a little boost. Short of a quote, buying a copy and sending it to a friend is the only leg up I can think of. Enjoy." Yes, it was fairly shameless.

"Well, I fucking love the thing," Bruno continued. "I had my assistant call Chancery to find out who the agent is, and they said he has no agent. Either he's a genius or an idiot. And the publisher says that this Benjamin fellow doesn't want to sell the film rights."

"That's his right, I guess."

"You've got to help me get to this guy. I have to make a film of *Time's Pulse*. Chancery is your publisher, after all. Maybe they'll tell you how I can contact him. I'm ready to put my own fucking money up to buy it. I've got to do it."

"Let me nose around and see what I can find out."

"You're the best. Call me as soon as you find out anything."

. . .

Over the following month, as *Time's Pulse* hung on the bottom of the best-seller list, I got a call almost every other day from Bruno Mortice asking if I had located Chambers Benjamin yet. Luckily, the calls finally stopped when he signed on to direct a remake of *Double Indemnity* starring Sharon Stone and Harrison Ford. It was a truly terrible idea, but at least it got him off my back.

One night, as I was about to get into bed after a dinner out at a Thai restaurant, I found a box wrapped in silver gift paper sitting on my pillow, like a bedtime mint at a hotel.

"What's this?" I asked Tina, who was reading, her stomach gently tenting the quilt like a small geodesic dome.

"Looks like a gift."

I ripped open the paper to find a thin silver tray the size of a book. There, engraved on it, was the *New York Times Book Review* bestseller list with *Time's Pulse* at number fifteen.

"I love it, honey," I said, leaning over and kissing her.

"I thought we could use it for Ben's Q-Tips. Or something like that."

"But I thought it was for me."

"I'm sure you're going to get a lot more silver trays."

"Why's that?"

"Because I know there's going to be more Chambers Benjamin books. So Mr. Benjamin, King, or Konigsberg, or whatever you're calling yourself tonight, could you come over to my side, please? This big mama needs a back rub real bad."

Forty-three

The weeks and months slid sweetly by. Tina looked more beautiful each day and by now couldn't see her toes. Little Ben seemed to be practicing tae bo, or some other arcane exercise program, judging by the activity that I could feel when I touched Tina's belly. My Chambers Benjamin novel, though no rival in sales to the Steven Konigsberg work, was still percolating along nicely.

I hadn't missed a Wednesday session with Sal Rigano since we started. Sal had finished his book, and the portion of the book he had rewritten was now tight and the voice fresh. He was also devouring the books I gave him. Sal had an innate appreciation of literary style and nuance. Though he expressed this with a vocabulary that wasn't generally heard in comp lit seminars, his analyses were invariably perceptive and original. The sessions had turned our teacher-student relationship into a simple one of true friendship. If Ben's books had brought me riches and fame, fear and threats, they had also resulted in important friendships with Dexter Parch and Sal Rigano.

Our usual routine was to work line by line through three to four pages, discussing everything from dialogue and punctuation to grammar and use of adjectives and adverbs. This would lead us into parallels with some of the novels and stories that Sal was currently reading. After a few hours we would break for lunch, generally either Thai or deli, then come back for another hour or so. We were finishing up one day when Sal invited me and Tina to his house in Bensonhurst for dinner.

"Just Teresa and the kids. I guarantee you a great Sicilian meal. Five-star."

"You know, Sal, Tina still has no idea about you, Wayne Woodley, the whole thing."

"Of course. How could I be so frigging dumb."

"But, hey. We're both writers. Let's use our imaginations and figure out a way to handle it."

Sal came up with the first part of the scenario, and I developed the second. Here's what we decided I would tell Tina: I had gotten to know Sal because I needed someone to help me with research for a character in my next book, who was a homicide detective in Brooklyn. How did I meet Sal? Through Stuart, of course. A few years back Stuart had represented a former police commissioner who wrote a book. He recommended Sal as the perfect person to give me the ins and outs about what it's like to be a homicide detective. There was little chance that Tina would check this out, since she hardly saw or spoke to Stuart.

"Just stick to your story and you'll have no problem."

"I think I can handle it."

Who the hell was I kidding? Lying and subterfuge were second nature to me by now. If it came to spinning a tapestry of lies to Tina or anyone else, I was aces.

"Steve, I have a rule I absolutely follow. Never tell the wife everything. 'Everything' is a word that can suck you in deeper than quicksand. It's a word that leads to confusion and danger. You know what I tell Teresa? I tell her what she needs to know. That's why we have a good marriage."

Tina accepted my story about Sal, and was pleased that I'd told him about the baby. She loved the idea that I had gotten to know someone like him. When I mentioned the dinner invitation, she was delighted. To have dinner with "real" people (i.e., not fancy Manhattanites), to go to a "real" home (i.e., not an expensively decorated town house or apartment), and to do all this in Brooklyn was heaven-sent. The last time I remembered Tina this excited about a dinner was the first time she met my parents. Her only problem was how to dress for our trip to Bensonhurst. She didn't want to appear too fancy, so she spent more time selecting her outfit than usual. In the end she looked, as usual, natural and beautiful.

The drive to the Bensonhurst section of Brooklyn took a little over a half

hour. Tina peppered me with questions about Sal, most of which I was easily able to answer. My mind, however, was not really focused on Sal and the
dinner, or on Tina's questions. As we emerged from the Brooklyn Battery
Tunnel, I realized that this was the same route I had taken to meet Wayne
Woodley that night so long ago in Coney Island. Where would I be today
if not for Sal? Probably indicted and awaiting trial for manslaughter, if not
murder. Once again, I thanked God for Sal Rigano.

The Riganos lived in a three-story house on Seventy-sixth Street between
Eighteenth and Nineteenth Avenues. The house, like all the others on the
block, was well kept and appeared freshly painted. Sal and Teresa, along
with their two kids, Sal Jr. and Marie Anne, lived on the top floor. Sal's in-
laws, Rocco and Gloria, lived on the first, and Teresa's sister and her family resided on the second.

After hugs were exchanged, Tina and I joined the Riganos in their large
dining room.

"I know the two of you are used to real good fancy food," said Teresa,
"but I hope you'll like the simple meal we're going to have."

"Jesus, Teresa," said Sal, "give it a break. You're a great cook and Tina
and Steve will love it. Now, how about some wine?" he said, holding up a
wine bottle without a label. "My father-in-law makes this in the basement,
but it's real good. He even grows the grapes in the backyard." Tina, of
course, abstained, but the rest of us, including the kids, who had small
glasses, partook. The wine was soft, with a smooth, fragrant taste. "And
you, Junior, what gives with wearing that Mets cap at the table? You think
you're at Shea Stadium? Get that off right now."

Our first course was prosciutto and figs. The figs, Teresa explained, were
also grown by her father.

"He wraps those trees up for the winter as carefully as a mother would
protect a baby in Alaska."

The second course was a heap of blue crabs that had been steamed, then
served with a spicy oil dressing.

"You're going to have to work hard to get the meat out," said Sal, pounding one of the crabs with a wooden mallet, "but once you do, you'll see that
the effort was worth it."

"We can thank my brother-in-law, Aldo, for these," added Teresa. "He
goes out crabbing every chance he can."

The crabs were followed by *pasta con le sarde*, thick pasta tubes that were slathered with a sauce of fresh sardines, fennel, onions, raisins, and pine nuts. It, too, was delicious.

"Before you ask," said Teresa, "Aldo didn't catch the sardines. But I guarantee you that they're fresh."

I looked over to Tina, who was beaming over a cleaned plate, expecting, like me, the next course to be espresso. But, no, Teresa wasn't finished with her "simple" Sicilian dinner. We were then served a salad of sliced oranges, olives, and mint. After that, finally, came the espresso. But it didn't come unaccompanied. In the center of the table she placed a platter of small confections made of almond paste and stuffed with pistachios. These, Teresa told us, were *frutti di Martorama*.

"Look at them closely," said Sal proudly.

We each held one close and saw they were all made into the image of a book. And there, on what would be the cover, in tiny letters of pink icing, were titles of my books.

"This is fantastic," said Tina.

"As was the meal," I added as I leaned over the table to kiss Teresa.

When we were about to leave, Teresa left the room and came back carrying a large carton.

"We thought this could come in handy," she said as she lifted it onto the table and opened it. Inside, it was filled with neat piles of baby clothes. "These were all Sal Jr.'s. I knew someday a friend could use them. I'm happy it's you. It'll give you a head start."

"She's a real pack rat," said Sal. "The basement here looks like a warehouse."

As we finally got up from the table, the doorbell rang and in came Teresa's parents and her sister and brother-in-law. We were then presented with more figs, wine, and, in a Styrofoam container packed with dry ice, a batch of blue crabs. We needed help to get it all downstairs to our car. Of course, before we left, out came copies of all my Steven Konigsberg books, which I happily autographed, including one to Father Vincent Amalfi, Sal Jr.'s teacher at St. Ignatius Junior High.

"God, that was great," said Tina as I drove onto the Belt Parkway.

"Aren't they terrific? And that meal. I loved it."

"There might be a lot of people like Teresa and Sal in Manhattan, but I sure haven't met them. The Riganos are real. People who are interested in life, not appearances. They're the kind of people we should be with."

Surprisingly, I found myself agreeing totally with Tina. Maybe getting out of New York was the thing for us to do. Not right away, but someday soon, after little Ben joined our happy band. Though we were ridiculously full and contented, we found room on the way home to toast the Rigano clan with a few more succulent figs.

Forty-four

Tina and I were a week away from our first Lamaze class. We had watched an instructional video, and now I went around panting when no one was listening except Chester. He would look at me like I was nuts, then join me with an inspired howl. My overall mood ranged from good to great. *Time's Pulse* was now off the *Times* list, but it had had an excellent run. The French and German editions were set to come out in the next few months. They would be delivered to my office, not the apartment. Here, in my library in the apartment, Fred carefully kept all the Steven Konigsberg foreign editions arranged alphabetically by language (yes, Steven Konigsberg was even published in Urdu!) on two long shelves. But to see my own work in another language would be a true thrill. And I had heard another piece of news from Dexter. Quentin Bass had told him over lunch that as a member of the fiction panel of the National Book Awards, he was pushing hard for *Time's Pulse* to be nominated. He felt that a couple of the other judges were leaning toward the book, too. I was amazed to hear that Quentin was on the panel, but the man who headed it was a former, very sympathetic colleague. Quentin's assignment to write the review for the *Times Book Review* came about in a similar fashion. The editor who gave it to him was someone he had once dated at Iowa. He had treated her poorly, but she still considered him a talented writer. It was hard to conjure up. Me, Steven King, becoming a National Book Award nominee. The bartender gets a look at the summit: "Hello, Phil Roth. Hi there, Mr. Updike. It's me, Steven King. No, not the monster bestseller from Maine, but the fairly young guy from Elmira. Save a place up there for me. I'm on my way."

It was a Tuesday and I had decided to take the day off. Tomorrow I'd be working with Sal, so I wanted to review the section of his novel he'd be showing me. I had been a teaching assistant when I was going for my master's at Iowa, but that never really placed me in a true teacher's role: grading papers is not teaching. For the first time, I understood the potential joy one could get from it.

I told Fred to screen my calls. I didn't want to waste the morning talking on the phone. Fred did a good job, telling all callers, "I think he went out, but let me check." I took a call from Stuart for one reason only: I had found out from Dexter that Chancery had sent a large royalty check (read that as almost seven figures) to Stuart six weeks ago. I hadn't yet received my eighty-five percent of that. Why the hell was he sitting on it?

"I just found out about it, Stevie. I'm terribly sorry. I've fired the fucking bookkeeper. How was I supposed to know the guy developed a coke problem? But don't worry, he didn't steal a cent. The fucking check was sitting on his desk. I've replaced him, of course. Now I have a Hasid who's dynamite. You'll be receiving your check by messenger on Friday. That's a promise."

I didn't believe a word about the bookkeeper, but what was the point of ripping into him again? He was my cousin, and I was stuck with him.

"Do you have a minute?" he asked.

"Yes, but just a minute. And not one word about the film rights to the kids' book."

"I told you I wouldn't bring that up again, but Disney and DreamWorks are still on me like a hooker who's giving it away. I've just gotten a very interesting proposition."

"What is it? Make it fast." I had long ago lost my patience with Stuart and treated him like a child who was up past his bedtime.

"I've been approached by a large corporation who's willing to pay significant money to have their company mentioned in your next novel."

"What are you talking about?"

"Okay. It's Coffee Nation. They're a new firm competing against Star-bucks. They've offered two hundred and fifty thousand to be mentioned four times in the book. And I think I can get them up to at least three-fifty."

"My next book takes place in the forties, Stuart. That's probably before the guy who started the business was even born."

"Maybe you can have a flash-forward. I've seen that in a few books."

"Tell them where they can stick their latte. Good-bye, Stuart."

An hour later, as I was about to take Chester for a walk, Fred came into my study to tell me that a woman named Vera was on the phone. She had told Fred it was important.

"At least I think it's a woman. The voice is awfully deep."

I told Fred to close the door, and after taking a deep breath, I picked up the phone.

"How you doing, Mr. K?"

I knew immediately that this was Vera. Her voice had the timbre and strength of a midway pitchman. This was a big woman with a voice to match. The sound seemed to boom out—then I realized she was on a speakerphone.

"I'm fine, thanks. You sound like you're fully recovered."

"What are you talking about?"

"Your car accident. Isn't that what put you in the hospital?"

Vera's laugh was almost as scary as her voice. It was the kind of laugh I suspect gladiators waiting to die heard in ancient Rome.

"That's funny. My sister is something. You've got to love her. So she told you I was in the hospital? That's great." She started to laugh again. "Thank God I wasn't, because I never could have kept up with my workouts. The food in jail sucks, but the weight room was pretty good."

My mind raced through scenarios of what put Vera Bowers behind bars. I didn't have to guess very long.

"I've got to watch myself now. If they bust me again, I could do some serious time. Though if another cop jabs me with his finger again, I'll prob-ably break that one, too. I don't take shit, Mr. K. The fucking anger man-agement course I had to take inside was a joke. I don't have a problem with anger so long as people leave me alone. Now, tell me, are you following my diet?"

"Religiously."

"I think you're shitting me. What do you think, sis?"

"I think Mr. Konigsberg's an honest guy."

"Except when it comes to putting his name on a book that was written by someone else."

I let that slide.

"Where are you calling from?"

"Frankfurt. I've got a competition tonight."

"Well, good luck."

"Luck has nothing to do with it."

"We're coming to New York soon, Mr. Konigsberg," said June.

"That's great."

"Cut the bullshit," said Vera, her voice echoing. "I've had my sister make some inquiries on what our little manuscript might be worth. Tell him."

"I talked with Sotheby's and Christie's. They're both very interested. They said they'd give us a guarantee. A big one. I also spoke to the University of Texas. They have a very large manuscript collection of contemporary writers. They want us to come down and talk to them. There's also great interest from–"

"But I believe it might be worth more to you," said Vera, cutting in. "I kind of think you'd be willing to top any offer that's made to us."

"What do you want?"

"I'm putting that together. I'll lay it out for you when we're back in New York. But right now I need another hundred K wired into the account. I expect the money to be deposited by tomorrow morning, ten A.M. Pacific time. If it's not, you'll make me very cranky. And sometimes I get physical when I feel that way. Do you understand me?"

"Yes," I said.

"And I can't wait for you to see my little sister. She's not so little anymore. She's not like me, but she's getting there. Right, sis?"

"I never miss a workout. You're really going to see a difference."

My hands were shaking when I hung up the phone. It wasn't what was said, exactly, or the fact that June's voice now was a lot deeper than I remembered; it was something else that scared me: the implicit threat behind everything Vera said. A darker threat, much darker, than I'd ever experienced. I was dealing with true lunatics, and strong ones.

. . .

I spent the rest of the afternoon going over Douglas Tern's report again. The call from the Bowers sisters had served as a splash of icy water. Who else was waiting to pounce on me? When I went through the report again, I decided to investigate one of the people who could be a possible threat. Lorenzo Buffman lived nearby in Snedens Landing, a small community across the Hudson River. The report said that Buffman was retired, though he published a newsletter, the *Sitcom Savvy Sheet*. I dialed his number and he answered on the first ring. I was so rattled by the call from the Bowerses that I used the name Steven Konigsberg.

"*The* Steven Konigsberg?"

"I guess so."

"I just have to tell you that I love your books. I read them as soon as they come out. I can't believe I'm talking to Steven Konigsberg."

"Well, you are, Mr. Buffman. Is there any chance I might come out and see you? It's about Ben Chambers."

"God, I haven't heard that name in . . . it must be thirty years."

We quickly agreed on Thursday at ten in the morning. He wanted to make me lunch, but he had a doctor's appointment at twelve.

Lorenzo Buffman lived in a small turn-of-the-century house set back from the road. A rutted driveway led to a garage in need of paint. I had just stepped out of my car when he opened the front door and waved to me.

"Right this way, Mr. Konigsberg."

Buffman looked like an old shore bird. He was wearing shorts, and his long, thin legs, pale as sand, were like stilts. He had a Jewish 'fro of silver hair, like a pillow of cotton candy. I followed him into what must have been his office. Two walls were lined with battered old file cabinets. Half the drawers were open, overloaded with papers and scripts.

"My life's work," he said, gesturing toward the file cabinets. "Over fifty years of scripts, treatments, ideas, you name it."

I told Buffman that I was in the process of putting together a complete listing of everything Ben had written.

"How is Ben, anyway?" he asked.

"I'm sorry to tell you, but Ben passed away."

"That's a shame. He was a great guy."

Then I got down to the subject at hand. Did Buffman, by any chance, possess some of Ben's work? A chapter of a novel, a fragment of a story, anything.

"He was always writing, Ben was. But he never showed me a word. I was a top sitcom writer in those days, and I would show him everything I wrote. Great editor. Whether it was comedy or drama, he could spot in an instant what wasn't working in the piece. I branched out at one time, did several *Have Gun Will Travel* scripts, and he was just as sharp with them. He had an amazing critical eye."

"So you don't have anything?"

"Not a postcard. Everything he wrote he kept in two beautiful wooden trunks, each locked tighter than a chastity belt. I don't know if you knew that he was a great furniture maker. I begged him to give me a look, but he would just smile and tell me 'someday.' But that day never came."

Buffman then went on to give me the long version of his career, covering every script he'd ever written, from *My Little Margie* to *F Troop*. I pasted a smile on my face and bobbed my head like a doll in the back of a gypsy cab. Finally, I glanced at my watch and saw that it was almost twelve. Thank God.

"Didn't you say, Mr. Buffman, that you had a doctor's appointment?"

"Please, call me Lorenzo. You're right. I have to get going. I sometimes get carried away when talking about the old days."

"I found it fascinating," I said as I got up from the chair.

"By the way, you know why I think Ben never showed me a page of his work? Because it was probably shit, and he knew it."

As Buffman walked me to my car, he asked if I could do him a favor.

"Of course. What is it?"

"I'm almost finished writing a comic novel. It's a lot like Evelyn Waugh, only it's American. Could you take a look at it?"

I handed Lorenzo Buffman my card, then backed out of his driveway. As I was driving on the Palisades Parkway heading back to town, a huge black cloud that had been blocking the sun parted and the road exploded into light. I took it as a sign that the other two people in the report would be as easy as Buffman. I put on my sunglasses and started to think about where I could go for lunch.

Forty-five

Around the corner from our apartment, a small, cozy restaurant had recently appeared, in a space formerly occupied by a string of failed Italian trattorias, all of which had started with either "La" or "Il." A few days earlier I had read the menu posted next to the door, and it had passed muster. It was Mexican, always a favorite of Tina's.

As we entered the restaurant, I greeted the maître d' and gave him our name.

"Right. Konigsberg. Reservation for three."

Tina give me a strange look. "Who's meeting us?" she asked as soon as we were seated.

"Our guest is already here," I said, looking pointedly at her huge frontage.

She looked down or, really, over herself, as if she were surveying a mountain from a plateau at the top, then giggled. "You're so cute, Steve, but the next thing you know, it'll be for real. Ben will be with us. Really with us. And we'll take him out to sample his first Chinese restaurant, where there are always babies. He'll have his bottle and we'll have moo shu pork and shrimp with black bean sauce. I can't wait."

"Neither can I, darling," I said. Reaching out for her hand and pulling her closer, I resisted the urge to wrap my arms around her, then and there. I forced myself to sit back in my chair and in a serious manner, as if I were

attending a conference on obstetrics, I said, "Two more weeks at Spence"–
Tina nodded–"then a couple of more weeks after that, and then"–I did a
little drumroll on the table–"welcome, Mr. Ben." Tina nodded vigorously.
She had insisted on working close to the end and seemed to thrive on it.

"The girls love feeling my stomach when the baby kicks. I line them up
and they come up one at a time. They're going to miss it. The ones who
have younger brothers or sisters are the old pros. They've gone through this
with their mothers, but they're all in awe."

I toasted her with my Coke. I had resisted ordering a margarita, since
Tina couldn't drink.

"Steve . . . ," said Tina in what I recognized as one of her worried tones,
"do you really have to go to Miami?"

"I think I do, darling. The bookseller I'm doing the reading for is special,
one of the best of the independents. He started the Miami Book Fair–I
think I told you that–and he's always been great to me."

"But what if something happens?" She avoided saying what the "something" was, as if we didn't both know.

"If that something you're referring to is little Ben, it won't. Remember,
I'm not going down for a while, and when I do, I'll be back on an early
flight the next day. Tina, sweetheart, believe me, I wouldn't leave even for
a moment if I thought there was any chance of his making an appearance
without me here to cheer you both on. The little guy will probably be safe
in his crib at our apartment before I go."

I was doing my best to reassure her, and I was doing a pretty good job.
Her face relaxed again, and she smiled.

The reason for my trip to Miami had nothing to do with the bookseller,
but with meeting the next-to-last person on Detective Tern's list of people
Ben Chambers knew, an editor who had been in business with him and
then retired to Miami Beach. I was betting on establishing quickly whether
the man knew anything dangerous about Ben's books (dangerous to me,
that is), and I was betting that he didn't. But I had to be sure.

Tina was trying unsuccessfully to suppress a yawn, which sent me down
the same path.

"I can barely keep my eyes open," said Tina. I thought of flagging down
a taxi, but we were only a few blocks away from the apartment and the air
was bracing.

Almost as soon as we got home, Tina was in bed. I snapped Chester's leash on to take him for his night walk and bent down to kiss her on the cheek. She was nearly asleep and mumbled something sweet but indecipherable.

Chester and I had our favorite spots. One of them, near our apartment, was an overgrown area shaded by a stand of hemlocks, with a path winding through it. There were so few people ever there that it had a private feel to it, almost as if it were part of the land surrounding our house in the country. Tonight it was deserted as usual.

I was walking along, letting Chester set the pace, when I heard footsteps right behind.

"Hello, Mr. K," a voice called out. "I hoped we'd find you here."

I turned around reluctantly. I had never met her before, but I knew immediately it was Vera. Of course, I had seen her picture from several clippings June had sent me, but the reality, even under the dim park lights, was more impressive and truly frightening. Dressed in black sweats topped by a black watch cap, she looked like a massive ninja. She was even bigger than I had imagined. June stood behind Vera, a lot larger than the last time I'd seen her; but she looked scared, too.

Vera reached down, petted Chester, and then gave him a dog biscuit. I protested that it was too late to feed him, but he had already swallowed the biscuit and was looking up, hopefully, for more.

"Do you know why we're here?" Vera asked. I shook my head. "Because you don't listen. Right, sis?"

June nodded. She seemed very nervous and kept looking, back and forth, between her sister and me. Suddenly, Chester collapsed onto the ground.

"Chester!" I cried out, dropping to my knees. He was out cold, his eyes rolled up, his body limp.

"Don't worry. He'll be okay. He's just taking a nap. I put a small amount of a crushed sleeping pill in the biscuit. Baked it myself."

"Why?"

"So we won't have the fucking dog barking while I pound you!"

Vera belted me in the gut. I doubled over but not before she kicked me in the groin. I was in agony but struggled to stand. As I did, she punched me hard in the face and knocked me down. I felt the place where her fist had landed already swelling.

"I better lay off your face, Mr. K. You might have to do a signing soon. Your livelihood is ours, too."

She started to work my body, the punches like hammerblows. I felt myself slipping into unconsciousness.

"That's enough, Vera. You're going to kill him," I heard June call out. As I fell to the ground, I saw her struggle to pull her sister off me. Vera pulled free to kick me once more, then leaned down and said, "We're off to a competition in Winnipeg, so you won't hear from us for a while. But when I tell you to do something, you do it. If you don't, maybe your fleabag mutt won't wake up next time. And you might not, either."

I don't know how long I lay on the sidewalk before Chester, now revived, started licking my face. I pulled myself slowly to a sitting position and then stood up, balancing myself against a small tree. I hurt more than I ever had in my life. I calculated that I had to walk three hundred yards to get out of the park, then two blocks south, to get to the apartment. I didn't know if I could do it. Then I spotted a sturdy branch lying on the ground that I could use as a cane. I slowly limped along like a street beggar in Calcutta, until I was opposite our building.

Leaning against the stone wall on the park side of the street, I stared at the entrance and pondered whether I could get past the doorman without setting off a groundswell of gossip and speculation about what had happened to me.

But I got lucky. A limousine pulled up to the front canopy. I knew that it belonged to a very old lady who always had to be helped out of the car by the doorman. Sure enough, he rushed forward and bent inside the car. This was my moment, perhaps my only moment, to get inside without being spotted. With Chester's leash in one hand and my cane in the other, I hobbled as fast as I could across the street and into the building.

I had made it.

I opened the door of our apartment cautiously and then looked into the bedroom. Tina was out cold. After throwing down a handful of Advil, I stripped my clothes off piece by piece, fighting the pain, then lay down on the bed, placing the side of my face that was bruised against the pillow, out of sight. I invited Chester onto the bed to sleep at my feet. After all, if he hadn't nudged me awake, I might still be lying on the pavement in the park. Almost immediately, he began to snore, and soon I joined him.

Forty-six

When I woke up the next morning at ten, Tina was already at Spence. I could barely get out of bed; my ribs felt as if they had been beaten like a carpet, and in a way they had been. Slumped over like a mendicant, I shuffled to the bathroom, where I had a scalding-hot shower. I don't know how long I was in the shower, but when I finally got out, not only was the bathroom mirror fogged thickly, the walls were wet, and droplets hung like ornaments from the ceiling. I toweled off the mirror and saw a huge bruise under my left eye, as dark as a cloud before a thunderstorm. I kicked my writer's imagination into high gear to come up with the scenario I would tell Tina later about why my face looked like something in an outtake from *Rocky*.

"I was just in my superklutz mode, honey. I turned quickly and bashed into the door of the armoire."

Not bad, but I could do better:

"Oh, the bruise. It's a combination of thinking about my new book and Chester. What do I mean? Well, I was walking Chester in the park. I was thinking about this chapter that I've been stuck on for a few days. It involves a character the reader's only met once at the beginning, and who suddenly reappears. All of a sudden Chester saw a squirrel and made a dash for it. I followed him for a few steps before I looked up, and there right before me was a tree. When I got up off the ground, I saw the little plastic marker that said 'Black Oak, *Quercus velutina*.' Take my word for it, old *Quercus velutina* is one hell of a sturdy tree."

That sounded better. The identification of the tree was a nice touch. I looked down at my ribs, and thankfully they didn't look bruised. If Tina noticed me wincing or moving around the apartment like a crab, I'd tell her that I had lifted something the wrong way and wrenched my back. People did that all the time.

When Chester came into the bathroom looking for me, he was moving slower than usual, still feeling the effects of Vera's knockout biscuit. That miserable bitch. I'd get her for what she did to both of us. But how? Strangely, I didn't feel frightened. Maybe I should thank Wayne Woodley for that. Having a gun pointed at you is a lot scarier than being pounded by a psycho female bodybuilder. Should I hire a bodyguard? That would be harder to explain to Tina. Wayne Woodley had made me an old hand at handling shakedowns and threats. I knew Vera Bowers wanted only one thing: money. The only accolades Vera wanted were trophies for bodybuilding. But what if I was reading her wrong? She seemed to be having fun when she was punching the hell out of me. Maybe the beating would trigger something bigger next time. No, that didn't make any sense. I had to stop scaring myself. Now.

In Tina's bathroom I rifled through her makeup, scanning the jars and tubes, trying one, then another, on the back of my hand. Finally, I applied Bobbi Brown's Foundation Stick, Beige 3, to the bruise. Gone was the purple corona, replaced now by a less threatening color, like liver that had been cooked too long.

When I made it into the study, Fred automatically appeared with a cup of coffee and my call list. He did a double take on the bruise, which I handled with the story I had prepared for Tina. It went down well, even eliciting a chuckle from him when I got to the part about the tree's name. So far, so good. There were a half dozen calls, two of which were from Dexter. The first one had "Important" next to it, the other, "You've hit a game-winning double."

"Hi, Dexter. What's so important?"

"Let me hear you roar."

"I don't know where you're going, but I'm not in the roaring mood this morning."

"Well, you should be. The New York Public Library wants to make you a Literary Lion. It's quite an honor."

It was an honor. A big one. But not for me. I was a cub, Ben was the lion.

"Turn it down, Dexter. It's an honor, all right, but I'm not ready for it yet."

"That's ridiculous, Steven. Millions of your fans would wholeheartedly agree with me. You owe it to them to accept the award."

"I'm honored, but I feel the time isn't right."

"The time is always right to receive an award like this. And you deserve it. Will you at least think about it?"

"Okay, I'll think about it. What's the game-winning double?"

"It's your day for good news. Quentin Bass called me to say that *Time's Pulse* is going to be nominated for the National Book Award for Fiction. He swore me to a vow of silence that makes the code of *omerta* seem like a Cub Scout oath. But I see no problem in telling you."

"That's fantastic. I'm thrilled."

"Of course, this one you can't attend."

Dexter was right. No one knew I had written the book. The award I had always dreamed about, I could neither acknowledge nor show up to accept.

"I'm still delighted."

"As you should be. Now, what about your promise?"

"What promise?"

"That you'll think about becoming a Literary Lion."

"Right. That's a promise."

When Tina got home, she yelped at the first sight of the bruise; then she accepted my Chester-and-the-tree story like a pensioner buying into a penny stock scam. She even kissed my bruise. Then she asked me why I didn't want to become a Literary Lion. Dexter had called her at school, and she readily agreed to use her talents of persuasion on me; my friend Dexter Parch could do an end run as well as anyone in the NFL. I told her that I was still considering it. What I didn't tell her was that I was also considering not publishing any more Ben books for quite a while. I certainly didn't need the money, and now that I was soon to be a National Book Award nominee, the desire to pursue my own work had never been stronger. By not publishing Ben's work, the chances of flushing out another menace like Wayne Woodley or the Bowers sisters would be minimal.

I gave Tina the story about hurting my back, then retreated to the tub, where I soaked for over an hour. Then I went into my study and read for a couple of hours to prepare myself for my next session with Sal. I decided I needed a vodka, icy cold from the freezer, and was halfway through the first and feeling a lot better when Tina walked into the kitchen. She looked great. She was dressed up, really dressed up, in cute little black shoes that seemed to be made up of a few thin twists of licorice, a black silk top that tented over her amazing belly, and a short gray moiré skirt that just touched the top of her knees.

"I've never seen Julia Child cook in an outfit like that. You look sensational, but I thought we were eating in tonight."

"Plans have changed. Go make yourself handsome. I'm taking you out to dinner."

When we finally went downstairs, there was a shiny black town car waiting for us.

"I decided that I would be the wife of the famous Steven Konigsberg tonight. A chauffeured car for a change, not my usual gypsy cab. And since little Ben is almost in the departure lounge, I thought he might appreciate a smoother ride."

While I told Tina once again the story of my battered face (this time adding an elderly couple who helped me to my feet), the car headed to the West Side Highway, then south.

"Where are we going?"

"I'm the choreographer of this evening. You're just a member of the audience."

Tina told me that Dr. Scherer had said that Ben might arrive a bit earlier than the due date, which was five weeks away. Immediately, I slid next to her and kissed her softly on the neck.

"I don't think I've ever been this happy," I told her.

"It won't be long before you'll be even happier."

The car pulled up in front of Chanterelle, my favorite place in the whole city. The room, which only holds fifteen tables, has pale creamy walls and a high ceiling of pressed tin painted white. A huge arrangement of apple and cherry branches with irises set in like small flags sat on a table at the front of the room. The meal unfolded slowly, with course after course that looked so good on the plate that it was hard to believe it would taste equally good; but it did. Two hours later dallying over coffee and chocolate truffles, the waiter brought over a small package and placed it in front of me.

"What's this?"

"You have to open it to find out," said Tina.

I tore away the wrapping to find a book bound in soft red calfskin. Hand-tooled on the spine was the title, *Time's Pulse*. Below it was not the name Chambers Benjamin, but rather my own, Steven King.

"It's beautiful, Tina."

"This is our secret edition. It's not for any bookshelf. You wrote a wonderful book and you should have a copy with the real author's name on it."

I reached over, raised her hand, and kissed it, choking on a rush of emotion.

"I love you."

"You're my whole life, Steven. I love that you're so amazingly talented, but you're also such a good person. So generous. So loving. These are the things that matter between two people. Please, promise me you'll never change."

We didn't talk much on the drive back to our apartment. We held hands and looked out the window at a tugboat muscling its way up the river. I don't think I've ever felt more content and fulfilled in my entire life.

Forty-seven

About a week later I got a call from Dexter Parch just as I was about to leave for my office.

"How's my favorite Mr. Five?"

"What are you talking about?"

"I just got the word. It's official. You've been nominated to be one of the five finalists for the National Book Award."

I started grinning like an idiot: little Stevie King, finally up there with the big boys.

"Who else was nominated?"

Dexter reeled off the competition. There was a first-time novelist like myself, a writer I had heard about but never read, and then there was Joyce Carol Oates and Robert Stone. Not bad company for a bartender.

"I told our advertising people to run an ad tomorrow in the *Times*. Which picture do you want us to run?"

"Picture of me!" I shouted.

"Relax, Steve. I was just kidding. Your secret is secure. The public will find out who Deep Throat was before they learn the identity of Chambers Benjamin."

. . .

I had a good writing session at my office. I was up to page fifty-five of my new book—that is, Steven King's new book—and it was going very well. My ribs had stopped aching and the bruise on my face was almost gone. Since my encounter with Vera and June, I had made an important decision. Actually, two. The first one came from the realization that I was in terrible physical shape. Though I wasn't yet in the love-handles phase of life, my endurance and strength were minimal. Occasionally, I used the treadmill and sometimes pushed myself to do a few sit-ups. My main source of exercise, however, was walking Chester.

My first move was to get a personal trainer. I didn't know where to start, so I called Dexter, who had recently published a book titled *How to Have a Special Forces Body*, by a former major. I had seen him on TV and had been impressed. His name was Ivan Poole III, and he was known as Major Trey.

"What kind of shape are you looking to get in?" Dexter asked me.

"Good shape. I'm tired of believing Brooke Astor could take me in an arm wrestling contest."

"Major Trey is tough. Two of my editors started to work out with him and gave it up after a week. He calls his course Basic Straining, and from what they've told me, he's not kidding."

"I don't want to take a group class. Do you think he'd work out with me alone? You know, one-on-one?"

"Major Trey, like everyone else in America, is a star fucker. The chance to work out with Steven Konigsberg, the best-selling novelist, will be impossible for him to resist. And I guarantee you that by your second workout he'll ask for a signed photograph to add to his wall of stars."

As Dexter had predicted, Major Trey agreed to train me. We started the next morning. The major looked not only as if he had been sculpted out of granite but also as if a lot of chisels had been broken on him in the process. He was six-three and stood as if someone had inserted an iron bar in his spine. His eyes reminded me of a cobra with attitude. The major's favorite phrase was "That was great, Steve. Now give me five more, only slower." The regimen he put me through was worse than the beating I had received from the Bowerses. It was two weeks before I could get out of bed without pain, but by the end of that period I felt different—stronger and mentally tougher. I wasn't yet ready for the Special Forces, but inch by agonizing inch, the major was turning me into someone who had the strength to defend himself.

To learn karate, my second decision, the person I reached out to was Mike Ovitz. We had met a couple of times in Los Angeles, and he talked to me at length about the man, or rather master, who had taught him karate.

"Hey, Steve, good to hear from you," said Ovitz, who took my call immediately.

I quickly explained my purpose in calling.

"I have just the man for you. My instructor, Master Kobara, has a nephew who just opened a dojo in New York. His name is Master Katsua. He's terrific. I'll give him a call."

"You don't have to do that. I can call him."

I called Master Katsua an hour later. The next day I journeyed down to his dojo in Tribeca. Katsua was short with a round face and looked to be in his early thirties. Because the outfit worn while practicing karate is so loose, I couldn't tell if he had a muscular build. After my first three lessons, I realized that muscles aren't everything. Katsua could put me on my ass anytime he wanted to.

His dojo was located on the second floor of a narrow building just off Church Street. An attractive Japanese woman, who I assumed was Katsua's wife, worked silently in a small back office. When he asked me why I was interested in studying karate, I told him that I had always been interested in it, and thought it would be a good source of exercise. He looked at me a long time before smiling shyly.

"So, Mr. Konigsberg, you're not interested in being able to kick the shit out of someone who threatens you? If that's the case, you're a rare student."

"Well, maybe a little bit," I answered, smiling back at him.

"We have much work to do before you even learn how not to hurt yourself. Let us begin."

In less than four weeks, working out daily with Major Trey in the morning and Master Katsua in the afternoon, I slowly and achingly went from a lump who sat in front of a computer much of the day to a man who someday might be able to surprise Vera Bowers. And though it might be a way off, I couldn't wait for that day to come.

. . .

In the middle of the week, after a session with Master Katsua, I met Dexter for a drink at the St. Regis bar. He had been calling me every day for the past month, asking when I was going to deliver the new Konigsberg book.

"You know, I already have it in the budget," he told me for the twentieth time as he nervously stirred his kir with his index finger.

"I'm having a little trouble with the end of the book."

This, of course, was bullshit. I just didn't feel like retyping Ben's book. Between writing my own book and working out in the morning and afternoon, the idea of doing the rote work to produce a new Konigsberg held little appeal.

"You're not blocked, are you?" asked Dexter with the look of someone who had just received bad news from his doctor.

"A little."

"Jesus."

Why was I putting Dexter through this? He was my friend and didn't deserve it. Why couldn't I just come clean with him, hand him the fucking onionskin manuscript and let him have someone retype it? The reason wasn't complex. Living a lie leads you to an intricate net of other lies: I was like a spider weaving web after web, eventually not knowing why the hell he was doing it.

"I'm sure I'll come out of it soon," I said, trying to bring a little color to Dexter's cheeks.

"That's great. You had me scared for a second, Steven."

"Just relax. I'll be back on track in a short time."

"I'd like to have our art director start in on the jacket. Do you have a title for me?"

"It came to me just yesterday. I'm calling this book *The Way I Left Her*. It's my first love story. You keep telling me that most book buyers are women—why not extend my audience even further?"

"Brilliant!"

Dexter's mood had shifted sufficiently for him to order another drink and then to give me the full story about the new addition to his house in Watermill, from the first two fired contractors to the newly hired one.

Part

5

A LIFE OF MANY PARTS

What is written without effort is in general
read without pleasure.

—Dr. Samuel Johnson

Forty-eight

It was three in the afternoon, which these days meant only one thing to me: karate. When I arrived for my lesson, Master Katsua told me he was going to show me a new move, a blow called a *tsuki*, or thrust, but I knew the drill. First and always, we warmed up. If I hadn't yet become proficient with my moves, I was finally learning how to hit the mat and roll. In the beginning, every time Master Katsua threw me I landed like wet laundry tossed from a high window.

After I'd worked up a sweat, Katsua said, "I see a brown belt for you in the near future, Mr. King."

I laughed. "A black-and-blue belt is more like it."

"Don't be modest. You have the right attitude, you're alert, and your form is good. I have faith in you."

Master Katsua had just demonstrated the new blow when my cell phone rang. Normally, I didn't carry the damn thing, which I view as a modern scourge, but with Tina so close to delivery, it made sense. Sure enough it was my wife: her water had broken.

I excused myself to Katsua with a bow and raced uptown to our apartment, where Tina was ready, her bag packed, with a taxi she had called waiting in front to take us to Lenox Hill Hospital. What followed next was a whirlwind that made me dizzy with excitement. Always the teacher, Tina was calm in the eye of this exhilarating storm.

Our first stop was the labor room, where Tina started to try to control her contractions by doing her Lamaze panting. I panted with her, setting the pace as if we were running a marathon together. Whenever a wave of pain washed across her face, I squeezed her hand and picked up my pace, trying to distract her. Every twenty minutes Dr. Scherer appeared to monitor the baby's heartbeat and measure the opening of the cervix. After three hours we finally reached the finish line.

"It's time, Tina," the doctor said. "Start pushing. You're fully dilated. Really push! You're almost there." As he and a nurse wheeled her toward the delivery room, he called out to me, "The scrubs are on the shelf next to you, Steve."

Dressed all in green, like an overgrown houseplant, I crouched on the chair I had been given in a corner of the room. I stared hard at Tina. All at once the baby began to emerge, and within moments he was out, a brand-new human being for the planet, one born with more hair than my father. I sprang toward Tina. "Here, Steve," said Dr. Scherer, placing the surgical scissors in my hand, "cut the cord right between the two clamps." As the baby wailed, the doctor handed him to the two nurses to weigh and clean. Tina lay back on the gurney with a smile like none I had ever seen.

Dr. Scherer came over to us and took Tina's hand. "You were born to have babies, dear," he said to her. "Let me show you this little fellow." One of the nurses carried Ben over. "Here he is. Two hands, two feet, ten real pink toes, and all the other necessary equipment. Now, let's get this little guy weighed, measured, and cleaned up, then get you three up to your room."

I went out to the hall, took out my cell phone, and started making the happiest phone calls I'd ever made. First my folks, then Tina's mother, then Dexter and Sal, and, yes, even Stuart and Quentin.

When I brought Tina and Ben home two days later, the baby nurse, Mrs. Wingate, was there waiting. She was older, experienced, and, best of all, calm. She had been in the newborn game for nearly forty years. We were so uncertain that we didn't even know how to pick Ben up properly. She straightened us out fast.

A few days later Tina's mother, Gillian, arrived from Key West, and my parents drove down from Elmira. Gillian is a warm, soft-spoken woman who is a lot like Tina: intelligent but full of common sense, an all-too-rare combination. Widowed early, she raised Tina and her two sisters alone in

Ohio before moving the family to Key West to avoid the long winters there. She had a clutch of health problems, big and small, but never discussed them. I was very fond of her, as were my parents.

After the visitors came the presents. Little Ben harvested more gifts than a Little League team: a complete set of Beatrix Potter from Dexter; a kid's-size Grand Prix car from Stuart; another truckload of clothes from the Riganos; and even something from Quentin, a framed poem he wrote about the life that awaited Ben.

When the family cleared out in a few days, it was just Mrs. Wingate and the three of us. The three of us! Nothing could have sounded sweeter.

Mrs. Wingate would be with us for only a short time more. She finished her two-week tutorial with a word to the wise that I thought of often: "Whenever you think Ben will never stop crying, remember that babies are a lot like weather. It may drizzle, it may storm, but you can be certain it will soon end. The sun will come out, and you all will be happy, especially little Ben. Babies are very changeable creatures—that's part of the wonder of them. Nothing is forever with a baby."

Mrs. Wingate was on her way to another newborn, and Tina and I settled down to truly being full-time parents. Mrs. Wingate told us to relax: we were ready to go solo. The Riganos told us to call them anytime for advice, which made us feel good. We were now running the show, and it felt right.

Aside from tiptoeing continually into Ben's room while he was sleeping to stand by his crib and listen closely for the sound of breathing, the regular rhythms of our life took over. I resumed going to my office every day to work on my new novel, which I had now titled *The Journey So Far*. I kept the old onionskin manuscript of the next Ben novel on my desk as a reminder that I had to start retyping it soon. I looked at it from time to time and told myself I'd start as soon as I finished the next chapter of my own book. But I didn't set that in stone.

I also had some unfinished business that I had to attend to. Little Ben's birth had caused me to postpone my trip to Miami to talk with Ben's former business partner, Victor Gentry, but now was the time to go. Then there would only be Flo Wanger to see, the last person mentioned in the detective's report. I had a hunch she wouldn't pose a problem for me, but I had to check her out, too. If neither of them proved to be a worry, the only threat I had to deal with was the Bowers sisters, who'd been silent for a while: no cards, no letters or calls. I prayed that it would stay that way.

I was so happy about Ben's birth that it was difficult to think of anything other than Tina and my son. It mellowed me. For instance, when Stuart could no longer resist giving the news of Ben's arrival to Liz Smith, I wasn't angry with him.

The news rippled from Liz to "Page Six" to *USA Today* to *Letterman* and triggered another onslaught of presents, including one from the Bowerses, a tiny workout suit in Lycra, complete with sneakers and a pack of minia-ture power bars to nibble on when he got teeth. Tina thought it was adorable. It made me angry. I explained to Tina they were fitness instruc-tors whom I had interviewed during my search for Major Trey, who, not to be left out of the gift game, sent a chinning bar that fit over the top of Ben's crib. It was a deluge, but a joyful one.

Forty-nine

My flight to Miami was scheduled for seven-fifteen in the morning, so I had Fred arrange to have a car pick me up at five-forty-five. Before I left, I slipped into Ben's room. There he was, looking like a blue tadpole in his sleepsuit, his side tucked against the crib bars. I had been told that infants instinctively move themselves away from the center of the crib (the universe) so they can touch the security of the bars (the real world), and therefore not feel as if they're floating alone in a vast, uncharted sea. I looked down at him, his dark hair fanned against the mattress, and searched his tiny round face. He was very still: I could barely see his chest moving. When I tapped my fingers against the top of the crib, Ben shivered as if a small current had passed through him. Then he was sleeping peacefully. Was that a smile on his face? Definitely. What was he dreaming about? Being fed by Tina? I slipped out of his room, went back to our bedroom, where Tina was still asleep, and gave her a kiss.

On the flight down to Miami I looked over Douglas Tern's report on Victor Gentry, who was seventy-six and lived with his wife, Sybil, in a condo on Collins Avenue in Miami Beach. They had moved down there ten years before when Gentry had retired as a copy editor. Before that he and Ben had been partners in a company called Edit Express, Inc. There was even a Xerox of their business card. Under the company name was their logo, an inkwell with a pen sticking out.

I had arranged to give a reading (my alibi) that night at eight. The book-store owner was delighted. The demand for tickets had been so strong that they had to move the venue from the bookstore, which was quite large, to a synagogue nearby in Coral Gables. That left me plenty of time to see Victor Gentry. I had spoken to him the week before and told him I was Ben's executor. Surprisingly, he had never heard of me. My feelings were not hurt, of course, though that kind of thing didn't happen very often.

Though Gentry was retired, he worked as a volunteer three days a week at the Fairchild Tropical Gardens, where he drove a tour tram. I arranged to meet him in the greenhouse at three that afternoon.

"You can't miss it," he told me.

"Three it is. I look forward to meeting you, Mr. Gentry."

The driver that Fred had booked to ferry me about Miami until I left the following morning was named Tod. He was in his late twenties and sported four earrings and a small gold cross stuck through the side of his nose. Tod smiled a lot and, best of all, didn't talk. Our first stop was the Delano, where I registered as S. King. My room was small, the price was high, but fortu-nately, it faced the ocean. I quickly changed into a bathing suit and went down to the pool. I've always been a pretty good swimmer, but now with my partially chiseled body, I felt like I was really knifing through the water. After ten laps I got out, liberally applied sunblock 35, and spent an hour in a chaise reading the *Wall Street Journal* and the *Miami Herald*. I always read the local paper when I'm traveling. I saw I had quite a bit of time before my meeting with Gentry, so I decided to walk down to Lincoln Road and find a place for lunch.

I told Tod to take some time off and meet me back at the hotel at two. Lincoln Road had been turned into a pedestrian mall some years before and now was lined with shops and restaurants. It was a great people-watching place, with a constant flow of male and female sculpted bodies on bikes and Rollerblades gliding by like salmon spawning. I found an Italian restaurant and had a salad and a pizza *margarita*.

I had brought down a check made out to Victor Gentry for $10,000:

should I give it to him up front? Something told me that I should keep my powder dry. Then I asked myself if I should skip the meeting and just fly back home—if Gentry knew something, why hadn't he contacted me by now? Maybe it was best to let sleeping dogs lie. But I knew I couldn't back out. For if Gentry as well as Flo Wanger turned out to know nothing, I'd only be left with the Bowers sisters to contend with. What I was doing was simply dotting the i's and crossing the t's on the strange path I called my life. I knew that when I finished these investigations, I would sleep like little Ben.

As I rode out to meet Gentry, I read a pamphlet on the Fairchild Tropical Gardens that the concierge at the hotel had given me. The gardens had been started in the twenties, and it sounded like the kind of place Tina and I would want to visit if we were vacationing in Miami. Rare tropical plants and trees of every possible variety had been collected from all over the globe. Once a month, a tour of the gardens was conducted during a full moon. I'd remember that next time when I came down with Tina (and Ben, too, of course).

I arrived fifteen minutes early, which gave me a chance to walk through a few of the satellite greenhouses that came off the hub of the central one. From the desert to the equatorial rain forest, I peered at the nameplates of specimens as exotic as props from a sci-fi movie. As I left the jungle, my shirt plastered wetly to my back, I noticed a heavyset, older man in linen pants and a short-sleeved shirt standing by the entrance. As I got closer, I saw a plastic tag pinned to his shirt with the name V. Gentry on it.

"Mr. Gentry," I called out, smiling and extending my hand.

"I see you've been visiting our version of a Turkish bath," he said as he pointed to Rorschach blots of perspiration on the front of my shirt. "We can have a glass of iced tea in the cafeteria with lots of ice, or we can stroll about and maybe I could point out a few interesting things to you."

"Why don't we do both? Let's get something to drink, then walk around."

Gentry, who had been a volunteer at the gardens for almost four years, was a knowledgeable and articulate guide. Not only did he seem to know all the Latin names of the myriad flowers, shrubs, and trees, he knew where they came from and when they'd been brought to this country. When we finished our drinks, we sat down on a bench located next to a small pond.

"There's an alligator in there. It's pretty small, maybe five or six feet. Visitors get a kick out of it when it comes out and suns itself on the log." I looked across the pond, but there was no sign of the gator, only a couple of turtles the size of large ashtrays dozing on the log. "You know, Mr. Konigsberg, I liked Ben a lot. But I can't say I ever really knew him. We were business partners and never had an argument, but I always instinctively knew that one day he'd just pick up and move on. What's that song Dylan sings, about a rolling stone? That was Ben. Always talking and itching to go somewhere else and try something new—a real restless guy. Never found out where that came from."

Gentry told me more about the business he shared with Ben and how well it had been going. He was the inside man, the editor and production person. Ben brought in the business and did most of the writing. I let him go on about the details of Edit Express for a while before I got into the real subject of my trip.

"Did Ben ever talk to you about his writing?"

"All the time. That and Samuel Johnson were his favorite subjects."

"Did he ever show you anything?" I asked with a bit of trepidation.

"Are you kidding? I was constantly reading and copyediting his damn books. Believe me, it took up quite a bit of my time."

Uh-oh.

"Are you talking about his novels?"

"That's all he wrote."

Jesus!

"How many did you work on, Mr. Gentry?"

"Who the hell can remember? A lot. Certainly over a dozen."

What felt like a hot metal band started to tighten around my chest.

"Can you recall any of them? You know, the titles, plots, characters—things like that."

He turned, looked at me, and smiled.

"Thank God, no. I hate fiction. Never read the stuff if I can help it. The real world is so exciting, why waste time and read what some guy has dreamt up? As a matter of fact, all I can remember was that it was a hell of a lot of work to copyedit them."

The metal band sprang open, and I took a huge gulp of air. Then I pressed Victor Gentry for any other memories he might have of Ben's novels. Finally, he said, "I think one of them was called something like *Junior's Strut*. Or maybe it was *Junior's Song*."

That was as close to *Juno's Dance* as Victor Gentry could get. I wanted to hug him. Instead of handing him the check for $10,000 that was in my pocket, I took out my checkbook and wrote him one for $25,000. "Ben spoke fondly of you, and I know he would have wanted to leave you something," I said, handing him the check. He was, of course, delighted.

"Hey, look over there," he said as we rose from the bench.

Sure enough, there was the alligator. I felt so good I could have written him a check, too.

That night I gave a great reading. The audience was with me all the way. And though the crowd at the synagogue thought they were hearing sections from the next Steven Konigsberg novel, I actually read to them from my own book. A bit brazen? Certainly. Risky? Not really. If anyone remembered that the section they heard wasn't in the next Konigsberg, I could simply say I cut it out. As I usually did, I scanned the audience closely. Whom was I looking for? The ghost of Wayne Woodley? Vera and June? Precisely. When you look hard enough, you can generally find something. Sure enough, there, seventh row center, was a dead ringer for June Bowers. No, this woman had more fat than muscle, but the resemblance was unnerving. I paused for a long drink of water and continued reading.

When I got to the Delano, I stopped at the bar for a brandy. The drink, the successful meeting with Victor Gentry, and the reception I got at the reading helped erase the frightening image of the "twin" in the audience. I went to my room at a reasonable hour and slept very well indeed, with no nightmares to mar my serenity.

Fifty

I was flying high. For the first time since I'd put my name on Ben's manuscript, I felt that I had done the right thing. Passing myself off as the author of Ben's books had allowed me to write my own. And if Ben's name wasn't on the novels, it was on the foundation I had created. A lot of the money from the books was going into projects Ben would have been proud of. Chances were good that Flo Wanger, the last of my potential problems from Ben's past, would present no problem at all. I would pay her a visit soon, then be able to cross off the final name from Tern's list. Though I was slowly learning to defend myself, I wasn't under the illusion that I could win if it came down to a fight with the sisters. But they, unlike Wayne Woodley, seemed to be rational enough to eventually work out a deal with me. For the first time in a long time, the skies ahead seemed clear.

I had some time before Tod was scheduled to pick me up, so I decided to go shopping. I took a cab north to the upscale shopping mall in Bal Harbour, with its ranks of tony stores. At Saks I bought a beautiful (and expensive) cashmere sweater for Tina in a wonderful lush pink, the color of an exotic cocktail, and on the way out stopped to pick up a small stylish evening bag in black with the outline of a cat in small black pearls. When I'd entered the mall, I had noticed a Neiman-Marcus, so I stopped there next. I raked my eyes over the luxury goods assembled on the main floor and decided on scarves, buying Tina an amazing Missoni scarf as well as a tamer one for Mrs. Wingate. Her cell phone number was at the top of our emergency call list.

I had saved the best shopping for last: toys for Ben. But now I saw I had only minutes to spend on him. On the mall's directory I found a store a few doors away, and as soon as I went in, I could tell my luck was holding. There was a cornucopia of toys. I ended up with a pull-toy dachshund (for later), a teddy bear to munch on (with requisite cotton eyes, no beads to swallow), and a string of farm animals to hang over his crib (for batting practice).

Tod got me to the airport just in time. The ride was smooth and his conversation was nil. The combination moved me to give him a hundred-dollar tip. On the flight back to New York, I was seated next to a middle-aged man who greeted me with a cursory hello. I took out my book, Quentin's latest. He pulled out a book from the briefcase at his feet and started reading, too. I didn't need to see the front of the jacket to know that he was reading *Time's Pulse*. I always felt a rush of pleasure when this occurred.

When the flight attendant came around to ask for our drink orders, we started talking, and it turned out that my seatmate, Albert Casemont, was an American lit professor at Vassar. He was on his way back to Poughkeepsie after attending a symposium at the University of Miami on Faulkner, where he had presented a paper titled "Animal and Plant Imagery in the Early Short Stories." He didn't ask what I did, and I didn't volunteer any information. After the attendant took our lunch order, I asked him what he thought of *Time's Pulse*, saying that I had been thinking of buying a copy.

"One of the best novels I've read in years," he said. "I like to keep up with what's going on today in the literary world, because my students are more attuned to the new, in all the arts. I can't wait to discuss this with them. But I don't want this to end. It's that good."

When I got home, I rushed into the apartment, shopping bags in both hands, with Carlos, the elevator man, behind me with my suitcase. I called out to Tina, who came in from the kitchen a few moments later. I hugged her tight, but there was no response. "Something wrong?" I asked. "Ben's okay, isn't he?"

"I have something for you," she said, handing me a manila envelope. Her voice was cold.

I opened it quickly. What I pulled out was Ben's manuscript, the one I had left on my desk in the office. I was so stunned that the pages dropped from my hand and tumbled to the floor like confetti raining down on a parade. On top of the pile was the title page, staring up at me like an immense accusatory finger:

THE DARK RAINBOW

A NOVEL BY BENJAMIN CHAMBERS

Yesterday, Tina explained, she had received a call from the super in the building where I had my office, saying a water pipe had broken and that he had to get in to stop the leak. She had gone over with the keys to make sure someone was there while they worked, and it was then that she discovered the manuscript.

I didn't know where to begin. I felt I had been hit with a brick right in the face. For a long time I didn't say a word, and then I tried to dance my way out of it. Within a minute I realized I couldn't: there was no way to explain, short of writing a book about it, to make Tina understand the twisted path my life had taken since Ben's death. Incoherent sentences tumbled out like rocks in a landslide. I started to sob, which made my speech even more incomprehensible. Somehow I had to make her understand what had driven me to do what I did. Most of all, no matter how wrong my actions, she had to know I loved her—that was the most important thing. I went on and on, like a drowning man reaching for bits of driftwood, seaweed, anything to keep him from sinking. What I wanted most of all was to be forgiven.

"Did you really write *Time's Pulse?*" she finally asked.

"Yes. Absolutely. Every word of it is mine."

"It's hard to believe anything you say. But maybe that's the only thing that's true here."

"Tina," I cried out, anguished.

"You've been lying to me for more than five years. And to everyone else—your parents, your friends. How could you do it? Haven't you a shred of remorse? Of shame? How can I ever believe anything you say again? I don't know who you are. The man I loved and married is gone."

Ben started crying in his room and Tina went to comfort him. When she returned, she shut the door to his room.

"I don't know what to do," she said. "I need time to think. I'd like you to spend the night in your office. We can talk more tomorrow. Maybe."

"You can't leave me like this, Tina. At least say that you still love me."

"My love for you is made up of many things." She paused. "But the most important part is trust. Right now that doesn't exist."

Fifty-one

I spent two nights in my office before returning to the apartment with Chester (who had also been banished, since Tina didn't have the time to walk him). I couldn't stay away any longer. There was a note on the hall table: "Steven: I've realized that the convertible sofa in your office isn't very good, so for the time being I've decided you can stay in the guest room."

I noticed that there was no "Dear" before my name and that Tina hadn't signed the note. That first night I had tried repeatedly to tell her what had driven me to copy Ben's books and pass them off as my own. While she changed the baby, I explained the writing crisis I was going through at the time, how I never thought I'd ever be published. Tina kept her back turned to me as I spoke. Later, when she was bathing baby Ben, I tried to capture how low my spirits had been after Ben's death; that after reading the manuscript of *Juno's Dance* I felt the book had to be published. Why didn't I attempt to have it and the others published under his name? My answer was lousy: as a matter of fact, I think I gave her three different versions of why I did it. What I wanted to say was: "Tina, darling, I did it because I was weak. I kept at it because it was the easy thing to do. The more money I made, the more famous I became, the weaker I got. Why didn't I at least tell you my secret? After all, I love you more than anyone in the world. You're the mother of our child. Would you accept that I didn't want you to share that kind of secret with me? The truth is I was afraid to tell you, afraid of what you would do and what you would think of me. I'm not a bad guy, I just did a stupid thing. Okay, it was more than stupid. I did a terrible thing. But can't you help me, baby, to work my way out of this mess? I don't have anything if I don't have you."

What Tina told me again and again was that she wasn't interested in tramping through the slippery muck of my excuses: what she needed above all was time to think. Things were so bad that Tina told me she didn't want me in the room while she was breast-feeding the baby. I was depressed in a way that was totally new. In the past if I got depressed, I always believed that eventually I would be able to pop my head up and see that there was a world out there, with a blue sky and a sun that shined most of the time. This time I felt as if I had been lowered into a deep, cold cave. There was no hint of a sky above me. I was alone, very alone, and I was scared. Then I realized what I had to do. I called Dexter's office and told his assistant that I had to see him.

"Today's real bad, Mr. King. He's in budget meetings all day. How about tomorrow after lunch?"

"That's not going to work. I have to see him today. Tell him it's urgent."

I wasn't surprised when she got back on the phone and told me that I could see Dexter at four. When Konigsberg said it was urgent, time could always be found.

That afternoon when I walked into Dexter's office, I realized I hadn't given any real thought to what I was about to tell him. I looked down and noticed I was wearing the same shirt I'd worn the day before. I checked to see if my fly was open and was surprised to see that it was zipped up. It gave me small comfort.

"What do you think of these?" asked Dexter as he held up two sketches for the jacket of the next book. "I like this one," he said, raising his left hand. "The colors are stronger, and the balance between your name and the title is just right. What do you think?"

"It looks fine."

"Great. I'll have our art director do a finished version. Now, what's all this urgency stuff about, Steven?"

I cleared my throat even though I didn't need to and plunged in.

"I've decided that I'm not going to publish any more novels."

"What did you say?"

"I've written my last Steven Konigsberg novel, Dexter. That's it. I'm finished."

"What are you talking about, Steven? You're kidding me, aren't you?" I sat there, slumped in the black leather chair like a kid brought to the principal for tossing a water balloon. "You know how many advance orders we have for this book," he said, digging through a pile of papers on his desk. He finally pulled out the one he was looking for. "Look at this. We have 1,237,491 orders in hand. Why would you do this?"

"I can't explain now, but that's my decision."

"What are you saying? Is this because you're blocked? We can help you through this—*all* writers get blocked."

"I'm not blocked, Dexter."

"Then tell me why."

"I can't, but I'm serious. I'm stopping."

Dexter looked stricken, his face whiter than the pocket handkerchief he wore perpetually. "That's not good enough. You haven't answered my question, and I deserve an answer. Have you been unhappy here?"

"No. You've been wonderful to me."

"You know how much money we've already advanced you on this book."

"Don't worry. I'll return every dollar."

"That's not it. I don't want the money back. I want the book."

"I can't do that now—not ever."

"What about your fans, Steven? They're out there waiting for the next Steven Konigsberg novel. Do you have any idea how many people have signed up for a reserved copy at Barnes & Noble?"

"I can't help them."

"What about the contract you signed?"

"I said I'd return the money."

"That's not it. You're my friend, Steven, not just another author I publish. You still haven't given me a reason for this incredible decision. Does Tina know about it?"

"Of course," I said, lying with my normal ease. I got up from the chair and walked to the door.

As soon as I got home, I rushed into the kitchen, where I found Tina having a cup of coffee and reading the *Times*.

"I did it."

"Did what?" she asked without looking up.

"I told Dexter I wasn't going to publish another Konigsberg book."

"That's something you should have done before you let him publish the first one." She looked up at me, her face flushed with anger, her eyes glittering like a cat's. This wasn't Tina. And then I realized with a frisson of horror that this was the Tina I had created.

"There's nothing I can do about that now, Tina. I'm just trying to right things."

"Right things?" she said with a sharp edge to her voice. "Did you tell him that all those bestsellers he published were written by Ben Chambers?"

"Not yet."

She got up from the table, her face once more devoid of emotion, and put her cup and saucer in the dishwasher.

"I have to take Ben out for his walk."

"I'll come with you. Chester needs a walk, too."

"I think you should walk him alone," she said in her now familiar chilly tone.

I waited fifteen minutes after I heard the front door close to call Chester, who stood patiently while I put his leash on. Since my departure from the apartment, Chester had started to walk very close to me, his flanks constantly brushing against my leg. This was his way of giving me emotional support. He had cut way down on his street sniffing and barking, as if to say that he shared my pain.

As we waited for the elevator, I reached down and patted his head.

"Thanks, Chester. You're always there for me. I think we'll walk over to Citarella today. My crystal ball says there's a major veal shank bone in your future."

When we got down to the street, I saw a stretch limo parked in front of the canopy. The building was chockablock with investment bankers and real estate moguls, and this was their favorite mode of transportation. And then a window in the back slid down noiselessly.

"Could you please get in, Steven?"

It was Dexter Parch.

"I have to walk Chester."

"You can do that later. We have to talk."

"I thought we already did."

"Please. This will only take fifteen minutes."

I didn't want to have a long discussion in front of Boris, the doorman, whose small cupped ears, like satellite dishes, were taking in every word that was said.

"Do me a favor, Boris. Hold on to Chester for a few minutes," I said, and handed the leash over.

"Sure thing, Mr. King."

As soon as I entered the gloom of the huge limo, I saw that Dexter had company. There, slumped in the back, was Stuart, his face the color of smoked turkey.

"Hi, Stevie," he said weakly, trying to smile.

My cousin's face was slick, and I noticed that each of the hair plugs that ringed the top of his brow had a puddle of sweat at its base.

The limo entered the park at Seventy-second street. Silently and slowly, it began to circle the park. Dexter waited until we stopped for a light at Central Park South before starting in.

"First off, let me preface this by saying that this is not between a publisher, an agent, and a writer. This is about people who care for each other. You understand?" I nodded. Stuart reached for one of the cut-glass decanters of liquor that were on a shelf on the side and poured himself half a tumbler. "I want to sketch for you what the loss of your books will do to Chancery. First, there will be layoffs. We can't avoid them. I don't think a department will be spared. You've made a lot of friends in the company, and, sadly, quite a few of them will wind up on the street. Then I have to face what Axel Guderian might do. He's a very bottom-line-oriented guy. Might this even push him into putting Chancery up for sale? Your guess is as good as mine. Now for the personal side. My new contract still hasn't been signed. It's with the lawyers. The details are small ones, so there shouldn't be a problem. But that was before you decided not to write any more books. Will Axel think the fault lies with me? Stranger things have been known to happen. I, too, could wind up on the street, Steven."

Now it was Stuart's turn. He had finished the first tumbler and was now working on his second. I sensed that there was some choreography here. Not good cop, bad cop exactly, but rather two desperate cops working in concert.

"I don't know where to begin, Stevie. I've never talked much to you about my agency, but now you're basically it. I lost some clients because they felt I was spending too much time on your books, and I lost others because they believed their work didn't excite me the way it used to. They were right, I guess. I have to confess something to you, cuz. I'm really in a deep hole now. A bunch of commercial real estate investments I made in Arizona have turned sour. I've had to sell my boat. You know how much I loved that boat. Now, someone could say, 'Stuart, you made a lot of money representing your cousin. Where the hell did it go?' That's a legitimate question. You know what my father, your Uncle Sol, would always tell people when they asked what I did? He'd say, 'My son, Stuart, is an organic chemist. He turns money into shit.'" Stuart drained his glass before continuing. "I'm talking now to you, Stevie, as cousin to cousin. We're family. I don't know what I'll do if you stop writing the novels." He pulled a rumpled handkerchief out of his pocket and attempted to dry his face. We had almost finished the loop of the park and would be turning off at the next exit.

"You know how much I care for both of you," I said finally. "I just can't see how I can continue to write those books. It's very complicated, but that's how it has to be." We were approaching my building. I could see Chester, his leash tied to the canopy post, Boris standing alongside. "What I can see doing is to continue writing as Chambers Benjamin for Chancery." At the mention of the name I didn't detect a look of surprise on Stuart's face. Obviously, Dexter, at this time of extreme crisis, had told Stuart the whole story of *Time's Pulse* and its secretive author.

"Thanks a fucking lot, Steven," said Dexter angrily. "That'll really help. It's like telling Radio City Music Hall that a Russian film about life on a collective farm will bring in as large an audience as the next Disney film. Give me a break. Chancery needs a sixteen-ounce porterhouse steak, not a damn literary tea sandwich. And you still haven't told me why you're doing this." When I didn't answer, he slammed his fist against the door. "Am I doomed forever not to know why my company's biggest asset is quitting?"

"Will you please think it over for at least a day or two?" pleaded Stuart as I got out of the car.

I felt so sorry for both of them that I nodded my head and mumbled that I would. Chester and I watched the limo melt into traffic, then we crossed the avenue and entered the park, walking as close and in stride as a ballroom dance team. "Chester," I said when we were alone on the path, "how did I get into this?" He looked up at me. I could swear he understood what I was saying. "But more importantly, how do I get out?" He licked my hand, and with tears in my eyes we continued walking.

Fifty-two

In terms of comfort, I couldn't find fault with the guest room to which Tina had exiled me. Everything was there that a guest might want: soft, silky sheets, a luxurious bathroom with a Jacuzzi, a comfortable armchair, a sweeping view of Central Park. I had everything but the wife I loved. Whenever I emerged from the room, the temperature around me dropped. Tina and Ben gurgled and cooed to each other, but I was chilled by neglect, as unwanted as yesterday's newspaper. Since Tina scarcely had a word to say to me, I spent an increasing amount of time in my office. Through it all, I wrote every day; go figure.

Piling up in the apartment was a pyramid of invitations, requests for readings, foreign contracts, galleys from publishers seeking jacket quotes, memos on this and that from those on the Chancery staff not yet in the know about my decision to stop publishing. All this would keep Fred busy when he showed up later. I had given him a week off starting tomorrow so he wouldn't be a witness to my season in Coventry. He was smart enough not to question a gift from above and was happily headed out at dawn the next day to Wellfleet with his girlfriend.

When I got home from the office, I would read my e-mails. Gone was the good news and gossip, replaced now by pleas and anguished urgings from Dexter and Stuart.

Dexter: "Think of Chancery. Think of your audience. You said we've been wonderful to you, and I believe that's true. Without you, of course, we wouldn't be having this discussion, but how can you quit at this point? Your decision may destroy Chancery. And I say this as a personal friend as well as your publisher—it may destroy me as well."

Stuart: "What about me? *Me!* Your own flesh and blood. Do you realize you're dropping your first cousin into a boiling pot of problems the size of an Olympic swimming pool? I could be facing bankruptcy. Do you have any idea what that will do to my mother, your beloved aunt?"

Even Axel Guderian got into the act. He e-mailed that he was coming next week to New York to talk to me. Or better yet, how would I like to visit him at his *Schloss* in the Black Forest? He was sure he could make me see the folly of the course I had undertaken. Tina, of course, was invited, too. After a few days of this bombardment I stopped reading my e-mails, listening to phone messages, and even opening the mail.

We were just beginning the second week of our new living arrangements when I woke up to find two suitcases sitting in the front hall. I ran into Ben's bedroom, where I found Tina dressing him.

"Ben and I are going to Key West to stay with my mother. The car will be here in a few minutes, so don't get in the way. I have things to do."

"How long are you going to be gone?" I finally found the courage to ask.

"I don't know."

"Can I come down to visit you and Ben this weekend?"

"No."

"When?"

I was beginning to feel a panic attack coming on. Was the most important part of my life now going on life support?

"You don't get it, do you?" She searched my face for something she didn't find, then continued. "I need time to sort this whole thing out and decide where I want to go from here. You better do the same thing. What kind of life do you want with Ben and me? Will you finally be able to level with us?"

"Tina, help me," I pleaded.

"I can't. You're the only one who can wipe the blackboard clean. Maybe there's still a chance for the three of us to get back to what we once were and to what we saw for our future. You're the only one who can put it back together again."

The doorman rang the buzzer to let us know that the car was there to take Tina and Ben to the airport. I didn't try to kiss her, because I knew it wasn't in the cards, but Tina did let me bend down and kiss Ben on his fore-head. Then they were gone, and there I was alone. Once when I was three years old, my mother took me to see Santa at Elmira's one big department store. Something caught my eye, and I sped to a display case to see what it was. When I turned to tell my mother what I was looking at, she was gone. I stood there bewildered. I suddenly felt lost and very small, terrified I would never see her again—just the way that I felt now.

It was late in the afternoon when it dawned on me that I had not eaten lunch, nor had Fred shown up for work. In fact, I was still in the same spot on the couch that I sank into after Tina and Ben left that morning. I realized that I was more than depressed: I was sitting shiva for my soul.

The sound of a key opening the front door made me spring up from the couch. Maybe Tina had changed her mind! When I raced to the door, I found Fred on crutches, a bandage over a welt on his right eyebrow that made him look like a club fighter after a ten-round bout.

"Jesus, Fred. What happened to you?"

He laughed, or at least tried to.

"As they say, only in New York."

"What do you mean?"

"I was on my bike riding through the park," he said as he collapsed onto a chair in the hallway, "heading here, the way I do every day. I was men-tally going through a checklist of the things to do today. I was feeling great. I was only a couple of hundred yards from your building when two women the size of battleships jumped out of the bushes—literally out of the bushes—and jammed a hockey stick in the spokes of my bike. I went down hard and bounced along the pavement for twenty feet or so. Then these two massive head cases started to laugh themselves silly. Did they try to help me? Are you kidding? They even threw the damn stick at me as they skipped away."

The sisters! They were obviously sending me a message, and as Dylan once sang, "you don't need a weatherman to know which way the wind blows."

Fifty-three

I woke up, and for a moment everything was fine. I was in our king-size bed, a band of early morning sunlight scissoring the blanket. Down at the foot, Chester was busily gnawing on his hind legs, a morning routine for him. But then it hit me—things were still shit. I was alone in this enormous bed. Tina was in Key West with Ben, and I had no idea when, if ever, she'd come back to me.

No one knew that Tina had left me except her mother. I probably would have told Dexter, but we weren't speaking. If I told my folks, they would go into shock, then descend on me. I thought about sharing it with Sal, but I didn't want to burden him with this particular trouble. Thankfully, Fred, back from his vacation, showed no signs of thinking anything was amiss. Everything was the same, except everything was different.

As usual, after reading the *Times* while drinking my orange juice, I took Chester downstairs for his morning walk. Now that I was getting in shape, I was wearing shorts and a T-shirt so I could alternate the walking with some running. It was good for Chester, too. I was about to cross Central Park West when I saw them: Vera was in an electric-blue spandex warm-up suit sitting on one of the benches in front of the low wall that circles the park. Next to her in a matching outfit, June looked much bigger than the last time I'd seen her. They were both smiling and waving at me. Immediately, I turned around and took the elevator back to my apartment, opened the door, and walked Chester into the hallway.

"I'm doing this for you," I said to him as I undid the leash. "Who knows what those two freaks might try to do to you? You've eaten your last knockout biscuit." He rubbed against my leg and gave me a reassuring bark. "As soon as I find out what they're up to, I'll be back for you."

"You're looking good, Mr. K. Never knew you had abs before," said Vera as I approached. "Working out is a good thing. It's nice to think that maybe my little butt-kicking might have had some positive influence on you."

"What are you doing here?"

Though it was only a couple of months since I had last seen Vera, she looked immense. Grapefruit-size muscles, from calves to biceps, bunched under her warm-up suit. I also noticed that she now had what looked like the beginnings of a mustache.

"We thought anyone could sit here. Including you, Steve. Take a seat. We have things to discuss," said Vera, patting the space next to her.

"I have to leave."

I turned and started to walk back toward my building.

"We don't have a lot of time to fuck around. We're leaving for Mexico City tomorrow, and we want to finish up our business with you when we get back," she continued. "So cool it and take a seat. We've decided to set up a foundation. It was June's idea."

"Sounds great," I said, sitting down next to Vera, resigned to playing out another edgy scene with the Bowers sisters.

"It should. All the money is coming from you. We're going to call it the Bowers Foundation for Physical Excellence. How does that sound to you?"

"Do you really want an answer?"

"No," said Vera. "We just want an answer from your checkbook. And make sure you have a pen with a lot of ink. We're looking for quite a few zeros before the decimal point."

"You see, with the foundation, which will benefit young athletes—"

"That's us, by the way."

"—we won't have to pay any taxes. It'll be just like having our daddy be-hind us—that is, if our daddy understood what Vera was trying to do."

"I'm not a tax lawyer, but I don't think it will play with the IRS," I said.

"You're not even a writer, so keep your opinions to yourself," said Vera. "By the way, why didn't you bring that old flea hound with you? Afraid we'd give him a Jim Jones biscuit?"

"I'm going to walk him later."

"I don't believe that for a second."

"I don't give a damn what you believe."

"Better watch that language when you're around the little boy," Vera said. "We don't want him to develop any bad habits. By the way, where is little Ben? As a matter of fact, we haven't seen much of your old lady, ei-ther. Hope they're all right."

"So you spy on me now," I said, almost spitting with anger.

"It's just our way of keeping an eye on our investment," said June. "You're very important to us, and so are they. You know this park can be dangerous. Something bad happens here almost every day. You wouldn't want anything nasty to happen to them, would you? He's really a cute lit-tle guy. There are loads of families that would give almost anything to have a kid like yours."

"If you ever try to hurt my wife or—"

"Take it down a notch, Mr. K. You're really scaring me. And seeing you in your cute running outfit reminds me I haven't done my roadwork yet. You ready, sis?"

"Sure, Vera," said June, standing up.

"You know, it's great having my sister as a training partner now. The day the Bowers sisters compete together is not far away. I'd ask you to run with us, but I do a five-fifty mile, and I doubt that you could break nine minutes."

Then they were off, Vera in front, legs pumping high, running like the wind. I stood there and watched them disappear into the park, wishing, like a child, that a hole would open in the earth and swallow them. If only this were a novel, I'd know how to write their demise. But this was all too real.

Fifty-four

"How's my boy?"

It was my father on the phone. I was working in my office, and only a few people had the number.

"Hi, Dad."

"Surprise. I'm in town. Got some time for the old man?"

"What's up?"

"Came in for the fiftieth reunion of my old outfit in the army."

My dad had served in Korea. Though he was in the Quartermaster Corps, and the only combat he saw was when he was caught in the middle of a brawl at a bar in Pusan, the war had always loomed large for him. His rite of passage, I guess. Was I going through mine now? If so, how would I survive it?

"How about a drink later?"

"I was thinking about something earlier. I'm meeting up with a couple of the guys for drinks before the dinner. How about we rendezvous at the Guggenheim? There's a Calder show there your mom told me I had to see. I'll see you out in front at three and we can take a walk in the park. Okay?"

. . .

I arrived ten minutes early to find my dad dressed sharply in a blazer over a dark blue shirt with a red and gold rep tie. His shoes were shined to the luster of bullion, and his gray slacks had a ruler-sharp crease. He prided himself on his wardrobe, and it always made me feel good to see him dressed well. But then I noticed something else: a cigarette between his fingers. He pulled on it deeply, then quickly took another puff. He had stopped smoking almost ten years earlier.

"What gives with the cigarette?" I asked him.

"I like one once in a while when your mother's not around. Hey, I'm a big boy, Mr. Bestseller. As your nephew, Alex, tells me all the time, 'Cut me some slack, Gramp.' " He put the cigarette out and gave me a hug.

As we walked down Fifth Avenue, he brought me up-to-date on how the King and Stagg stores were doing (down eight percent from last year); my brother's golf game (he just won the club championship again for the third year in a row); Elmira politics (two people on the city council were indicted the month before for taking bribes); and the cruise he and my mother were going to take in a couple of months (seven ports in eight days).

"Is there anywhere around here we can get a cup of coffee?" he asked as we neared the Met. I remembered the sculpture garden on the roof of the museum.

"I know the perfect place."

The roof was almost deserted, and the sculptures currently on view stretched upward like steely supplicants. We took our coffees and sat on a bench in the sun.

"Tina and the baby all right?"

"Fine, Dad. They're in Key West visiting Gillian."

Some visit. Tina had left me the way people in the Middle Ages fled the plague. I wondered if my father could sense the desolation I was feeling.

"You know, Stevie, I don't want to worry you, but I'm a little concerned about your mother," he said as he lit another cigarette.

"What's wrong?"

"She's been having a little trouble with her heart."

"Like what?"

"It races sometimes. Skips some beats. Dr. Emmett did an echocardiogram last week. He thinks she might need a pacemaker down the road. Who knows, maybe even angioplasty."

"Why didn't you call me about this?"

He took a long pull on his cigarette, then exhaled two even contrails of smoke from his nostrils and gave me the standard, maddening parental mantra, "I didn't want to worry you."

"Worry me? Are you kidding? We're talking about my mother. You can't keep me in the dark. I'm not a kid anymore."

"That's why I didn't tell you. You're a worrier. She's going to be fine."

"I want to fly her here. I'll have her see the best heart specialists in New York."

"Dr. Emmett is a good doctor."

"Yeah, for Elmira."

"Your mother trusts him. She won't come here. I know her."

"Then you have to convince her."

"I know what will help her." He stood up and looked down at me. "Stevie, her outlook will be a hundred percent better when she has your next book in her hands. She loves your books. They mean the world to her. That's the best medicine you could give her. Forget your fancy New York doctors. What she needs is a Steven Konigsberg novel to read."

Of course, a Konigsberg novel is not just a great read. It's much more than that. It's the answer to coronary problems. A Konigsberg novel can get the lame mamboing and the blind making jump shots beyond the three-point line.

When I got back to the apartment, I called Dr. Emmett. He had been the family doctor since I was a kid and was now, of course, a great fan of mine.

"Thanks, Steve, for sending us the signed copy of the last book. Miriam and I loved it. We have all your books in a special section in our den."

After answering a few questions about the movie version of the last novel (he liked it, but liked the book more), I got into the subject of my mother's health, particularly her heart.

"She's fine. A little angina, but it's totally manageable. You know she told me that your grandmother lived to be ninety-seven, and your mother has the same genes. I'd say the only threat to her health is if she buys too big a Cuisinart and falls in. You're going to have her around for a long time."

How could my father do this to me? I wanted to rush out, and . . . do what? Hit him? Scream that he had lied to me? As wrong and misguided as he was, I knew he'd done it out of love. And he hadn't come up with the scheme on his own. Stuart's fingerprints were all over this brutish plan. Of course, he was the villain in this piece.

I rushed downstairs and took a taxi to Stuart's office. My anger at Stuart could probably be read on the Richter scale. I knew that part of it stemmed from my feeling of helplessness with Tina. Finally, I had an outlet for the anger I had been storing up since Tina's discovery of Ben's manuscript.

When I walked into Stuart's office, he was on the phone. He motioned me to sit down. "I'm not here to sit. Put down the damn phone. Now." The office was a shrine to the Konigsberg industry. Photographs of me—signing books, speaking, appearing on television, throwing out the first pitch at a Mets game—lined the walls. Floor displays of my books, in hardcover and paperback, were crowded into every corner of the office. Everywhere you turned was another artifact of my fabulous, and totally dishonest, career.

When Stuart put down the phone, the first words I said were "You miserable motherfucker." I didn't get any further because he started to cry. They were big summer-rain tears. Within moments his face was as wet as if he had stepped out of the shower. He came around the desk and got down on his knees in front of me.

"I didn't mean to scare you, Stevie. You have to believe me. My desperation is driving me, not my mind. It was wrong for me to talk to your dad, but I didn't know what else to do. I feel like I'm in a movie where the walls keep caving in. I'm being crushed."

Still on his knees, again he recounted his crumbling financial life. The bad investments, the loans that were past due; every detail adding up to a picture that resembled Berlin after World War II. I had to get out of there.

"Have your accountant contact me when he figures out what it will take to keep your head above water. I won't let you go under."

"I don't want a loan, Stevie. What I want is what you were born to do—write. Give me another novel. That's what we all want: Dexter, your parents, your fans. Don't turn your back on a gift that was meant to be shared with the world. Please."

Stuart struggled to his feet, bracing himself against the edge of his desk. I don't know why I did it, but as soon as he was at eye level, I shoved him with all my might. He dropped to the floor, where I left him, then I headed for the door. His cries of "Please, Steven, please . . ." echoed behind me as I ran for the elevator.

Fifty-five

I started the day off by calling Tina, as I had every day for the past two weeks. Of course, I was never able to reach her. I told myself that she had given up answering the phone for Lent. It would pass. Instead, I spoke to Gillian, my special envoy who was working valiantly to bring Tina back to me. But so far her assignment had proved as difficult as brokering peace in the Middle East.

"No progress, Steve."

"Not a glimmer?" I asked, like a condemned man who keeps wondering if the governor had called to commute his sentence.

"I don't want to feed you false hopes. I've never seen her like this before."

"Is it hopeless?"

"Don't even think that. I love Tina, but I love you, too, Steve. We're all going to get over this. You two belong together. You have to be patient."

"I've never felt this miserable."

"Stay strong. We'll talk tomorrow."

I can't account for it, but I was still able to write. Every day the pages came. And the work was good. *The Journey So Far* was going to be a better book than *Time's Pulse*. Most days I stayed in my office till late in the afternoon so that when I got home, Fred would have left. I was sure that by now he knew something was wrong between Tina and me. Fred was a sensitive and caring soul, but the one thing I couldn't face was a heart-to-heart with him about my marital woes.

I had only one outlet for my spiritual funk: Chester. He was with me all the time. At the office he would put down his chew toy and listen to me attentively whenever I went on about Tina. Sensing when I was particularly sad, he would shuffle over and rest his head on my lap and stay there until I revived enough to start writing again. We needed each other, but I definitely needed Chester more.

When Chester and I got back to the apartment, I checked the messages, though I answered few of them these days. There was one from my mother reminding me for the third time to put the date for my niece's bat mitzvah on our calendar. This was for an event that would take place in seven months! Hamilton Cray called to say that they were close to deciding on a date for the dedication of the Benjamin Chambers Reading Room. He also looked forward to seeing me at the foundation board meeting next month. Sal called to say he loved the Hemingway novel I had given him to read and would see me tomorrow at the office for our usual session. Then there was a call from a man named Osborne Brulee to remind me of the panel discussion on the future of the novel in which I had agreed to participate at the Morgan Library at eight that night. Dexter Parch was the moderator, and the event, he said in rounded, pleased tones, was a sellout. Could I get there by seven for a group photograph for the *New York Times*? As much as I wanted to duck the evening, I saw no way out. I couldn't call Dexter and explain, as I once might have, that because of the problems Tina and I were having, I wouldn't be able to make it. To beg off would be seen by Dexter as yet another act of betrayal.

"When are the clouds going to part?" I asked Chester. He didn't have an answer, but he was smart enough to go into the bedroom and come back with his leash between his teeth. Chester was right. We both needed a walk.

I arrived on time to be met with a warm hello from Osborne Brulee and a frosty nod from Dexter. All the panelists were already there (a *Times* photo op always does wonders with attendance among the lit crowd), including

Quentin Bass, who I sensed had opted to fortify himself with a brace of Tanqueray before tackling the rigors of the panel discussion. The group was made up of four novelists (including me), a critic, and an agent. Aside from Quentin, I hadn't met the other two writers before. One was an elderly man who hadn't published in years, the other a militant lesbian whose books always included the mandatory slaughter of several men via hideous and bizarre means. I also didn't know the agent, Tara Jeckel, though I had read a lot about her. In her mid-thirties, she was called the Pythonette by the tabloids for her ability to squeeze out big advances from publishers and extract writers from the clutches of other agents. Her list, both literary and commercial, was one of the best in the business. Jeckel was always coming on to writers she didn't represent with ideas for books, dangling huge sums before them that she guaranteed she could get from a publisher. It was said that every author had two agents, his own and Tara Jeckel. She was a tall woman with an expanse of cleavage that was formidable. Tara Jeckel wore her long red hair ("It's red everywhere, my friend," she was once quoted as saying seductively) swept up in a dramatic fashion that resembled a wave about to crest.

The panel proceeded at a predictable pace (the old writer going on endlessly about today's lack of publishers like Alfred A. Knopf, the lesbian almost hissing every time she used the word "man"), until I was shaken out of my sad fugue state by a question that Dexter directed at me.

"What do you think is the author's obligation to his audience, Mr. Konigsberg?"

He smiled at me, but it was the kind of smile a man wears when he kicks a dog that's bitten him.

"Well," I said after pausing for a long swallow of water, "I believe an author's main obligation is to the integrity of the work. If that's not there, then there is no work and probably no audience." Pure sophistry, but it was enough for Quentin to weigh in on the base fickleness of readers.

"A writer has only one true fucking reader," he said, slurring his words, "and that's himself." Then he knocked over the carafe of ice water, drenching a woman in the front row. Finally, like the gates of a prison opening after a ten-year sentence, the panel was over. But it really wasn't: I was still obligated to attend a dinner afterward for the participants. After signing fifteen or twenty Konigsberg novels as I made my way out, I felt Quentin's arm snake around my shoulder.

"You were great. Integrity. That's what it's all about. Absolutely fucking on target. Do you think there's a bar at this dinner? I really could use a drink."

"I guess so. They said it's in a private room in an Italian restaurant across the street."

"Well, let's get going."

While Quentin ordered his drink at the bar, I walked to the back of the restaurant to see where the dinner was to be held. I prayed I wasn't seated next to Dexter. When I entered the room, there was Tara Jeckel changing the place cards. Cool as can be, she looked up and smiled at me.

"I just wanted to make sure you had an interesting person next to you. Namely me. They had you seated between the old fart and the bull dyke. Trust me, I'm a lot more fun."

And Tara Jeckel was right. She was funny, always interesting, and at times shocking.

"Your friend Quentin slipped me a note saying that he might be interested in being represented by me. Know what I said? I told him I don't take on clients who are midway between the remainder table and a detox clinic."

"You're pretty tough, Tara," I said as she poured more wine into my glass.

"Just tough enough. By the way, is Stuart still your agent?"

"You know he is."

"I hear he's your cousin."

"First."

"Then why does he charge you a full commission? That's a crime."

"What do you mean?"

"Steven Konigsberg doesn't require a lot of work to sell. All you have to do is have the patience to listen to Parch make higher and higher offers until he comes up with the one that's his ace card. That's all there is to it. If I represented you, Steve, I'd charge half of what Stuart does—seven and a half percent."

"I'll keep that in mind. But to me blood is thicker than saving seven and a half percent."

"You're a rare man, Steve."

For all her brashness and in-your-face intensity, I began to like Tara. I guess the wine didn't hurt, either. When the dinner ended, I found myself on the street, leaning against her, hailing a taxi. It turned out she lived at the

Dakota, which was just a couple of blocks away from my place. When we pulled up in front of it, she asked me if I'd like to come up for a drink and I said, "Sure," at the same time thinking, what am I doing? I'm not horny, I'm just miserable and drunk. This is a big mistake.

We got out of the elevator, and I followed her down a hallway lighted as dimly as a wine cellar. When she stopped at her door, she quickly turned and pinned me to the wall, her lips pressing against mine.

"You taste good," Tara said as she moved away from me for a moment.

I knew that was my only chance. I had to get away. If Tara got me into her apartment, the treacherous slope I had recently been living on would become as steep as Mount Everest. Any chance I had of getting my family back would melt away like butter in a hot skillet. I pushed her off, and without a word I staggered away. Knowing she would snare me if I waited for the elevator, I took the stairs, two at a time, almost falling headfirst several times. Once on the street, I took a couple of deep breaths and slowly made my way home. Chester was waiting for me at the door.

"Chester," I said to him, "would you give me a pass on your walk tonight? I really don't think I'm up to it. In fact, I don't think I've got it in me to make it to the bedroom." With a final lurch I made it to the sofa, where I passed out promptly.

Fifty-six

The next morning, feeling hungover and guilty, I called Key West. After four rings I heard this message:

"Hi. Tina, Ben, and I are out today, heading north to Islamorada to visit Uncle Dennis. We'll probably be back tomorrow afternoon. Please leave a message and we'll get back to you, except for Ben, of course. He doesn't like to use the phone."

Dennis was an old, gnarly guy who had lived in the Keys most of his life, leading bonefishing excursions through the shallow gin-clear waters. He was Tina's favorite uncle. To say he was a man of few words was to call a Trappist monk loquacious. But he smiled a lot, showing an expanse of gum, which more than made up for the lack of talk.

The phone was ringing as I got out of the shower. Generally, I would let the machine pick it up, but it was early, and my brain was barely in neutral.

"I've had men turn me down before, Steve, but that was the first time I had one flee. I'd like you to call me when your courage returns."

"How'd you get this number? It's unlisted."

"So is Bob De Niro's. I make a point of giving a substantial Christmas gift to a couple of people I know in the phone company. You ever want a number, let me know."

"I'm married, Tara."

"I love married men. I find they're generally looking for the same thing I am."

"Well, I'm not."

"You're quite the Boy Scout. You can't be tempted to have a little fun, and you're loyal to a cousin whose other clients have either left or are in the process of leaving."

"You described me perfectly. Now, have a good day. And if we meet again, I'll pour my own wine."

I was about to leave for my office with Chester when the doorbell rang.

"This just came for you, Mr. King," said Carlos, the elevator man, handing me a large envelope. Spotting the name Bowers in the upper left-hand corner was enough to make my pulse quicken. I ripped it open and found a couple of dozen photos of Tina and Ben taken with a telephoto lens, with a note:

> Hi, Mr. K. We're back in town and ready to wrap up our business. Give us a call at 555-5774 and don't sit on your hands. Got it? By the by, where're Tina and Ben? All these snaps are out of date. We have some ideas for new photo ops. Much more exciting stuff. XOXO, V

I shoved the note and the photos into my jacket pocket, where they felt hot enough to burn a hole, and headed to my office. Vera was ratcheting up her threats—where was she going? I couldn't focus and walked like a blind man, letting Chester set the route and the pace. I had been unbelievably dense to dismiss the sisters simply because they were out of sight. I fooled myself into thinking they were no more dangerous than hyperactive trick-or-treaters. I knew now that I had a much bigger problem than I had imagined. At least Tina and Ben were nowhere near the Bowerses' playing field. What had been a terrible absence (temporary, I still prayed) had become a plus.

I was ready to leave to meet Sal at my office when the phone rang. Fearing it was Tara, the agent from hell, I didn't pick up until the third ring.

"Yes."

"This is June."

"Hi."

I thought I was losing my mind because her voice now sounded as deep as her sister's.

"I'm calling on my cell phone. Vera's showering. I don't want her to know I'm speaking to you."

"What's up?"

"I'm having trouble controlling her, Mr. K. A lot of trouble."

"What do you mean?"

"She gets . . . angry. Real angry. All the time. Even with me." I heard a voice in the background and then June said, "Got to go now. She's calling me. Just remember to do what she asks you to. Don't upset her. I don't know what she might do."

And then the line went dead.

As always, Sal was waiting for me. His novel was almost ready to show to Dexter, but that was on hold for the moment. I was interested in hearing what he thought of the Hemingway I had given him to read. After running through the whys and wherefores (all positive) of his reaction, he tied it up neatly. "Tough but tender is how I would sum it up."

"Sal, you have the makings of a literary critic. Ever thought of switching professions?"

We both had a good laugh, then turned to a small but knotty problem in Sal's own fiction. I was grateful for the distraction. We made such fast progress on it that we decided it was time for a lunch break. Each time we met, Sal brought along heroes his wife had made of provolone, soprassata, and hot and sweet peppers, tasty enough to console even me.

Sal must have sensed that something was bothering me other than Tina's and Ben's absence. I had told him about that but hadn't explained why it happened.

"What's wrong, Steve? Someone trying to shake you down again?"

I had bottled it up too long. "Yes," I blurted out, then launched into an account of the sisters, highlighted, of course, by a complete one-eighty from the truth about *The Dam and the Pocket*. I didn't want to lie to Sal, but I couldn't get into the real story with him at this point.

"The shakedown artists," I said, "are a pair of sisters who are body-builders. One of them is real serious about it. They're in their thirties, and the one that's nuts about bodybuilding looks like Popeye after three courses of spinach."

"Sounds like they're ready for *The Howard Stern Show*," he said, chuckling.

"This isn't a funny story. I was doing a book signing for *The Dam and the Pocket* at a Barnes & Noble when towards the end of the signing a woman passed an envelope to me. Inside was a manuscript of the book. My book. I couldn't believe it. It looked exactly like the original. Then she told me to meet her at a gym in a hotel downtown. I went there later that day. After foisting a ghastly health drink on me that looked like bile, she showed me the manuscript again. It was exactly like the original of *The Dam and the Pocket* I have in my safe-deposit box. When the story came to me in a burst, I was so excited I wanted to sit down and write it at once. But I had a prob-lem—I had broken my hand playing volleyball on the beach. So I dictated it to Ike, a friend I knew could help me. It took less than an hour, and when we were finished, he gave me the original. I had him make a copy because I thought I might need it."

It was at this point that I realized my story was as filled with holes as a target at a shooting range. What had happened to my ability to whip up elaborate, ornate falsehoods that were polished and rock solid? I just had to plunge ahead.

"I have no idea how they got hold of Ike's copy. Now they're threaten-ing to sell it at an auction house like Sotheby's. The big problem is that my name isn't on the manuscript. Either copy. How can I prove I wrote it? They've been on my case for months, and every time they show up they raise the ante. And the worst of it is they've begun threatening Tina and Ben."

Though my tale made no sense (a manuscript without the author's name on it?), I saw that Sal had bought it completely. He was both my friend and my protector. He'd follow me into a burning building to help if need be.

"Those bitches," he said in a tight voice that was almost a snarl. Sal's face began to redden, and his hands balled into fists.

"Their latest ploy is secretly taking photos of Tina and Ben, which means they're following them."

After a few moments he regained his control. He put his hand on my shoulder. His black eyes burrowed into mine. "You're not alone with this any longer, Steve. I'm going to handle it. You're going to call them and set up a meeting as soon as possible."

"How about right now?"

"Okay. I'll be at the meeting with you, and we'll take it from there."

Fifty-seven

With Sal on the other phone, I called the Bowers sisters. Sal and I had spent almost an hour rehearsing what I was to say.

"June?"

"It's Vera. Can't you tell us apart by now?"

"Hi, Mr. K. I'm on the other line. Are you ready to wrap this up?"

"That's why I'm calling. Meet me at one tomorrow at the pier by Christopher Street." Sal wanted the meeting to be in a place where there was little chance of me being recognized.

"We'll meet, Mr. K, where we tell you to meet," said Vera. "You don't call the plays here. Meet us at 17 Mott Street, in Chinatown. It's a restaurant called Hop Gar. They serve the best congee soup in town. I love congee. And I've gotten my sister to like it, too."

Sal nodded okay to me.

"What time?"

"Twelve-thirty. Be on time." Then the line went dead.

"Boy, does she sound like bad news," said Sal as he hung up the phone.

"That's nothing. Wait till you meet her."

"I don't care if they look like extras from *Jurassic Park*. I'll handle them."

. . .

You enter Hop Gar by descending a flight of worn stone stairs. As soon as we entered the restaurant, we spotted the sisters, who were dressed alike in violet turtlenecks, black gym pants, and high-top sneakers. Though Vera seemed to be almost ready to explode out of her sweater, June didn't seem too far behind. She had gotten way bigger since our last meeting, and now, like her sister, had a visible shadow of a mustache. Her smile was gone, and her once bright eyes seemed dull as buttons. She didn't even look up at me. In front of each was an enormous bowl of gray liquid, the surface as shiny as a newly frozen pond.

"Take a seat, Mr. K," said Vera, looking up from her bowl.

They were seated side by side in a booth near the kitchen. Steam from large boiling pots spilled like fog in a cheap horror film. I slid onto the banquette opposite them, with Sal right behind me.

"Who the fuck said you could bring someone with you?"

"This is Sal Rigano, my business manager."

"He looks more like a cop to me," said Vera.

"They have a better health plan than the one Steve provides," said Sal, extending his hand across the table. The sisters kept their hands on their spoons and continued to eat.

"We don't really give a crap who you are. This is totally on the up-and-up, anyway. We're selling something that's legally ours. If you don't want to deal, we've got other buyers," said Vera, whose name, I noticed, was stitched on her sweater.

"Like Sotheby's, Christie's, and the University of Texas," said June.

"What is that?" asked Sal, pointing at the soup.

"Congee."

"What's in it?"

"The important point, Mr. Business Manager, is that it's perfect for building body mass. Any other questions?"

"We're here to wrap this up. Do you have the manuscript?" I asked.

"Of course not. It's in a safe place, and you'll get it when we finish our business," said Vera, who signaled to the waiter for two more bowls. Sal started to say something, but she silenced him with a raised palm. "We can talk when we're finished. Eating to us is the same as a workout. It's not a time for talking."

When they finally finished, they set down their spoons like drummers sounding a final beat.

"The foundation's papers will be ready in a week. So we'll meet seven days from today at the Chase branch on Fifty-seventh and Sixth at noon."

"You'll have the check with you, certified, of course," added June.

"You haven't told us how much," said Sal.

"One point two million. Want to know what we're going to do with it?"

"Vera means what the foundation will do."

"First off, we're going to hire us a full-time coach, fitness trainer, nutritionist, and masseuse. We're going to need an easy way to get all of us to competitions, so we're going to buy a time share on a G3," she said, lifting her palm off the table in imitation of a jet taking off.

"We're also going to set up an office. We need a staff to handle bills, hotel reservations, things like that."

"Seems like you've thought of everything," said Sal, smiling.

"Being a bodybuilder doesn't mean a person's dumb."

"You don't have to tell me. I know some bodybuilders."

"Like who?" asked Vera.

"How about Lou Ferrigno?"

"You know Mr. Lou?"

"He's my first cousin's best friend."

"He went head-to-head with Arnold. Almost beat him a couple of times," mused Vera with the worshipful look of a Yankees fan remembering DiMaggio.

"I saw them go at it once. Amazing."

I just sat there quietly, watching Sal become Vera's best friend. Gone were her suspicions that he was a cop. She was chuckling at his stories of his cousin and Lou Ferrigno, listening intently to his description of his cousin's failed attempts in the world of bodybuilding, roaring at his jokes.

"I enjoyed this," said Vera, looking at her watch. "We would like to continue to shoot the shit with you, but we have a workout in a half hour. You're okay, Sal. When I say you're okay, that's a big fucking compliment."

"I feel the same way," said Sal, who tapped his balled fist against theirs.

They started to get up, then glanced at each other and sat down again.

"You seem like a guy who knows his way around. Maybe you can do us a favor," said Vera, leaning in and dropping her voice to just above a whisper.

"I'll certainly give it a shot. What can I do for you?"

"Know anything about the juice?" asked Vera.

"Steroids? A little."

"We're running low, and we don't have anybody here to write a scrip for us."

"What are you looking for?"

"We'll take either Deca-Durabolin or Equipoise. In a pinch Oxandrin will do."

"The Ox is the only one that's oral, right?"

"You're the man, Sal. Is there anything you don't know?"

"I get around. Expect a call in the next day or two from Terry. I think he'll be able to set you up."

"You got a good man here, Mr. K. Treat him right," said Vera as she stood up.

"I'll do my best," I said.

After the Bowerses left, Sal motioned for the waiter.

"We'll have some spareribs, beef lo mein, and kung pao chicken."

"No congee?"

"Absolutely not," said Sal.

Sal wasn't ready to talk until we finished the ribs.

"You're right, Steve. They are pretty scary. It's partly the steroids. One minute they seem fine, the next they're ready to bite the head off a cobra."

"How did you learn about steroids?"

"I did seven years in narcotics. The girls are playing with very dangerous shit. My sense is that Vera's been doing it for quite some time."

"I'll call my business manager this afternoon and have him start to get the money together for next week."

"I don't know if that will be the end of it."

"What do you mean?"

"After I left you yesterday, I went into the station house and checked them out on the computer. In addition to spending seven months in jail, Vera Bowers has had some serious problems—two indictments for assault and battery and a reckless endangerment charge. She beat all three. Seems her old man paid off the victims. She isn't just scary, she's dangerous."

"What do I do?"

"Let me work on it. There's always a way to handle a problem. Let's stay cool and we'll figure this one out." Like Vera said, Sal was the man. I trusted him implicitly.

Fifty-eight

The next morning before I had even pulled myself out of bed, the phone rang.

"Steve?"

"Yes?" I answered guardedly.

"It's Gillian," said my mother-in-law. "Did I wake you up?"

"No, no," I answered quickly. "I got up a half hour ago." Then I realized how early it was, and I got scared. Maybe Ben was sick. "Is everything okay?" I asked, holding on to the phone like a lifeline.

"I didn't mean to give you a scare." Gillian paused, and I could hear her quickly puff on her cigarette. "In fact, everything's more than okay. I'm calling with good news. I think now might be the right time for you to come down. I have no idea what came between you and Tina, but I know you love each other. You've got to find a way to work your way through this and get back to what matters. What I do know is that Tina's been very hurt, and she's terribly lonely. She's still angry, but it's beginning to melt away. She needs you."

"I've been waiting for this call a long time, Gillian. Do you really mean it?"

"A mother can sense these things. And Ben is fine. He's learned to push himself up from his stomach and look around. He smiles all the time."

The word "smile" hung in the air like a helium balloon, and Gillian latched on to it.

"Steve," she continued, "you and Tina need to learn to smile again. At each other. Come down here and give it a try. You've been away from each other for three weeks now and that's too long."

I almost shouted, "I think I can get down there by this afternoon."

Fred wasn't in yet, so I rang up the business jet company I generally use to charter planes. Then I put the phone down. I realized that arriving in a Gulfstream was the wrong signal to send—way wrong. Better to fly commercial. On the next flight out that I could make, there were no first-class tickets available on American—only coach. I took the seat.

Before I left the apartment, I swept my money clip, the key to the safe-deposit box that now contained all of Ben's manuscripts, and a jewelry box from the top of the bureau. Inside the box was a slender gold necklace I had bought the other day on Forty-seventh Street. Though it looked very simple, this was going to be the most important gift Tina had ever received from me.

A few hours later, still smiling, I crammed myself into my coach seat between two men so fat they would make a Weight Watchers franchise salivate if they enrolled. My connections were perfect. By midafternoon I was cruising over the Keys in a two-engine plane that flew from Miami to Key West. Below us was a string of low keys set against an expanse of blue-green water. I could see small boats thread their way through serpentine channels.

Within minutes of landing I was at Gillian's house in the old section of town. It had a trellis in front overflowing with bougainvillea, and on every other inch of the tiny yard green tropical plants, their leaves gleaming as if they had just been waxed. Tina had once told me her mother pruned them religiously each day in a struggle to keep them under control, but, like whiskers, they seemed to sprout again overnight.

When she heard the taxi door slam, Gillian appeared, holding a glass of lemonade. "Your wife and son are not here," she said, "but they'll be back soon."

We sat under the trellis, and within minutes I saw them.

"Hello," called Tina softly as she opened the front gate.

I almost tripped over my feet rushing to help her in with the carriage.

Tina gave me a sweet smile and, I prayed, a forgiving one. I was as tongue-tied as a child giving his first school recital. I stood back, not daring to touch her, afraid to break the spell; but there was my adorable son in her arms.

I reached out for Ben and picked him up. He took one look at me, screwed up his face, and began to cry. He didn't recognize me! Tina and Gillian stood arm in arm, laughing at my dejected face. Then I started laughing, too, and Ben gurgled and waved his hands. Gillian took Ben from me, saying it was time for his nap.

"Tina, will you and Steve do me a favor and go over to Pepe's? I forgot a couple of things I need for dinner. Plain bread crumbs and some lettuce, Bibb or romaine."

It was a blatant excuse to get us together. Bless you, Gillian. We walked together in silence, until I could no longer hold back my feelings.

"Tina," I said, wanting to grab her, though I didn't, "I came down here for only one reason. To tell you I'll do anything, anything, to bring you back into my life. I've been thinking of nothing else. I know only one thing: my life is meaningless without you. What can I do?"

"You asked me that same question before I left. It's up to you to supply the answers."

"I have them. Absolutely."

"The most important thing is, have you changed? Can you show me you've changed, and can I believe you? Do you remember how I felt when I realized your life was a lie? That nothing about our life was what I thought it was? I was in pain, Steven, physical pain. I didn't know where I was going or where you were going, or how to pull us back together, or even if we should try."

"Yes," I said, almost choking on the word. "I remember."

"I've thought about this a lot, and I know the only way we can get together again is if you change your behavior. Behavior! That's putting it nicely. I mean really change, big-time."

"I swear, Tina, I'll do anything to bring you back to me."

"Okay," said Tina, stopping in front of a large tree, searching my eyes for something I prayed was there. "One, all the money you've made goes to the foundation. Two, you sell the apartment, the house in Connecticut, and we move out of New York City. It hasn't done either one of us any good. And, three, most important of all, you stop publishing the Konigsberg books. I mean forever. Can you do that?"

"Yes, Tina. Yes. I'll do it all. I just want you and Ben back . . ."

"This is not a time for fast answers. Give it some real thought and we'll talk again later."

Before Tina started down the sidewalk again, I touched her arm. When she turned, I took the jewelry box out of my pocket and handed it to her.

"What's this?" When I didn't answer, she continued, "It's too early for presents."

"Please open it," I said, almost pleading.

As she pulled the necklace from the box, she saw the key dangling from it.

"What's the key for?"

"It opens the safe-deposit box that holds all of Ben's manuscripts. It's the only key."

She looked at me and then at the key, then back again. Slowly, she reached out and put the necklace around my neck. "This will never work unless we trust each other," she said. Then she stepped forward and embraced me.

That evening the three of us had dinner on the back porch. Gillian's Sublime Meat Loaf, with a hard-boiled egg in the middle just like my mother's, was the main course. I think it was the best meal I've ever had. I had bought some wine at Pepe's, inexpensive but nice. And the conversation was easy. Tina and Gillian did most of the talking, while I basked in the presence of Tina. She looked at me most of the time with a soft, hopeful look.

That night, without discussion, I slept in the guest room. The next morning I caught a flight back to New York, and this time I had all three seats in the row to myself. Though I was prepared to sit between mating hippos with good cheer, I took the empty, spacious row as a good omen. For the first time, I allowed myself to believe my life might actually be turning around.

Fifty-nine

The next morning I hit the ground running, waking up at six. After shaving I took Chester out for a walk. I had to rouse him, since Chester is not an early morning dog, but he quickly caught the change in my mood and bounced happily alongside me. I started to hum, which he answered with deep, companionable barks.

My first order of business was to find two real estate agents: one to sell the apartment and office, another to handle the house in Connecticut. I had met a number of real estate agents in the country, so lining one up there was no problem. I picked the one who had never asked me to autograph a copy of a Steven Konigsberg novel. For the New York apartment it took a few more calls, but by late morning I thought I had found the right one. Then I called Marty, my business manager.

"Marty, I need a check. A big one."

"No problemo, Steve. What's up?"

"It's for a contribution I'm going to make. A contribution to peace."

I left out that the peace would be my own.

"How much you need?"

"A million two."

This elicited a soft whistle.

"Will do. Actually, you do need a big deduction. You've had a hell of a year."

"Could you please send it by messenger to the apartment today? And make the check certified. I'll write in the payee."

"Then I'll deliver it myself. Wouldn't want a messenger to wind up with a condo in the Cayman Islands."

Though I didn't need the check for another few days, when Sal and I had our meeting with the Bowers sisters, I wanted to have everything in order to conclude this final messy episode. I had one other thing left to do: to see Flo Wanger. From my bedroom, behind a tightly closed door, I called her number. Fred was working, as he always did, on the myriad housekeeping aspects of Konigsberg, Inc. I had vowed to myself that I would find him a good job, and short of that to give him a year's severance and full medical benefits for at least that long.

Flo Wanger's secretary put me right through. After introducing myself, I plunged in.

"Would it be possible to see you tomorrow?"

"Why not?"

"How about one o'clock?"

"That's fine."

"Do you know what this is about?" I asked.

"I think I have an idea."

Her answer more than intrigued me. However, now that I was in the process of severing the last Konigsberg connections and threats to my life, I wasn't frightened about what she might reveal or ask for. After all, I was now out of the plagiarism business.

I met Flo Wanger in her office at C&W Fine Furniture. Located on the edge of the industrial section of Northampton, Massachusetts, the corporate offices were housed in a large Victorian painted a deep burgundy. The factory occupied two squat corrugated metal buildings, painted the same color, that sat on either side like bookends.

On the drive to C&W I thought a lot about Ben. According to the detective's report, this was the business that Ben started with Flo twenty-five years ago in Palo Alto, which she'd been running alone since he left.

A secretary showed me into her office. Flo Wanger was in her mid-seventies but looked ten years younger. She was short and sturdy, with bright almond eyes and a stylish short haircut that would have fit in nicely in St.-Germain-des-Prés. One look at her and you knew she could handle anything, from a family spat to a tough labor negotiation.

We shook hands, and I sat down on the other side of her desk, surprised by what surrounded me. Antiques! And they seemed like good ones, though all I knew about the subject was garnered from an occasional viewing of *Antiques Roadshow*.

Flo laughed. "No, we don't manufacture 'antiques.' I just like having them around. Our stock is completely contemporary, from Philippe Starck and Andrée Putman knockoffs to Ikea-style basics."

Then she stopped abruptly. She stared at me as if I were in a police lineup.

"You know, Steven—and since I'm old enough to be your mother, I think I can call you by your first name—I've been expecting you for some time. We both know you didn't come up here to see the beauty of the Berkshires."

"No."

"I guess you might want to know how Ben and I started this little venture. It happened the way most things happen—by chance. We met at a party. I had just gotten a divorce and was at loose ends. Same for Ben, though little did I know then that this condition was the norm for him. After falling in love like teenagers we decided that it would be fun to work together. The furniture idea was Ben's. I had an M.B.A., and Ben, without any training, was a natural designer. We were a hit right from the start, and we could barely fulfill the orders. Then just like that, Ben left. He told me he would always love me, but he had to move on. He promised that one day he'd come back to me. But he never did. The heat of anger can transform a person. I hired lawyers who were essentially mako sharks in suits and sued him. But Ben didn't even contest it. I wound up with the business, but not with Ben. So here I am. Very successful and very lonely."

"Did he ever talk to you about his writing?"

"Are you joking? Those books were the center of his life. I read every one of them."

I didn't know what to say next, but I had to say something.

"Did you like them?"

"I loved them. Just as much as I love Steven Konigsberg's novels."

I looked at Flo, who was smiling as if she had swallowed both the cat and the canary.

"So you know."

"Right from *Juno's Dance*."

"Do you want to know why I did it?"

"I'm too old to be interested in why."

"Believe me, I'm sorry. I guess I've done a terrible thing."

"You've done what Ben didn't have the guts to do."

"Do you really mean that?"

"Listen, Steve, since Ben left me, I've spent enough money keeping tabs on him to send five kids through Harvard. I know he made you his sole heir. The books belong to you."

"Then why didn't you contact me?"

"That's not the way I operate. I knew eventually you'd find your way here."

"And you really believe that Ben wanted me to publish his books?"

"Yes."

"Under my own name?"

"I don't think he gave a damn. Any name but Ben Chambers."

I sat there, opposite her, for a long time. I felt I had just digested a meal of too many courses.

"I need to push on back to New York," I finally said, standing up. "Thanks for your time." I reached into my pocket and pulled out a check for $25,000 made out to her. It was my good-bye gift to the people who had crossed Ben's life. She took one look at it, ripped it in half, and let the pieces drop onto her desk.

"Thank you," she said. "The thought was nice, but the amount is way off." I just stared at her. "I want you to write out a check for one million dollars. Make it payable to the Northampton Hospice Center. I know what you've made from Ben's novels, and this represents no more than the cherry on the top of a sundae for you. Think of it as a gift Ben would have approved of. The center is very important to me, and I'm sure he would have felt the same."

I had my checkbook in my jacket pocket, and without saying a word I wrote the check. Flo Wanger took it and put it in the center drawer of her desk. Then she stood up and came around the desk.

"Steve," she said, "we share something very special. We both loved a beautiful, unique man. All Ben ever wanted was to do good. Don't ever forget that. He would never have intentionally put you in a position that would harm you." Then she kissed me. I closed my arms around her, and we stood that way, unmoving and silent, like mannequins in a store window.

Sixty

"Have you ever been to Italy, Steve?" asked Sal as we sat at a small table in a coffee shop off Sixth Avenue.

"Once."

"Remember what the coffee tasted like there?" He glumly stirred his cup of espresso. "First off, they don't put that much espresso in the cup. What they give you is sort of the essence of espresso. It's so thick it almost sticks to the spoon. Every sip is like tasting—and excuse me if this sounds a bit precious—the soul of the coffee bean."

"I know exactly what you mean."

"The shit they serve here is nothing like it. You know why?"

"Don't have a clue."

"It's the coffee they use. That's the number one, two, and three reasons. There are a couple of places in my neighborhood that do a pretty good job, but it's still not quite what you get over there." He finished his cup and looked at his watch. "Time to put this show on the road. Got the check?"

I patted my jacket pocket. "Just the way they asked for it. Made out to the Bowers Foundation."

"Don't hand it over until I tell you to."

We were only two blocks from the bank, so we arrived five minutes early. Twenty minutes later the Bowerses were not there.

"I sure as shit would show up on time if I had a monster check waiting for me," said Sal.

"They're flaky. Nothing they do surprises me."

Fifteen minutes later they still hadn't shown up.

"What the fuck gives? I don't get it," said Sal.

"Neither do I. Do you think this is some kind of ploy to get more money?"

"I'm going to call them. You wait here in case they show up."

"Why don't you use your cell?"

"That's department property. All my calls can be checked. I don't need that. I'll just go outside and use a phone booth. Got a quarter?"

Sal returned a few minutes later. "Very strange. Hotel operator says they're not taking any calls."

"What should we do?"

"I'm going to the hotel to see what's up. You go back to your apartment and wait for my call."

"Should I give you the check?"

"Sure. Maybe I can wrap this up without your coming back downtown."

I wasn't back in the apartment for more than a few minutes when Sal called.

"Something's come up," he said in a low voice.

"Is it a problem?"

"I can't talk now. I'll see you when I finish up here. Everything's going to be fine. But I don't want to meet you at the apartment. Go to your office. I'll join you there."

"How long–"

"Can't talk now." His voice was so low I could barely make him out. "See you later."

I stood there holding the phone, suddenly feeling very scared. Why did Sal want to meet at my office? Why was he whispering? What was going on?

As I left, Chester appeared at the front door, his leash in his mouth.

"Not now, Chester. I have to go alone this time. We'll take our walk later."

I patted him on his warm back, then watched him go back to his pillow bed in the kitchen, unhappy but accepting. When I got to the office, I tried to write and couldn't. Then I reread my last chapter and found myself staring at the page as if in a trance. When would Sal show up? Maybe I should go out for a bite. But he might arrive while I was gone. I called Fred at the apartment to see if Sal had called me there. Nothing. I gave Fred a long list of small tasks that didn't need attention, but at least it gave me something to do. Finally, I went back to my book and spent an hour writing a paragraph that I threw out. And then I heard the doorbell.

"What happened?" I asked as soon as Sal walked in.

"This happened," he answered as he handed me a large envelope.

I tore it open to find the sisters' copy of *The Dam and the Pocket*.

"Great."

"And I also have this for you."

He handed me another envelope. I opened it to find the check.

"I don't understand. Why didn't they take the check?"

"They couldn't. June and Vera went to the big tournament in the sky. They both overdosed."

"That's unbelievable. From the steroids?"

"No. The sisters apparently liked to party." Sal took off his jacket and sat down on the sofa. "I went up to their suite, but there was no answer when I knocked. I got the housekeeper to let me in. There they were, one on the sofa, the other on the floor, blue as gum balls. One still had a spike in her arm. Terry, the dealer I put them onto, was there, too. It looked like he was trying to get to the phone. He probably knew pretty fast the stuff was a lot hotter than he'd thought. Won't know until the lab report comes in, but my guess is that it was heroin. When I called headquarters to report what had happened, since Terry was one of my regular snitches, I told them that Terry was arranging to make a big sale to the sisters. That's why I was there. Unfortunately, I got there late."

"I don't know what to say, Sal."

"Just say thanks. That'll take care of it."

"Of course. It's just that . . . I guess I'm too shocked to absorb it all."

I looked at Sal while holding the manuscript tight. A voice inside me was screaming, "Sal killed them for you, Steve. The problem is gone, but now you're an accessory to murder. Three more people dead because of you."

Sal stood up and put his hands on my shoulders.

"Steve, listen to me closely. I can see it in your eyes. You think I had a hand in this. Like maybe I gave Terry that bad shit. Believe me, those three mutts killed themselves. I had nothing to do with it, and neither did you. It's too bad, but the world is well rid of them. It was just luck. Theirs was bad, yours was good. There's no connection to you, and now, finally, this scary chapter in your life is over." I wanted to hug Sal, but he was already on to other things. "You know what I want to do now?"

"What?"

"Get some Chinese food and discuss that book you gave me last week. I see now what you mean by building a character."

Sixty-one

The *New York Post* had a field day with the deaths of the Bowers sisters. They played it big for three days. The old newspaper maxim "If you have a picture, you have a story" was proved in spades as they displayed photos of Vera, oiled and massive, posing in competitions from Jakarta to Capetown. June, the number one fan, always standing at her side, smiling rapturously at her sister. As Sal had predicted, the results of the autopsies on the Bowerses and Terry, the dealer, came back as death by heroin overdose. Oddly, the heroin that killed them was known on the street as Golden Touch, which prompted the *Post* headline, "Sisters Cop Their Final Gold."

Tina and Ben were due back in a couple of days, and I was almost finished with the dismantling of the best-selling supership, the SS *Konigsberg*. I instructed Marty to sell all the securities in my account. I hadn't yet told him to transfer the proceeds to the Benjamin Chambers Outreach Foundation, since he had trouble understanding why I wanted to liquidate my portfolio. I gave him the totally unconvincing reason that I thought the market was going to crash. After a half hour of listening to his assurances that there was no chance of that happening, I simply told him the money was mine and that he should sell the stock, or I'd get someone else to do the job.

On the real estate front things were moving ahead smoothly. I had accepted an offer on the Connecticut house and had received close to acceptable bids on the apartment and the office. My real estate holdings seemed to be selling as well as Ben's books. After seeing Flo Wanger I had debated with myself for a couple of days about whether or not to tell Tina what Flo had revealed to me.

"You won't believe this, Tina, but it's true," I told her in my mental scenario.

"What, Steve?"

"Ben wanted the books to be published. Flo Wanger, the woman whom he loved and almost married, told me that."

"Really."

"Yes. And he didn't care under whose name they were published. So what I did was actually what he wanted all along."

I wasn't able to take this imaginary conversation any further because I knew where it would lead: Tina would head straight back to Key West. She wouldn't care whether Flo Wanger was telling the truth. Tina expected–no, demanded–that I stop my masquerade. And getting her back was more important than anything Ben's books had given me. What I had to persuade Tina to agree to was not to give every last dollar of my tainted fortune to the foundation. I sort of knew where I wanted to move and the amount of money it would take to buy a house there. After all, some money was due me for promoting the books and making bestsellers of them. I didn't want a lot, just enough for the down payment on a house and enough to tide us over for a year until I could finish my new novel. What I was asking for wasn't unreasonable, but I knew if Tina objected, I'd give in to her. I put this matter at the top of my list of things to discuss when she returned.

My final piece of business concerned Dexter and Stuart. I was leaving them in the lurch and that wasn't right. How to balance the scales a bit was a problem I hadn't yet solved. And what about Sal? I owed him big-time. What could I do for him?

As I did every morning, I headed with Chester to my office, grappling with these problems. With me at the word processor and Chester on the sofa, we put in three productive hours; working straight through, I produced a decent page and a half. Chester fell asleep immediately, snoring and snuffling without letup. Before leaving for a walk and then lunch, I decided to take a look at the contents of my safe. The manuscript that Tina found was there, held together untidily by two thick red rubber bands. The copy I was making was stacked below. As I was about to close the safe and spin the dial, I noticed a folded piece of paper in the back. It was my original list, cataloging all of Ben's manuscripts. As I scanned the titles, memories of first reading them back in Boothbay Harbor came at me with the power of a rogue wave. Of course, I had periodically read the list to decide which of Ben's novels I would transmute into the next Konigsberg opus.

Looking over the titles was a sad exercise for me: so many terrific books that no one would ever read. Then at the bottom of the list I saw *The Third Suspect*. I remembered both the story and the book's protagonist, Teddy Grammas, as if I had read it the day before. Teddy was a young New York police detective who lived in Astoria, Queens. His parents ran a small Greek restaurant there, and Teddy, like everyone else in the family, pitched in to help from time to time. Why hadn't I offered up this book to the Konigsberg fans? Of course. I realized the moment I finished reading it that if I had published *The Third Suspect*, there would have been an immediate demand for a sequel. And then another, and another, until Teddy Grammas would take over center stage. After all, even plagiarists have egos.

I was about to put the list back in the safe when the idea hit me. Here was the way to pay back Sal, and at the same time do something for Dexter and Stuart. I hurried back to the apartment with Chester, shaking himself out of his sleep and trying to keep up. I then took a cab to the bank where *The Third Suspect* manuscript was stashed. I went directly back to my office. Then, in a reprise of my marathon effort retyping the first of Ben's books, I plunged in. Aside from a few breaks to go out for sandwiches and coffee, I stayed at it until three in the morning. The next day I went to the office before Fred arrived at the apartment and worked until midnight. I did the same the next day. Luckily, it was one of Ben's shortest books and, as usual, I didn't change a word or move a comma. My final act was to type out the title page:

THE THIRD SUSPECT

A NOVEL BY SALVATORE RIGANO

The next day I went to see Dexter. He gave me a cool "Hello" when I walked into his office, then actually smiled when he saw the large envelope under my arm.

"Have something for me?"

"Indeed I do."

"Might it be a novel?"

"Actually, two."

Dexter's smile now was that of a lottery winner. "I knew you'd eventually change your mind."

"Actually, I haven't. These were written by a friend."

The smile was now completely gone.

"Oh, so you decided to become an agent. It's quite a crowded profession, you know," he said bitterly.

I knew that I had to avoid our shooting darts back and forth, so I quickly launched into who Sal was, my relationship to him, and what the two books were about. I tossed out comparisons to Robert Parker and Patricia Cornwell for one book, and Joseph Wambaugh and Scott Turow for the other. I stressed that I was talking to him because I felt an obligation. There wasn't a publisher, I told him, who wouldn't kill to sign up these books. By the end I got through to him. I could see that Dexter was interested. Very interested.

"Well, I'll take a look," he said, extending his hand for the envelope.

"You have to promise me something first."

"A good salesman knows when to stop selling, Steven."

"This is something else. I want you to read them yourself. No xeroxing copies for the editorial board."

"Agreed."

"And I want you to read *The Third Suspect* first."

"Is that it?"

"One last thing. I want you to clear your calendar and start reading them now."

"I have a business to run. They can wait until I get home tonight."

"That won't play. Either you start right now or I'll take them elsewhere."

"Jesus, Steven, the Pentagon should have had you interrogate their prisoners. But okay. I'll do it."

"I expect to hear something from you by tomorrow afternoon. Understood?"

He nodded, and I handed him the package. As I walked out, I turned and saw that Dexter had already started to read.

At five in the afternoon the next day, Dexter called.

"I read them both," he said.

"And?"

"When can I start negotiating? I assume it's Stuart?"

Yes, I thought, as soon as I bring him into the loop. "I'll have him call you. They're real good, aren't they?"

"Not as good as Steven Konigsberg, but they're pretty good."

As luck would have it, the following day was my Sal day. We met at the usual time, but Sal was surprised to find two flutes of champagne on my desk instead of a stack of books and his manuscript.

"What gives?"

"We have something to celebrate," I said, raising a glass.

"I'm all for that," he answered, clinking his glass against mine.

"To Sal Rigano, a soon-to-be-published author."

"What are you talking about?"

"I showed your book to my publisher. They want to publish it."

"But we haven't finished polishing it."

"It was ready. Chancery's wanting to do it proves that."

"Jesus," he said, sitting down on the sofa. "Imagine that. Me, a guy from Bensonhurst, getting his book published."

"Now, Sal, your book is only part of this celebration."

"I don't think you can top that."

"Let me try."

I had been rehearsing this speech since I connected *The Third Suspect* to Sal. I started by telling him that I was going to stop writing novels under the name Steven Konigsberg. In fact, I was abandoning altogether that type of book.

"What! Are you serious?"

"I am."

"I don't understand."

"I want you to, and I'll try to explain. You'll see why."

"I love your books, Steve. So do millions of other readers."

"I know that. It's just something I have to do. Also, Tina and I are going to move out of New York."

"Where?"

"I'm not sure. It'll be close enough that we'll be able to visit each other without hopping a plane."

"I guess that's something," he said dejectedly.

"When you read *Time's Pulse*, you told me you thought it was my best book. Do you remember that?"

In addition to Tina, Stuart, and Dexter, Sal was the only other person who knew that I was also Chambers Benjamin. Sal and I shared so many secrets that entrusting him with that one was like giving pocket change to an investment banker.

"Of course I do."

"As a writer yourself, you can understand why I don't want to go on writing two completely different types of books."

"I guess so."

He didn't sound too convinced, but I knew I had to move on. Here was the tough part. I told Sal I owed Chancery one more book, but that presented a problem—a big one. I had promised myself that I was finished with Steven Konigsberg. I had already buried him. And here was where Sal could help me out.

First, I told him some of the plot of *The Third Suspect*. Then I got into the character of the young detective, Teddy Grammas. I could see I was getting to Sal.

"He sounds a lot like me. Thinking that he knows a lot, but all he has in his suitcase is a bit of courage and a lot of innocence."

"This is what I want you to do." I went to my desk and handed him a copy of *The Third Suspect* that I had made the day before. "I want you to go home and read this."

"That's all?"

"No, that's step one. If you like it and, in all modesty, I think you will, I want you to agree to something that will really help me out."

"I don't like where I think you're going."

It was time for the closer.

"Yes, I want the book published under your name."

"How can I do that? It's your book."

"Here's how. Number one, none of the money earned on it will go to you. It will all go to a foundation. I'll tell you more about that later. So you won't really be benefiting from the success of the book. Number two, you're a writer, Sal, and this will give you a better chance to leave the department and write full-time. Why am I saying that? Because the hardest thing to write is the second book. Teddy Grammas can become your character. Believe me, there are a lot of books that can feature him. All of those books will be yours. Really yours. And the money, too. Now, go home and read the book."

The next morning Sal called.

"I love it. Teddy is like my twin. I can already see his next book."

"So it's a deal?"

"Yes. Now only you and I know about this, right?"

"Not even Tina. And we both know how to keep a secret."

"Why are you doing this for me?"

"For one reason. You gave me my life back, Sal."

Part

6

A LIFE

How **vain** it is to sit down to write when you
have not stood up to live.

—H. D. Thoreau

Sixty-two

My name is Steven King and I'm a writer. As you can see from the spelling of my first name, I'm still not the guy from Maine, though this story now ends there. In the three years since I abandoned the fabulous shell game called "The Steven Konigsberg Explosion" (*Time*, December 9, 2001), a lot has happened. Tina and I moved back to Boothbay Harbor. We live in a large Victorian house on the west side of the harbor that we run as a B&B from April to the end of foliage season. Ben is not so little anymore and has just started preschool. He also has a sister. Lizzie is seven months and has already captured everyone's heart, including Chester's.

My second novel, *The Journey So Far*, again written under the pseudonym Chambers Benjamin, though this time with my picture on the flap, was just published by Chancery. The jacket even has a quote from the real Stephen King. He's a generous guy and we've had dinner twice. Reviews so far have been even better than for my first book. Foreign rights have been sold in twelve countries, including Israel *and* Egypt!

Two days a week I drive to Portland, where I teach creative writing at the University of Maine's campus there. I love it. I'm still famous, though in a different way. Like Salinger, I'm viewed as the quintessential "writer kook." Of course, I'm not reclusive like old J.D., but no one can understand (especially my parents) how I could walk away from eight-figure advances and legions of adoring fans. The tabloids still speculate that either I have a drug problem or I'm about to join a religious cult. I've had my TV bio done by both the History Channel and A&E. The versions are remarkably similar. One reason for that is they both use eight-millimeter footage of me as a kid that was supplied by my folks: selling lemonade in front of our house in Elmira; smiling like an idiot at my bar mitzvah; accepting a trophy for archery at summer camp. And they reach the same conclusion as to why I turned my back on fame and fortune: I just couldn't take the pressure. I went too far too fast. They show back-to-back videotapes of my readings as Steven Konigsberg and as Chambers Benjamin to prove their point. The Konigsberg readings are in large packed auditoriums, while my Benjamin turns are in small bookstores. When the camera zooms in on me as Konigsberg, I look serious, maybe even dour; as Chambers Benjamin I'm smiling as if auditioning for a toothpaste ad.

Even before I sold our apartment, the word had gone out, via Stuart, of course, that I was abandoning the Konigsberg oeuvre. Stuart was talking to everyone, and in no time the gossip columns and their TV equivalents were filled with my curious tale. The revelation that I was also Chambers Benjamin came from Dexter. Though he was happy to get Sal as an author, and loved both the books, the pilot light to his anger was still on. A number of people, including Quentin Bass, felt wronged. I tried to explain things, but the word that came back from Quentin, which was scrawled on the back of a letter I sent him, was short and not so sweet: "As the great Isaac Bashevis Singer once said, 'When you betray someone else, you also betray yourself.' By the way, go fuck yourself."

Dexter published both of Sal's books in the order I recommended. The first, Ben's book, hit the *Times* list at fourteen, moved as high as eleven, and stayed on for five weeks. Sal's own book did even better, getting as high as eight. My own book, unlike the first, never hit the list. My father thinks it's because of the lack of advertising on Chancery's part. He wanted to write a letter to Dexter, but I talked him out of it.

Last month Stuart quickly completed a three-book deal for Sal to continue the series. The advance was close to what a baseball player with a lifetime .275 average would get as a signing bonus. Sal quit the police force and bought a house in the horsey section of New Jersey. He also bought houses nearby for his in-laws and brother. He comes up to visit me every month. I work with him mainly on plot and character development. His writing is now focused and spare, and it generally needs very little help from me.

Tina and I spend a lot of time on the Chambers Outreach Foundation. We now have board meetings (Tina, Hamilton Cray, and me) every month. I persuaded Tina that it wasn't wrong for the three of us to take a modest salary ($40,000 a year) for our work. Between this, my teaching salary, the B&B, and money from my writing, we're doing fine. I doubt if I'll have to tend bar again. The foundation is the seventh largest in the state. We concentrate our efforts in the Boothbay area, but we've made grants as far south as Brunswick and as far north as Port Clyde. We've recently underwritten a low-cost loan program to enable young lobstermen to buy their first boat. The addition to the library is a big success, and Ben, our son, goes there twice a week for storytelling. We're now in the process of building the Benjamin Chambers ice-skating rink and a new firehouse. The firehouse will be named for Ben's parents.

Am I happy? Yes. Actually, very much so. Do I miss some aspects of my Konigsberg life? Yes. (Does Tina? No.) It's not the celebrity thing of being recognized, asked for autographs, of getting the best tables at the hottest restaurants, of flying on the Concorde and staying at four-star hotels that I miss. As crazy as it might sound, what I miss is the excitement of living on the edge. Those years as the super-best-selling writer Steve Konigsberg were a time when all my senses were jungle keen, particularly after Wayne Woodley appeared on the scene. My metronome was constantly bouncing from scared shitless to wild, fence-jumping exhilaration. If I tried to paint those years, I wouldn't use pastels or watercolors: my palette would be made up of thick oils ranging from sun yellow to tar black. Like the barroom trick of trying to balance an egg on its point, my old life had been an ongoing attempt to play Hamlet with a new script each night. This improvised life might have been exhausting, but at times it was also damn exciting. If Tina hadn't discovered Ben's manuscript that day, would I have called it quits one day on my own? I still haven't been able to answer that question.

A week ago I drove to Wiscasset for a foundation meeting. As usual, we met in Hamilton Cray's office. Tina couldn't make it because Lizzie and Ben were busy sharing a fever. Hamilton's office, complete with a rolltop desk, is on the third floor of a nineteenth-century brick building and looks out over the Sheepscot River where a dozen lobster boats rocked gently against their moorings. It had rained earlier, but now the sky was brightening, and a trail of sunlight lassoed the boats. Our first piece of business was to review the foundation's finances. Thanks to Hamilton's Yankee conservatism, the foundation's money had been invested for the past two years in bonds and CDs, and though the returns had not been spectacular, we'd avoided losses. We then reviewed a half dozen applications for grants, from organizations in Boothbay and Bath. We rejected all but one, a shelter for abused women in Bath. Hamilton would contact the group in Bath and ask for a more detailed plan that we'd take up at our next meeting. The last item was to approve raises for the foundation's secretary and bookkeeper. Our two ayes brought the session to a close.

"I have something for you, Steven," said Hamilton as he went to his desk. He opened a drawer and took out an envelope. "I think you know what this is." From the handwriting on the front, I could see it was from Ben. "You should know that this is the last one."

I mumbled "Thanks" and headed down to the street. Everything in me wanted to rip the envelope open and immediately read what was inside. But standing in the street or sitting in my car wasn't the right place. I drove back to Boothbay Harbor, the letter lying on the passenger seat. Would Ben finally tell me what I should have done? I could feel my heart racing. I turned the car radio on, then after a minute turned it off. I wanted to go out on the water on *Boswell* and read the letter alone, but I couldn't. Whatever the letter said would be as much for Tina as for me. When I arrived home, the children were sleeping and the house was quiet.

"I have something for us," I said as I led Tina outside to our front porch, where we sat together on the front step.

"It's from Ben," she said, recognizing the handwriting.

"It's the last one."

With hands that were not surgeon steady, I opened the letter and started reading aloud.

> *Dear Stevie:*
>
> *It's been a while since my last letter (that is, if Hamilton followed my instructions, which knowing him I'm sure he did). I told him to let you know*

that this is my last missive from "beyond." I don't want these letters to wind up as the basis for an episode of The Twilight Zone. *You'll notice that I didn't date this letter. Though I'm writing it only a little more than a month since the first letter, the time interval is not nearly as important as a decision I've made since then. And what may that be? Finally to be honest with you, with the world as I know it, and, most importantly, myself.*

Do you remember that lunch we had in Portland after dropping Tina off at the airport? I talked to you that afternoon about my brother, Tom. I told you that Tom died in a car accident. That was true. What I didn't tell you was that I was driving the car that night. Yes, the road was wet and slippery, but more to the point, I was drunk. I went through a lot after that, very little that was good. It took me many years, and many different occupations, and constant moving from here to there and back again, before I understood what I had done and who I was. I've been trying to make up for what I did that night. Not an easy assignment.

Now to set the record straight—I didn't write those manuscripts in the trunks. Not one of them. They were all written by Tom. Tom taught in the history department at Bowdoin, and he was a natural writer. It just flowed from him. But he never wanted to publish. Totally uninterested. He thought it would get in the way of his academic writing. I tried to convince him that it wouldn't have any effect on how his research papers on fifteenth-century political thought (his subject) were received. No argument of mine could sway him. Though I loved Tom, I was also somewhat competitive with him. So during all that time when Tom was writing novel after novel, I decided that I'd become a writer, too. My writing, though I kept at it for years, was lousy. My stories were trite and my characters wooden, the complete opposite of Tom's work.

So there I was after Tom's death, the custodian of his legacy. What to do? I desperately wanted to see the books published, but how could I do that? That would go directly against Tom's wishes. I thought about publishing them under a pseudonym and putting all the money that was earned into a foundation to do things that I thought Tom would have wanted. In the end, as you know, I just kept them. I built those trunks and stored them there. Wherever I went, the trunks went with me. Then why did I lie to you and tell you I wrote them? Honestly, Stevie, I wish I knew. Though the books weren't mine, I guess I began to wish they were. Once, I even had one of Tom's books retyped by a guy in San Francisco. Later, when I was tutoring two sisters, I read to them one of the children's books that Tom had written. They loved it. Why did I have to tell them it was mine? They were just children, for Christ's sake!

   Stevie, I've told you a lot, but I haven't told you what to do. That's because I believe that you'll know. You're made of good stuff, my friend. Make sure you take good care of Tina. She's very special. Wherever you are now, and whatever you're doing, always remember that I love you.

   Ben

P.S. Boswell *has been showing a tendency to slip out of gear recently. I think eventually you'll have to have the transmission rebuilt. Don't put it off. They have a saying in the harbor: "There are only two kinds of boats: sound boats and sunk boats."*

When I finished reading the letter, we didn't say a word. Then we walked down to our dock, where a gentle chop slapped softly against the pilings.

"You know," said Tina, "the fact that Ben was weak, too, doesn't justify what you did."

"I know that," I told her. "Someone had to break the long sequence of lies. You did it, Tina.

"I'm just so grateful to be where I am right now," I continued, "with you, the kids, our life here. There's only one thing missing."

She knew what I was thinking. Tina went down and picked up a small stone, polished smooth as a marble by the tides, put it to her lips, then tossed it out into the water.

"That's for you, Ben."

Slowly, we walked back to the house. It was time to wake the kids.